Penguin Book

Cast But One Shadow and Winter Love

Han Suyin was born in Peking. Her mother was half
Dutch, half Flemish, and her father was Chinese. She
was brought up in China, and learned English after
she was ten years old. She attended a Chinese
university in Peking, and later went to Europe. In
1938 she returned to China with her husband and
lived in the interior during the Sino-Japanese war.

In 1942 she returned to England, and after the death
of her husband completed her medical studies at
London University. She then returned to Asia.

Her other books are *Destination Chungking*, about
the war in China, written in collaboration with an
American woman missionary; *A Many-Splendoured
Thing*, the story of what happened to her on the
'sea-wet rock' of Hongkong, and *And the Rain my
Drink*, about Malaya during the Emergency of
1952–6. The last two are both Book Society Choices
and published in Penguins. *The Mountain is Young*,
which is to be filmed, is about the coronation of the
king of Nepal, which Han Suyin attended in 1956.
The Four Faces is her most recent novel.

Cast But One Shadow
and Winter Love

Han Suyin

Penguin Books
in association with Jonathan Cape

Penguin Books Ltd, Harmondsworth,
Middlesex, England
Penguin Books Pty Ltd, Ringwood,
Victoria, Australia

First published by Jonathan Cape 1962
Published in Penguin Books 1965

Copyright © Han Suyin, 1962

Made and printed in Great Britain by
Richard Clay (The Chaucer Press), Ltd
Bungay, Suffolk
Set in Monotype Bembo

Cast But One Shadow

Cast But One Shadow

A Cambodian village, any one of the many hundreds of Cambodian villages. A huddle of wood houses on stilts, with roofs of Cambodian-made oval small tiles glowing gently pink and grey.

The house of the astrologer is like all the others. There is a veranda round the house, and steps in a staircase to ascend from the ground to the veranda. The inside of the house consists of two rooms, spread with mats. There are also, for show rather than for use (because sitting on mats is so much more comfortable than sitting on chairs), two rattan armchairs, placed on either side of a table covered with a flowery Japanese cloth. Upon this stand two glass vases bought in the market, with artificial flowers of silk made in China. These flank a picture on the wall, a framed picture of the Lord Buddha, garlanded with more artificial flowers. Also on the table is a radio, made in England.

Outside this house are the other houses, all alike in a family portrait way, for Cambodia is a country where there is no great wealth and no great poverty; ninety per cent of the people own their piece of land, cultivate their fields, and have enough to eat . . . rarity in Asia. The school is also such a house, slightly larger, and so is the communal hall, which also serves as a resting place for travellers.

Cutting the air, eager messengers running to the village, are the erect poles and shining new wires of that wonderful, miraculous proof that reality is infinitely more subtle and rich than imagined, seen, and heard by man: electricity. The light that turns night into day was recently installed in every village house. A single bulb, it hangs from a thread in the middle of the two rooms, though some extravagant villagers have two. The bulbs are often naked; but some already wear, like a bishop's cope, the opaque white glass of a shade.

In the house of the astrologer, the astrologer sits on a mat in the centre of the living room, whose wide open front looks on to the veranda and the village and the marvellous serene landscape of Cambodia: rice fields and palm and coconut trees, cotton fields and kapok trees, and lakes and rivers, and a continuous slow procession of clouds. A gentle, serene, and eternal landscape, to humble the proud and make the humble intrepid.

Facing the astrologer, on other mats, the courtesy coloured mats woven and reserved for important guests, with tea in Cambodia-made plastic cups (the tea is Ceylon tea), are seated two Europeans from France. One is older than the other, but neither is above thirty-five. They are unable to sit in the comfortable lotus position which the astrologer employs, but they manage to huddle their knees to their chins, and do not appear too uneasy.

Underneath the house, between the stilts which support it, two bullocks chew. They have necklaces of beaten pewter and brass for ornaments. They look at the landscape in stolid rumination.

On the road there is stationed the black sports-car with red upholstery (a Mercedes-Benz) in which the two Frenchmen came.

The astrologer said: 'I predict the fate of those who ask of me; with brainless mandarin bird piping and dead dice rolling, with cynical calendar of days like squares aligned in a schoolchild's text-book, each square fomenting the number of its ministering planets, I interpret events, advise movement of tongue and hand, gestures to counter the hostile effluence of the all-knowing obdurate sky. Yet I myself do not believe in fate, since I, like bird and six-faced dice, have a share in its making.

'Yet I harm not those who desire to be lulled by my lies, for they come in doubt, and I, reading their character from their faces, chart for them a course of action or restraint which suits their bones and muscles best. I, who talk of spirit, am the one true materialist. You cannot blame me if sometimes I read amiss. For what I read is not the mindless, voiceless stars, but the starfish yearning of men and women rapt in their own luck.

'It is not their fate I predict. It is their own choice I reveal, and part of their choosing is their choosing to come to me. I replace them in mapping the mainway of their lives, become the heavenly telegram from the unheard gibbering void. Yet I am perturbed, though my birds soothe me (I feed them after each prediction, it makes them sing more willingly). I am perturbed, not by what I tell them, but by what has not been said, for the word is without mercy.

'And each decision abolishing the conditional silence is like a sword cut, each sentence a long line of assassins stabbing their what-could-have-been, the other choices, unmade, dead before birth. Some who consult me have only one foetal other choice to murder, but most have two, three, or more possibilities in themselves. Each one of us is a patchwork of becomings, a reverberation of other selves unchosen, a guilt of the unknown.

'Choosing then implies guilt, and it is my guilt too, since I advise, counsel, guide, and help to kill. A slaughter of the unchosen, the unborn, the might-have-been, maledictions casting their shadows upon the elected, the manifest, the substantial. This is my guilt, to be borne gratefully, with knowledge that in the Almighty Compassion of the Buddha I shall not be damned, for it is not within me to do anything else.

'Luckily in my country there is not, as in yours,' said the astrologer, turning a laughing face upon the doctor, 'original sin, unborn guilt uncommitted, hardened jelly like the hump of the ox, aquiver upon its spine, exactly fitted that the yoke may hold fast. Only sin past and sin present, to be expiated in future sins. A more logical arachnoid thread through the temporal labyrinth of existence, Buddhism than Christianity, don't you think?

'But even so, I *feel* guilty (though with the reassuring reservations I have elaborated) because those who come to me demand solemnity, an assurance of mien like a mask, to pursue their becomings in one way and one alone, and to lay into graves the many other lives that I see waiting for them to live. I would starve if I told them of all the other-ones in them; if I said, you can do *this*, or *that*, or *that*, and yet be none the worse for it, they would stone me. No. I sell inevitability, and live.

'You are a doctor, a medicine man of the West, as inevitable as I am in the East, and you have come to me to ask me about this girl whom we Cambodians call Devi, and whom you the French call Sylvie. You and this other white man, who you tell me is mad, are demanding of me a resurrection. But I am an honest man, a punctilious materialist. How can I decipher the past without the equivocation of syllables? The future, which is so much easier, escapes only with one metamorphosis, for the pointing voice of the unknowable is a machine-gun puncturing its files but sparing one copy for show. You think telling the past will really heal your friend's present madness?'

The doctor said: 'My friend has also lived in an air fraudulent with words, but unlike you they are the only beings he knows. He has lived, devouring his own articulated feelings, because he was wealthy, he had everything, everything except himself. The mind needs hunger. Having no other hunger, he devoured his own soul, and his soul was made up of feelings, syllabled emotions. Hence he is a little, though not entirely, mad. No more nor less than anyone who reads the newspaper and looks at television and believes that his mind has been informed. Then came Sylvie, whom you call Devi, and upset this manger arrangement, so that he has nothing left to consume except the vomit of the past.'

'Ah,' said the astrologer, 'that is why my days of singing truth-fragment have a reward too, in that for a time perhaps I appease the cannibal feast within each man. But at what cost? What cost to myself? Guilt, a feeling of guilt, I who was born guilt-free, being a man. Your friend should have come to me earlier. He looks a far-advanced case to me. And what is he holding in his hand?'

'He is holding a spool,' said the doctor, 'a spool upon which the voice of the past is wound. Now, having no soul left, he is mad, ravenous, a frenzy of inanition, needing to devour something else, the past of Sylvie, his most beloved only sister. Therefore I have brought him to you.'

'To devour the past of Devi-Sylvie dead, whose voice is alive upon this spool, the days gone like the cohorts of Angkor and of Rome into cosmic time,' said the astrologer. 'I understand perfectly. Those are the ways of what, with shabby innuendo, with licentious decency, many call love. Yet love is more than a mirage of water for thirst, a dream of shade on the head, and your friend's disease will not be cured. He will need another prey, after what I can give.'

'Yes,' said the doctor, 'I know it. But I need time to heal him. And you are wise, and I must try everything.'

'I spent three years in a monastery, learning the Great Compassion,' said the astrologer, delighted with the word wise. 'I have been many things in life, a clown and a mountebank, a workman and a male prostitute, a bureaucrat and a husband, and also a soldier who killed, which was bad but my lot, hence forgiven even before I raised the rifle. I know many things. For instance, I know how to keep breathing when sunk in rice-field mud, breathing and alive when all of me is submerged, for at least three hours.'

'How?' said the doctor, forgetting his mission, the mad friend by his side who turned in his Holbein-pale, sweating hands the tape-recorder spool.

'A stem of the lotus,' said the astrologer, a yellow glee-beam upon his face. 'Hollow it is already, then put it in your mouth, let its upper end reach the air, sink below the glass bed of the mud, and live. Some of my friends endured thus many more hours than three, while all around them the hunters searched, those brothers with other uniforms on skinning them into foes. If your mad friend had done this, only once, he would not be mad now.'

At this the madman began to mutter fretfully: 'Jacques, Jacques, you promised he would tell me. I want to know ... everything ... everything. I have a right to know. More than anyone else, I have a right to all of her.'

'Yes, Philippe,' replied the doctor, 'this man will tell us what he knows.'

'I want the truth,' said the madman.

'The truth, as I have explained,' replied the astrologer, frowning with one eyebrow, 'is more difficult to recount about the past, than to surmise about the future. Ask me the future, not the past, and relieve me of responsibility, though you can do nothing about the guilt of the unworded. You are the first of my clients in many years to ask me to tell all the past, and yet ask nothing of the future as well.'

'My friend lives wholly in the past,' replied the doctor. 'But there are many nowadays like him among us whom you call the whites. We have become as we imagined the Chinese used to be before the Great Change came to them. Many of us flee backwards, burrow in the scooped-out shelters of the never-again, walk as Lot's wife of the turning head, seeking shadows of flames in a night sky. This man listens to a voice that was once bone and nerve, blood and flesh, and is now a magnetic wave on a tape, as eternal as its origin was transient. He feels strongly, in his madness, that only the past endures, and of course he is right, since only the past is irrevocable. But apart from this madness he is quite sane in other ways. He is a great and astute banker and businessman, though he fancies himself as a patron of the arts and a would-be poet with no time to write. You should see him in his office. He makes more money in a minute than you in a lifetime or I in a year. He takes great decisions in the instant required for a cicada to breathe, as your Cambodian saying has it. He has no fear of killing his hundreds and his thousands so long as he does not see the blood drain from their mangled limbs. He weeps over good music, and becomes indignant when a man beats his wife. In short, he is perfectly normal, except on this one point.'

'The past will be expensive,' said the astrologer meditatively. 'I will have to charge you double price. Because I am honest I must tell you that truth cannot be guaranteed, even if you were to give me all the money in the world. It is disastrous to seek the secrets of another human being's actions, and even more disastrous to believe that truth can be found in words, chat of corruption, human breath, dangerous wind scattering babble-gravel. I see he is a man who needs an air pestilent with words, and I shall give him words, but you must pay me double price.

'Now,' said the astrologer, shifting his legs into an even more meditative posture, so that the serpent of life coiled in his loins might easily ascend to the brain, opening up along his spine the lotus flowers of enlightenment, 'before I start on the film of the past as regards Sylvie-Devi, your sister, I must tell you of an analogous event which happened somewhere else, in another time. For events repeat themselves, though never completely in the same manner, never twice the same for any time, any individual, only sufficiently alike to bear some elements of comparison. Nature never remakes the same face of an ant. Only the machine, man-made, imprints an unnatural likeness upon all its progeny; yet even there, even there, differences occur, for between the births of two identical objects has intervened the cosmic flow of time-space-event, and this truth the Lord Buddha knew and tried to teach.

'I shall first tell you this other story, as one would tell the synopsis of a film. For now that I see your friend handle this spool my mind goes into the level of our technical century, and must handle this human material as if it had come out in ribbon, smooth celluloid, to be projected as shadows on a screen, images in a linear procession of polysyllabic skeletons. We live today in the middle of the shadows we have created; in the middle of electro-magnetic waves of our own making, waves which nothing will stop, matter nor time nor space, but which go on to the ends of the universe, pursuing the stars to the confines of heaven. And all these become shadows for our vision and for our ears, shades of shades that we call reality. So let me project the eternal shadow of another event, which may now be commented on in Andromeda and Orion, upon today's discourse.

'This story also began during the war, the same war as yours, World War Two. But it was not in Cambodia, our beautiful Khmer land, that it happened. It happened in Indonesia. Here there were Frenchmen at that time, lording it over us, for we were then a colony, which we are no more. There it was the Dutch who were the masters, and they too are gone.

'And there, as here, the Japanese came. Before them the white men fled or capitulated, and we rejoiced, thinking the Japanese liberators. But after a while we understood that another master had come, trying to replace the old. And because the Japanese did not have Right Intention and Right Action, which the Great Compassion of the Buddha enjoins upon all men, they too were defeated.'

'I am not interested in Buddhism,' interrupted the madman, Philippe.

'In Indonesia,' said the astrologer, unheeding, 'there lived a Dutch family, very much like the French family of your friend. A father, a mother, some children. They fled before the Japanese, left behind a little girl, Bertha, about five years old.'

'My father was killed, murdered,' said Philippe. 'He did not run away. He was of the Resistance. He refused to collaborate with the Japanese, as other businessmen did in Indo-China, the Vichy lot. He was murdered, and so was my mother.'

'There are differences, as I said,' replied the astrologer. 'Killed or fled, the family disappeared and a child was left behind. In each case, a little girl. Your sister was called Sylvie, this little girl Bertha.

'Bertha's parents went away, and Bertha was left to be looked after by an Indonesian woman, a servant in her parents' house. This Malay woman thought that Bertha had been given to her as her own daughter. Malays and Indonesians, we Khmers, and many other Asians, easily adopt children, making no difference between those born of our flesh and those born of the flesh of others. And so this woman, whom I shall call Fatimah, thought the child given to her by Allah the One and Only God, and being Muslim brought the child up as a Muslim; and when she was fourteen betrothed her to a young man, the best she could find, agreeable, religious, well-educated, a school teacher.

'But by the time Bertha was fourteen the war was over, and her parents returned to Indonesia. The war had taught some men that all need freedom, as the bird needs to fly, but not all had learnt this lesson, certainly not certain governments. The French came back to Indo-China, the Dutch returned to Indonesia, and for a while they tried to go against the great flow of the cosmos which is for ever forwards, both in the stars and in the affairs of men. And it took much blood to make them go away again.

'Bertha's parents now came to Fatimah and claimed Bertha back. Fatimah refused to give up her daughter. The case was taken to an English judge in Singapore, who ruled that the child Bertha belonged to her flesh-and-blood parents. And because of this judgement the Malays rioted for three days, the streets of Singapore ran blood, thirty people died or were maimed, and some are still in prison. Because of Bertha, who is now a Dutch housewife.'

'But here,' said Philippe Bergerat in a choked voice, 'only my sister died, my little sister, who had done no harm to anyone.'

'It is as I say,' replied the astrologer. 'A judge, any judge on a par with the English judge who solemnly gave judgement so many years ago for the Dutch girl, must quote precedent for what is, in truth, not only a cure but also a judgement. For as an English judge is conscious of the majesty of the law he represents, so must I, a Khmer, here in the shadows of the great Angkor, the past that was, render justice to your friend in my tradition, which is older than his.'

'Come, come, monsieur the astrologer,' replied the doctor, Jacques Rouvier, with a tiny smile, 'you are a wise man, but I believe that to establish your bona fides as a judge is superfluous in this instance. We have not asked for judgement, we have asked for some fragments of the past about Sylvie, Philippe's sister.'

'And how could you accept these fragments,' replied the astrologer, 'unless I first place them in their context, their historical relevance in the framework of the universe? Therefore I have quoted the case of Bertha Hertog in order to abolish one of the roots of your friend's disease, which is uniqueness. He is entirely self-centred, a world unto himself. He believes that no one suffers as he does, feels as he does. O separation of himself, ripped from the arm-in-arm reality that beats upon us as the sun does, all revelation is irrelevant to his ghost in armour thrashing the wind. I have only words to breach the visor affixed like a coffin-lid to his face. You must forgive me if, therefore, I become long-winded, like a magistrate in the best tradition.'

'Let him give his bona fides,' said Philippe suddenly. 'How dare you talk of my sister? Who are you?'

'In those days, for we are in the past,' said the astrologer, 'when my story and your story begin in the waywardness of past time, I was not a reader of the stars, the voice of unknowing through the material cloud of the knowledgeable, as I am today. I was a young monk, rescued from paederasty in a brothel for French and Annamite intellectuals by an old abbot, whose sensual loves had withered about his aged flesh, leaving dispassionate echoes he satiated with goodness. He taught me assiduously, as autumn delineates the leaf, moulded me with admonition, touched my heart with the golden hoariness of ancient sacred texts, and though I fell away later, yet now I return to him. Approaching the life-span of the penumbra, in the sunset shadow which lengthens thought, having committed and compounded the sum of evil which it was in me to determine, I too begin to gather goodness and young men about me, to teach them what I learnt. One day I shall become again a Buddhist monk.

'Meanwhile, let us go on with your case. I was not a good young acolyte, not like Prem, His Excellency Prem, who later tried to save your sister and her lover, Rahit, both from you and from themselves. After my protector died, I served a holy man who was a hypocrite, who abused me both in spirit and body, for he kept away from women but not from youths. It did not mar me, for I had learnt fortitude when I was a little boy sold by my parents for food. I could see life as a wholeness about me, as the Buddha and perhaps Marx enjoin us to do. Evil ran off me, like water off the swan's neck, I bowed to it and it did me no harm. I ran away from the holy man, and let my head, shaven for the priesthood, grow its hair, and roamed and starved, sold women at street corners by sidling up to French soldiers and whispering: "Would you like my sister?" Went to prison for pimping, and came out again none the worse for it, as is usual; became a guerrilla and fought and killed a man, ran away to hide in a plantation, and tapped rubber for a while on your father's plantation, and was there when the Japanese came.'

'I never saw you,' said Philippe. 'We had so many workers.'

'You owned so many workers,' replied the astrologer gaily, 'you never looked at their faces. You own many more today, for you are wealthier than your father. I wonder that riches have not yet killed in you the great need for words. Rich men, usually, have lusts and desires, but no needs. Here you come, to gorge at the banquet of my words. I wonder that incantation and magic have not yet been decanted out of words by money, that words are still for you louder than storms, greater than oceans, and certainly more valid than human beings.

'I saw that morning the Japanese come, a small horde on motor-cycles and in jeeps, bristling as insects do with projecting spines of rifles and bayonets and booted limbs, led by the sabre-trailing officer who in his spare moments wept over moon and rain and autumn *Haiku* verses, played the flute, and declaimed grandiloquent prose before the stone carvings of Angkor. He was a normal, good man, like yourself. I noticed him because he carried himself proudly, as proudly as in the sculptures of Angkor does Rama, head back, draw-ing a bow, riding the shoulders of the monkey god, Hanuman, leading his monkey cohorts to battle against the ravisher of Rama's wife. No doubt the Japanese officer felt Rama-like, out to right a wrong by killing the wrongdoers. Man's mind is a many-sided mirror, distorting what it wishes to fit what he calls his purpose.

'They rumbled up to the garden of your house, those jeeps, and I and the others, your hands, your workers, heard them among the green-grey trees whose wild milk, the latex, was your flood of gold. We heard the rumble and the roar, like a distant Niagara, and knew it meant catastrophe, though, ensconced among the greenwater stillness of the trees, not for us. And I, who was young and swift, ran with bowed head, zigzagging among the boles, and came to the barbed wire which fenced in from us your great white house and beautiful flower-garden, and saw. I saw the same thing happen to you' – turn-ing to Philippe – 'as happened to me, oh, rather more often to me than to you. I saw –'

'You lie. The man lies,' cried Philippe, springing up and radiating a fear-filled pallor through his sun-tan with its ooze of pale fair down. 'I was left for dead on the ground. It took months in the hospital before I was well again.'

Jacques Rouvier said: 'Calm yourself, Philippe. Calm yourself.'

'Really,' said the astrologer, surprised, 'I do not know why you should feel so crestfallen when I mention your having been raped, monsieur, by a Japanese officer. It happened to so many. It happens all the time. What those soldiers did to you and to your mother before she died is a pantomime exercise of power, a cliché of all wars, repeated through the millenniums by all soldiers, I assure you. There is no need for you to feel guilty.'

Philippe said: 'I tried to protect my sister, Sylvie. I stood and tried to hit them. I was left for dead.'

'As you please,' said the astrologer amiably. 'Refuge yourself in that phrase, if it comforts you. It is a small, obdurate block-house needing no demolition. Your sister Sylvie, whom we call Devi, also Moen, was saved by a Japanese soldier, a bow-legged, brutal-looking peasant boy with a delicate heart untouched by words, for his vocabulary was limited, his brain slow, his heart wholesome, a new recruit to whom massacre was unplumbed horror. While the others pillaged and slaughtered and raped, he, who had had to pretend to use your mother when she was already dead –'

'Leave my mother alone,' screamed Philippe, 'leave her alone. I do not want to hear this. Jacques, make him shut up.'

'Is this relevant?' asked Jacques. 'Monsieur the astrologer, you are exaggerating. There is no need to make this encounter more painful . . .'

'You wanted the whole truth, I thought,' said the astrologer. 'It is relevant, actually, for your friend knows all this already. When Kano, for that was the Japanese soldier's name, buttoned his trousers, he wanted to vomit, and instead of joining the others busy with the maidservant, her daughters, and the cook's pregnant wife, he ran into the garden and there found Sylvie, sprawled in the flower-bed, while you on the veranda were held by two fellow soldiers, maintained in the position which made your buttocks available to their officer while he rode you like a beast. I, having endured this before, felt no pity for you, but watched Kano pick up your sister, and had it not been for the fence between us, that fence erected by your parents to protect their property from our intrusion, I would have interfered. Savaging little girls is not to my taste. But this was not Kano's intention, although we did not know it and killed him later by mistake.'

'You killed him?' cried Jacques.

'Not I, but other hands. Sometimes I get confused as to who really did what. Milking the warm milk from those vegetable cows, all bent together with the gnats mazing their collective of stings about our faces, we sometimes do not know which pair of hands did what, so linked to each other do the poor become. Not I, but other hands killed him, with their rubber-tapper knives and their bark-gnarled hands, leaving a corpse to fester in the green milk light of the wayside bushes, until it turned to honey-drip for a million flies.

'And yet Kano had saved Sylvie, moved by a pity whose Right Motive we found only later, much later, when even his bones had become part of my land, as he is part of my remembering. He had seized her under his arm, while she screamed, and the officer, intent with you, did not hear. He mounted his motor-cycle and rode the air out of the plantation, until he came to the edge of the forest, and there, striding into the thigh-warm shadows, he put her down. Then he was back on his motor-cycle, and about half-way a tyre punctured. And those other hands, running away from the plantation, saw him helpless, bent over his machine, and fell upon him. When he was dead they rifled his pockets, took off all his clothes, and also what they could sell from the motor-cycle, tyres, lamp, and saddle – impartially unclothing both man and machine. And some months later I heard that one of us had found upon Kano a photograph, and burnt it, the photograph of a Japanese woman holding a little girl in her arms. Kano must have thought of his wife and child, and saved your sister because of his own child.

'I saw his name again later. A Chinese who ran a pawnshop and had amulets for sale, showed it to me. A Japanese amulet to exorcize sickness and protect from death, made of one thousand stitches by a thousand Japanese women; but the Chinese had counted only nine hundred and fifty stitches. It had the name of Kano upon it, and was twice as valuable now that its owner had been killed.'

'You are wasting my time,' said Philippe coldly, turning the spool over and over, 'telling me all this. I am not interested in the life story of this Japanese, Kano, nor in yours, nor in the fate of a Japanese amulet. I want to know what happened to Sylvie, my sister, an exact picture of what happened to her, her childhood, how she was found, what was done to her. I asked her, often, when she was with me. But there was so little time, and she did not want to speak of it. I know there must have been something, some little thing about her I could have used to prevent her going. Now I want to know everything.'

The astrologer looked with compassion upon Philippe, then at his own wrist-watch with its white cotton band, checking its time-telling with the sun's obliqueness, and remembered it was the hour at which he turned on his radio set to listen to Khmer Radio news. It was only a few months ago, and therefore a long time ago, now that time goes faster than it did and gathers speed as it runs, that the people of the village had stopped fearing the insubstantial Voice out of the box. Now they took it for granted, desired it, bought the voice when their savings allowed it. Destiny, the stars, owl-hoots, the cries of flying foxes, and their own dreams, were all confirmed by the bodiless voice dribbling oracle at the turn of a screw.

'You want a more succinct interpretation of events than the one I am giving,' said the astrologer. 'You are not interested in the life of Kano, the Japanese soldier who saved your sister. You do not care to know why he performed this act of mercy, incurring thereby subsequent punishment. Yet I would have wanted to know, since it was important . . . otherwise you might not be here today, sitting, waiting to know your sister's past.'

'For years I thought she was dead,' said Philippe. 'I could not forget. Whenever I approached a window, I saw someone in the glass, a drowned in dying face, turned to me, imploring, the mirror surface turned into mouth and eyes lifted to me, in need. Any window, any mirror, gave me back the horror, the blood on my mother's face, the blood and the pain of my own body. How can I be interested in a Japanese soldier and why he did what he did, when it is of my sister I want to know, all of her, all that has escaped me of her? Can't you see that?'

'Though you clutch her voice in your hands as if you were seizing her by the throat,' said the astrologer, 'you will not bring back to this life the already-born-again-through-death. But I have told you what I saw, and now it is someone else's turn. I will now call Maté, the mother, who took your sister and loved her until you came back and wrested her away. You remember, you came one day, looking for Maté, after your sister left you?'

'She was not there,' said Philippe, 'not in her house.'

The astrologer rose, went down the steps of his house to the ground, for it is consummate discourtesy to talk from one's house, throwing one's breath down upon the face of listeners on the road. He called one of the children sparrow-lingering there, and bade him call Maté, mother of sons, to come to him when she could, to meet the French who would speak with her of her daughter Devi, also called Moen the Lovely. This he told the child, to warn Maté,

23

so that her speech and face should be made intact, smooth, closed over the apertures of emotion to give no dent or cleft whereby her spirit could be seized by those who came as scavengers to devour memories. For the astrologer knew that everyone's face is also a shield through which come words, marshalled words, but that the spirit within must keep its supply of knowledge intact, as the ocean bed mirrors only a sky upon its surface, and not its own depths. Maté had much to guard, having had so much of life from Moen the Lovely One, Moen who was also Devi found-by-the-lotus, Sylvie Bergerat, sister to Philippe.

Up comes Maté in her work clothes, a strong woman with hair cropped short in the fashion of Cambodian women who fight in wars and shear their heads in widowhood and in sorrow. Her body is less slim than when she found her daughter Devi by the lotus pond, her breasts slightly fallen, but she still has a fertile suppleness about her, and in her square, high-cheeked face, the wonderful mouth, large-lipped, full-curved, gathered up into that ecstatic half-smile, a gaiety hovering on the edge of ferocity, a smile carved many thousands of times upon the figures of Angkor: a magnanimous mouth, withstanding the centuries. Up she comes, barefooted, and stands in front of the men.

Philippe and Jacques look at her, at her face, and suddenly are aware of their own faces: Philippe's narrow, a distinguished, pale, fine-boned dejection called elegance, with his sister's eyes, hyperthyroid blue, bulging, petalled with gentian irises; with a narrow, fleshy lower lip, a little Hapsburg (at least, he had thought so, watching himself in the mirror, noting the resemblance to the Velazquez King of Spain); Jacques's face, round, jaw well set, lips a little bleak, disappointing in the strong, good-humoured steadiness of the face; these lips are due to bad digestion and too little sleep after Sylvie's death.

The astrologer rises to salute Maté with folded hands, for Maté is a woman of power, elected to represent the village at the twice-yearly Assembly which is held throughout the country. Maté has now gone once to Pnomh Penh, the capital city, to settle a village lawsuit, an affair of wells' ownership, and she has led the village women with spades and baskets to build their own new road, and is it not because of Maté that the electric light has come to the village? And all this has happened after the death of Devi.

But Philippe sees none of this, for it does not interest him, it is not represented on the inner film he thinks the world, his world, nor is it on the tape he hangs on to like a child clutching the nourishing breast of his mother. He sees a woman ungrieving, and thinks: 'she does not know sorrow as I do', and this makes him rejoice. He clutches more strongly the spool in his hand, contentedly wrapped in a pain unshared and therefore, by connotation, valuable as an original Old Master: I loved her best, since I grieve the most. Even Jacques forgets about Sylvie at times, although he has actually killed her. I, Philippe, will not forget. My love will endure through Eternity, and evidence here it is, the redeemer in my hand, this slender plastic tape to eternity, redeeming my misery into unctuous, immortal blessedness.

'Maté,' said the stargazer, 'these men have come to ask about Devi. Their minds are troubled, and we must soothe their grief.'

'Even the vultures,' said Maté, 'do not overturn earth-filled graves. Why should they come? Have they not done enough?' But she spoke quietly, without the grimaces of grief upon her face, giving nothing away, and Philippe rejoiced even more, although now he was stalked by another desire, born on the instant, to make her suffer, to nibble with his eyes at the shadow-play of pain about Maté's mouth, for only the mouth would betray her.

'Do not be angry with us, Madame Maté,' said the doctor. 'It was fate, or destiny, that took her away from you, and see, we are here to beg your help.'

'I see,' said Maté. 'And so we must pretend a communion of the living, to bring forth our dead? Going together along the arduous long road of recall to make Moen the Lovely, Devi of the lotus born, live again in a little while of words? Of what use is this thistle exercise? Devi is dead many days, her spirit may be reborn somewhere else. And that reminds me. I want of you, astrologer, if you are worth any of the money which you get from me and from others so easily, I want of you the whereabouts of my daughter today, where and under what shape she is born, if born again, that I may go to her and find her and perhaps talk to her, and tell her: once I, too, was your mother . . .'

Said the astrologer: 'Maté, Mother Maté, do not ask of me more, I pray you. I have already done all I could about this affair of the future, and told you: Moen is reborn, that is sure. But it is far from here, in another land, and important though you are in our village, it is too expensive for you to travel so far.'

'You are a wily cabalist,' said Maté, 'and I do not believe you. The time will come when I too will travel to other lands, and also the time when no one will ask you any more for signs from the stars, for we shall all know much of cosmic geography and do our own divining. Give me some betel.' She took in her strong, brown hand the wrapped betel in its green leaves from the small acolyte who served tea, cigarettes, and betel, and chewed till her mouth ran blood with the red stain.

Philippe shut his eyes, for staring at Maté's mouth he saw the glaucous mirror face of his mother, blood upon her mouth, and heard his own screamings. And now he could not stop the unrolling pictures, sound and feel and sight, the breath of the soldiers heaving while his body was torn with unimagined pain, though at twelve a boy does imagine so much, especially when he has a small sister to play with who demands stories, and wants to be frightened, then soothed and cuddled and reassured. He could feel now, at the root of his tongue, words languageless, suffocated, choked in the with-held saliva in the box of his mouth. 'I have always lived expressing myself.' But now the betel blood choked him, his breath filled his lungs with fire, his skin was the enclosure of a furnace, where a myriad goblins, flames, spikes, sparks of fire glowed and danced in a world of silent fury.

Maté sat down in the courtesy way of the Cambodians, her two legs folded to one side of her, as if she were a mermaid tucking her fishtail neatly upon the rock floor, and straightened her body. Jacques, looking at her, seeing a solid woman only, now felt his heart somersault, for he saw Sylvie's gesture, movement in Maté. Now, any second, Maté would lift her arms and start combing her hair, the same lifting gesture that Sylvie had used, combing her hair with the ivory comb, its back inlaid with carved Cambodian silver; and he had watched Philippe, her brother, brush his sister's hair with the brush from the same set, and sparks flew off in the dry heat of the Cambodian winter, and somehow the whole scene, the three of them together, was disagreeable and delightful, unwearying in its obscene purity.

'So you want to unlock your grief with the keys of talk?' said Maté, eyeing Philippe with her great mouth. 'It is a monster you must live with, your grief. A pet monster whose death will leave you lonely. My friend the astrologer has hinted to me that you are a madman of time. Are you not mad because your time is created of words that fail to fit, that take up too much room within your small cage of self? An equation of the alphabet that is your monster's ungainly body, always demanding more A B Cs? That is what I thought anyway when I saw you: some feed mulberry leaves to silkworms, and the silkworms make cocoons and die in their own suffocation.'

'I never saw you,' said Philippe, 'and I do not understand entirely what you say, because it is the paraphernalia of a religion to which I do not adhere.'

'Not at all,' said Maté. 'I am not a religious person, neither is my friend the astrologer, nor are you, though you like churches and cathedrals and dim sepulchral melancholies, but only because of what you can say about their aura, or their architecture, or their organic perspective, anything that can be plastered like bird spit upon their surface so long as it appears that you remain unmoved, untouched, and unbelieving. But I have been sad and known bereavement, and it has taught me that man was made for beauty and gaiety, and sorrow and tears, and for being all the time buffeted like a sail clapping to the wind. You never saw me, it is true, but I saw you when you tore in your car to the village, when Devi had left you and you were pursuing her. You thought she had returned to me. But she was not here. You came into my house, up the steps, uninvited, moving as if on oiled hinges, impervious and opaque like the statue you wanted to appear. You asked a child the house, you asked for me. I hid, I did not wish to see you. You looked through the village, you found the headman and the astrologer. Before going you asked the astrologer to let you know if Moen returned, and gave him money, which he accepted, though he had no intention of saying anything to you. And now you are back, because in all the world there is no other place where you can be nearer to her than here.'

'Sylvie is dead,' said Philippe, grinding his teeth, which had a shiny concave surface. 'Dead. And you are responsible, just as responsible as we are, for her death.'

'As I am,' interrupted Jacques Rouvier, the doctor. 'Do not forget, Philippe, it was I who killed her. Unknowingly, but it was I who fired. It was an accident, but I cannot forget it, or forgive myself. Of all of you, mine is the greatest guilt, although accidental.'

'Good,' said Maté, spitting a long stream of blood-like betel

27

juice into a near-by shining green glaze spittoon, with a small whizz of her agile lips. 'Now we sit like a manacle of murderers, chained together by a death, and talk it over. Is that what you want? It is like tracing the moon's way across the sea, a bland, perilous highway, mirage of light in darkness, a tentacle waving us towards nothing. However, it shall be as you wish. Let me get my time right, first, for I am not out of mind with time, which is mind's overthrow, as you are.'

'Serene those whom time heals, like you, Maté,' said the doctor, 'but pity those obdurate against cure, as is this man.'

'His mind is at ease in the out-of-date wallow of his pet horror, as I said,' continued Maté. 'To cure would be to dispossess him, and he would be truly bereft. Look at the energy, the furious thin energy the man derives from this great hunt into the past. Were it not for him, we should all be gone to our siesta as by the sun and our Cambodian habit prescribed, but he and you will keep me up, awake and talking.'

'We can return later,' said Philippe contemptuously. 'We do not wish to disturb your customary repose.'

'No,' said Maté, 'for then I would be guilty of discourtesy, and rudeness is a real, true sin of social man. Let me but plant my feet into the past again . . . their soles feel mud. Yes, it was muddy where I found her that morning in the forest, muddy as only the lotus ponds can be. I was heavy then, carrying my one-before-last son. I believe a curse was laid upon me by a young man whom I had rejected as lover, that I bear sons only and no daughters. Although I did all in my power to have a daughter, I could only bring forth sons for other women's houses and other women's daughters, and had no daughter to own my house and rice fields and bring time round to make me young again in her children.

'That morning I was heavy with child. I had been anointed the night before with balm of woman-tree all over my body, and had walked to the house of a woman rich in daughters to steal her rice (with her pretence that she did not know, to deceive the wily spirits), as is our custom, a spoonful of rich-in-daughters-woman rice, and I had cooked it and eaten it. I went into the forest earlier than usual to cut leaves for my lying-in mattress, before the dawn could make visible a thread held between my fingers, and to call the spirit of my mother to help me in the birth to come, for she had often sat by the lotus pond and her memory could have lingered about its edges. And there I heard the wail of the child. At first I thought of forest demons and was afraid. My son was by my side, my son Rahit, and the child within my stomach kicked, and Rahit said to me: "I see a thing between the lotus leaves." I should have run backward away, but my body instead went forward, and I found her, Moen, whom I called Devi too in secret, although that name is royal and reserved for the children of Khmer kings. Her hair flowed like a white flame, and I knew her instantly, the daughter I had waited for, my daughter. I picked her up, seated her upon the unborn child, no longer wishing for a daughter. I brought her home, fed her, named her Moen the Lovely, Born of the Lotus, Devi.'

'I want to know,' said Philippe, bending his long face like an axe-gleam forward as if he would split Maté's round skull, 'what dress she wore when you found her. What colour?'

'What dress? What colour? It was the colour of our mud when I found her. I washed it carefully, but perhaps not carefully enough, for it tore. It may have been white, or pink, but it never turned into anything else but grey when I washed it. I could not get the lotus mud out of it. I cut it in squares and patched our clothes with them, and it all disappeared in the flood.'

'It was blue,' said Philippe, 'pale blue, smocked, with lace, and she had a blue ribbon in her golden hair. I can still see the ribbon, for that morning I had taken her on my back, playing horse to her, going round and round along the gravel walks of our garden, and I can still hear the gravel flying and hissing under my soles, and the ribbon slid off her hair and she cried, and I stopped and tied it back for her, and then I kissed her tears. Oh, Sylvie,' he cried, enraptured by his picture of himself under Sylvie in blue, in the sun in the happy garden by the white house, 'how lovely it was, our childhood, Sylvie. I shall never forget it, never.'

Maté drew on an Apsara cigarette. The betel was finished, her mouth was cleaned and happy with the burn of the lime and the sting of the mint she had chewed, and after puffing twice she went on: 'Moen was unhappy at first. She kept crying. Only crying.'

'Did she ask for me? Did she ever ask for me? Did she call my name, Philippe?'

'I do not remember,' said Maté. 'I do not remember her saying anything the first two days, only crying; and on the third she said

"Mama" to me, and then "Maté". I had to carry her everywhere, and at night she clung to me. Even when I gave birth she would not let go of me, I had her with me on the birthing mattress. The other children, with their father, stayed outside the curtain. I tried not to scream that she should not be frightened again. She held me tight, then she saw I was sweating. "Maté, you have water on your face," she said, and wiped my sweat with her small hands. And my pain left me at the touch of her love, and day came, the child was born, Chok, my fourth son, and he cried, a hardy, long, strong boy. Moen, who had watched with me, was no longer afraid. "See, Moen, I have made a little brother for you to play with," I said. As soon as Chok was washed Moen took him in her arms, for she had no doll, I had not had time to make a doll for her; but she had Chok as a doll.'

'Oh,' moaned Philippe, 'how dreadful it all is.'

'Philippe,' said Jacques, 'they have done their best, but of course they don't live as you do. I think it's rather beautiful myself.'

'I knew her better than you, Jacques. Sylvie was so sensitive, so delicate. To think of her, lying there, so frightened . . . And it was years before I could find her, give her what she deserved, what she was born to have.' Tears ran down Philippe's face. 'I kept her doll,' he muttered. 'They found her doll when I was in the hospital, and they gave it to me afterwards. It was a rag doll with fair hair and green eyes that opened and shut, and Sylvie called her doll Little Sylvie, her own name. Later when she came back I showed it to her, but she had forgotten, she had forgotten her doll.'

'Dolls only came with the electricity a few months ago to our village, after the police came to take Moen away from us,' said Maté. 'We now have Japanese dolls, and some have fair hair. But they are still too expensive for most of us. There is one for the school, and all the little girls play with it in turn.'

'Yes,' said the soothsayer, delighted, 'the world is larger now, we have electricity in the village, and radios even, and soon many other things.' He chuckled with satisfaction, and looked at his radio and at the bulb hanging from the ceiling.

'And independence,' said Maté, looking like a mother of revolutionaries.

'I see,' said Jacques, with irony, 'that our modern European diseases are spreading even to you and your village, O wise man. Your strip of individual loneliness has become too great for you, and your desires for objects to people the larger void you feel. Soon you, as we do, will call back for that ravishment, that seizing and losing of the self which gives us back a share of the paradise we lost, the paradise of the unconscious, of silent sociability with all things, away from the loneliness of too much individualization, away from too much defining, from the ambition of being exceptional and the horror of discovering one's own solitude. Electricity has come, as you say. The plague has come. The radio, your proud possession today, tomorrow will be the familiar property of every villager in Asia, and then you will stop thinking for yourselves. You will want the symbols of ownership rather than the possession of wisdom, ownership of gadgets to measure achievements in terms of the machine, that great socializer. And like us you will become its slave, slave to that master whose voice goes on, drip drip drip, moulding your spirit, wearing away its adamant to people the voice which haunts the cosmos for ever, the gibber in the middle of which we no longer hear ourselves. The great silence of the universe will be abolished, and the silliness of perpetual chatter replace it. You will no longer hear the smoulder of fiery metal in the stars, burning towards their own future. You will be deaf to that silent consultation of yourselves which we envy you without emulating you, for we are too much afraid of what we have done to listen to our consciences. All of you long to subject yourselves to that delicious, nefarious, haunting, disembodied sound which proves that you are not alone, and will take the place of friend, parent, village, will isolate you in your individual terror of loneliness. But you too will become like us, you too will go mad, O soothsayer, just as my friend, perhaps just as I am, as Maté will be now that she has begun to talk to us of the past. None will escape.'

'*Touché,*' said the astrologer. 'I see you understand, my friend, the dilemma with which the Lord Buddha wrestled. This confounded craving for more oneness, for restoring the merging into Life, balanced with this desire for asserting separateness, for being distinct from others, that is precisely what makes the Wheel of Life go on, the essential problem of each man, the one that makes him listen to the radio and consult the stars. The most tyrannical powers in the world proclaim loudly their great lust for power to serve the world; the Pope avers himself the least of the servants of the Lord, and what is humility but a more exacting tyranny to rule? I understand this as well as you do, but do not believe that I am a dupe of my own error. I know the mind has no neighbours, that the heart spends its love to draw men closer apart. All this was said twenty-five centuries ago, by the One who knew all words vain, yet still used words, the Lord of Compassion, Gautama Buddha. There is no end to this pendulum, my friend, and it is true that having talked with you we are all a little infected with madness. And we must all, leaving each other, find our salvation from this madness. I for one will retire to a monastery once again, and meditate in silence for six months. For we still have silence, you know, and even mechanical silence helps. I know now that I must break my beloved radio, or give it away. What will you do?'

'I don't know,' said Jacques. 'Am I mad? Is consciousness of aberration still lunacy? What will Maté do?'

Maté waved her head slowly about, meaning nothing. Then she answered Philippe: 'You say Moen suffered. It is true that at first she was not used to us. But later she was happy. When the floods came, and she lived, afterwards she was happy. Happy to survive, as we all are. She always wanted a little danger, a little fear in the middle of her happiness. She loved to hide, to run away, and to be found. Most children love to be frightened in order to be reassured, but she went on longer than most. She wanted so much to be loved. She still had to learn to love others, when you took her away.'

Philippe said: 'I could have taught her. She was beginning to love me, when she left. I think now that your son forced her, in the name of images of a happy past, a village paradise, a childhood together. He forced her with emotion.'

'He did not force her. She followed him. He was her brother, her friend, and her lover.'

'No,' cried Philippe, his face distorted with anger, 'I am her brother. I was teaching her, and she was learning from me. With me she would have learnt everything.'

'Everything? There was one thing you could not teach her, that my son gave her,' said Maté. 'The love of a man for a woman. You were her brother by blood; my son her brother by my love only. You could not marry her, not in this life. And you would have prevented her from loving any other man but you.'

'It is not true,' cried Philippe. 'She was my only sister. I wanted her happiness. I would have gladly seen her love someone who could make her totally happy. I would have given up everything to see her happy.'

'Everything except herself, Sylvie,' said the doctor, heavily. 'Do not pretend, Philippe. You know I loved her, and you tried to break that. I was the man who could have made her truly happy. But always you were with us, you never left us alone, and how cunningly you broke her early curiosity about another male. "Good old Jacques, *ce bon vieux*." "Old before his time." You turned me into a heavy, benign, fatherly figure of fun, and I put up with it, to be near her. But the necessary, delicate mystery which must exist between a man and a woman you broke, to make sure she would not love another man when you were there.'

'Oh,' said Maté, shutting her eyes so that only her mouth lived in her face, 'she must have suffered, Moen, suffered very much, caught between you with your constant talk, talk, talk. No wonder she tried to come back to me.'

'I don't believe it,' said Philippe. 'She ran away, but she did not return to the village, to you. I came here, I did not find her.'

'You came too early,' said the astrologer. 'Your sister was on her way back, back to the only refuge she knew, Maté the mother. But she never reached Maté. You killed her before she could reach Maté. All of you. Rahit, Philippe, Jacques, all three of you made her death.'

'Not Rahit,' said Maté, 'not my son. He loved her. He would never do Moen any harm.'

'Even Rahit,' said the astrologer sadly. 'I read the stars, and they tell me. Even Rahit.'

'I do not believe it,' said Maté. 'You cannot read the stars. You cannot even read all the words in a newspaper. I will die before I believe that Rahit harmed Moen.'

'As you wish,' said the astrologer. 'As a fish taken from water and thrown to dry land, your thought shivers to escape the dominion of truth, Maté. So be it.' And he looked solemn, and then a little anxious, somewhat deflated.

'Tell me of the flood,' said Philippe. 'Tell me what Sylvie did when there was the flood. She never talked to me of a flood. I want to know. What flood?'

'She was eight years old, and Rahit ten, when the monsoons came, longer and heavier that year than usual, and it rained without a stop for twenty days. The river swelled, its waves like dragons growling round the stilts of our houses. We burnt incense and we prayed; the old shaved their heads and went to the temple in the beating rain but the waters rose, every hour a little higher, higher, higher, so that the watchers by the river banks now fell back. One night the river broke, and charged across the rice-fields like a tribe of wild elephants. And the earth shook as the waters came stamping and roaring their mad roar, charging for our village. "Run, run," cried the watchers, and we ran. I carried Chok and another child, and Rahit carried Sylvie and my husband took the other two. In the confusion of the wind and the blind night, with the rain pouring upon us, we ran before the rushing waters. The Lord of Waters had gone amok, and the earth itself would be drowned. Beneath our feet soon there were no more fields, only water, water screaming about us, screaming for death. I heard Rahit shout, but could not turn back because of Chok and the other baby. My husband turned back, though he carried two sons, and it was then that they drowned, I think. I reached the upraised road, scrambling as it crumbled under me, and the waters washed over it and into the fields on the other side. But the road did give me a little more time to run, and there was a small hillock with trees and a shrine, and people had reached it and climbed on it; thick as the fish in the Great Lake when the barrages dam it and the fish rub their scales off on each other, the people of our village and another village crowded the hill.

'I put Chok and the baby down, then I went back and waded and swam, back to the road, but the road had melted away. I called: "Rahit, Moen, Rahit." Many were dying in the water, who tried to grab at me and called me, but I did not heed them. I went on shouting "Rahit, Moen," in the mouth of the wind, and suddenly I heard Rahit's voice, and there was Rahit, clutching a beam, for the houses were washed away now, the water was strewn with their wood. He said: "Moen, she is there, I hung her in the tree while I caught this beam." There was Moen, caught in the branches of a tree like a fish, by her hair and her clothes. We swam to her with our beam and pulled her on to it, and I thought she was dead, but she opened her eyes and said: "Maté", and I was happy, my heart swollen with happiness. I thought, this is not my daughter of my body, yet I love her more than if she were. Then I knew that the children given to us or born to us are truly the same, that Moen must have been my daughter in a previous incarnation, and given to me again, for what blessing and as a reward for what good deed I would never know. But thus it was. We swam about for hours, supported by that saviour wood, and I blessed it and still have it with me in my house. When dawn came we saw the hillock and climbed on to it again. That was the day I decided Rahit and Moen would marry each other, and I would keep my daughter in my house.'

'You decided,' said Philippe. 'You never asked her.'

'I did not ask her, because I knew it would be so. I knew that Rahit loved her. He looked after her all night long, and all the days we sat, waiting for the waters to furl their waves back into the river. Then it stopped raining, the sun came out, and we saw the corpses glistening like dead fish about us, bellies up, and through the days waiting for the waters to go down they stayed with us, the dead. And we hungered, except that Rahit went swimming out among the corpses to unhook fish from the tree tops where some were caught in the branches, but often he got none, for there were many of us on the hillock, some were strong men and women and they too went swimming for fish. And all the fish that Rahit caught he chewed for Moen and put in her mouth, for she was so ill, and he stood in the sun to give her his body's shade. Chok and the baby died, and only Moen and Rahit and I lived on, to watch the waters go.

'And Rahit already knew his mind, and I knew it too, and when Moen was better I said to them: "Your hearts must be a refuge for each other, for you have grown together, and now you have both survived the flood. So you must grow under each other's hands and eyes, more abundant and full of life through the years, giving each other life." And Rahit said: "Yes, that I shall be for her, shade in the sun and rice and fish in the pot, and our lives woven together from one incarnation to the next." And Moen laughed gently, for she was happy being loved.'

'What a hero you make of your son,' said Philippe. 'But Sylvie never mentioned him at all. Not once. All the months she was with me, getting used to the life that was hers by right of birth, and I could see her blossom, become really herself, her beauty growing in its proper setting, her intelligence developing, she never once mentioned Rahit. Now you would have me believe that they were

35

predestined for each other, that it was a Romeo and Juliet love begun in a flood. I find this difficult to believe.'

'They loved each other,' said Maté, 'and she left you because Rahit came to fetch her, and she followed him.'

'She left, yes, but in bewilderment, in confusion, submitting to some childish compulsion, nostalgia of the village she had known – even perhaps threats, who knows? She did not love your son, because Sylvie quite simply did not know what love was. Love of a woman for a man, I mean. In spite of what Jacques Rouvier says, who may know about women but does not know a young girl. Sylvie was pure, untouched, untouchable. She had real purity, and it made me feel I was nobler, more decent, when I looked at her. I, her brother, I knew my blood throb with her blood, I could feel the current between us, always . . . I would have known it, if she loved someone. Your son swept her off her feet with I know not what story, and she ran away. But he was not with her when my sister died, my little sister, all alone in the forest to meet her death.'

'She was coming back to me,' said Maté.

The astrologer said: 'You are both wrong. She was not going *back* to anyone. She was walking towards herself. Why do you think that on her way towards herself she was coming to you, Maté?'

Said Maté: 'She knew the refuge of my arms. I had saved her twice, given her a childhood, a house, brothers, and love, everything that makes a world. A world that everyone returns to, sooner or later. In that world she would have learnt to love Rahit. He loved her so much. No love like that can go unanswered. They were both returning to me.'

'Maté,' said Jacques Rouvier, 'at the moment you are being stupid, as if the inhibitions that attend us when we force ourselves into ordinariness had suddenly fallen upon you. You are afraid of exposing your son, Rahit. Afraid to blame him. Sooner or later, perhaps later than sooner, Sylvie would have left you too, as she left Philippe. Perhaps, then, she would have turned to me, for I was her only friend in all this, the only person who truly loved her and asked her for nothing in return but to become herself.'

'That,' said the astrologer, 'will be considered in its own place. Meanwhile, I would like to hear more from Maté. After the flood what?'

'My husband,' said Maté. 'And my two other sons. They were

drowned. I had almost forgotten them until now. That night I had forgotten about him, clinging with my two safe I felt happy, I did not think of the others. Such a strong man could look after himself. I had forgotten that the Water Gods take the ablest swimmer and spare the weakling. His corpse floated by many days later. I would not have recognized him, but Rahit did, or said he did. There were so many corpses, and the smell was so terrible after a few days that we could not mourn for them, only push them away with sticks. When the waters receded the monks burnt the bodies for us. Strange that it hurts me now to recall this after so many years, more than when it happened. It is this talk which forces one into emotions, feelings that are not real since the event is past. Suddenly I know myself old. I had five sons and a husband, and only Rahit is left, but he no longer is mine, and there is no man and no child in my house. I am alone.'

'You weep for yourself,' said Philippe. 'You are a selfish woman, it makes me glad.'

Jacques said: 'I realize now that neither of you know what it is to love. Each of you wanted Moen, or Sylvie, for yourself.'

'Who says so?' asked Maté. 'I wanted her happiness, and she was happy with us, because we loved her. When the school opened, I put her in school. Always she had the best food, the best of every-thing I could afford. I gave her more than to my own children. And Rahit is handsome and clever and loved her. And Rahit would have made her happy. What more can anyone have?'

'Not after she left you and lived with me,' said Philippe. 'My good woman, however handsome your Rahit, however good, she could no longer find him possible, for she became used to a higher standard of living. I could see her change, every day. With me she had all the things you could not give her: a large house, the most exquisite cuisine, servants, many dresses, and a modern life – much more than life in a backward village, Maté, where electric lights have only just come in. These things count, with a woman.'

Maté said: 'Then you were prostituting your sister with wealth. Perhaps it is true, that she changed a little, corrupted as only the rich can corrupt. But she left you anyway for Rahit, with Rahit. She was returning to me. This I know, and it cannot be changed, whatever you may say.'

'It would not have lasted,' said Philippe. 'I have proof, here in my hands, that she changed. I will play you this tape, and you will know. Do you wish to hear her voice again? For it is here, immortal.'

'No,' said Maté, closing her eyes and mouth.

'But you must,' said Philippe, joy flashing in his face. 'Here, whether you like it or not, you will hear it. I have brought the machine with me. I will play it for you.'

'Do not hurt me,' said Maté, 'more than I am hurt.'

'Ah, it is you now who fear pain,' cried Philippe, radiant. 'You are less strong than I thought. You fear a voice, a sound, the sound of your daughter's voice. I do not fear it, for I loved her.'

'He plays this tape to himself,' said Jacques to the astrologer, 'many times a day. He never gets tired of it. This is his road to Sylvie, tattooing loudly the pattern of his mortal pleasure and pain. I have never seen such obsessive actions, except in the insane. Hence I say he is mad, in part.'

'I should go easy on the word mad,' remarked the astrologer, conversationally, as Philippe fumbled with the machine in its leather casing. 'If I may say so, we are all in the same boat . . . and this metaphor, borrowed from your language, brings back to me an image of your Christian Middle Ages, of those *nefs des lunatiques*, vessels of the insane, lunacy afloat, the already-there of death, amiable in colours like a surrealist film of pleasure boat upon a pleasant river. The madman then was consigned to the waters, his boat's destination the sea. This image of madness makes me aware of the earth itself, our magnificent ship, peopled with madmen far more dangerous than your friend, with whom we have embarked towards what the stars hope will not be a universal disaster, the blood-laden seas of the Last Judgement. This Christian metaphor amuses me, we're all in the same boat.'

'I made clear,' said the doctor, 'that he was only mad in one way, otherwise as sane as anyone else. I mean, as normal.'

'You mean, otherwise within the dimension of the rational,' replied the astrologer, 'otherwise battered into rationality by words as continual as bells, awaking familiar echoes of compulsion. But, my friend, let me call you here nineteenth century, old-fashioned, in your choice of vocabulary. You as a physician should know that normalcy depends only on the administration of certain amino-acids, wherein the insane can become suddenly lucid and rational for hours together, until, with the exhaustion of the special nourishment their brain cells need, they fall back into dehiscence, incommunication. How do you know that I, who speak to you, am not a madman under the influence of a sanity beverage? How do I know that you are not an escaped lunatic with an ample temporary dose of methionine? No, go easy on the word mad, as on the word normal, I pray you. They are both elusive.'

'I would not have thought,' said Jacques, 'that in a Cambodian village I would have found articulate people as yourself, and Maté. I am utterly confused. I never thought this would happen.'

'Does it seem abnormal? Or merely irrational? And if so, why? At certain levels of consciousness the confines of the rational are effaceable,' said the astrologer, 'just as the limitations of time are ratiocinations to those who watch the behaviour of nebulae. Already in this world the centuries imbricate: in art the planes intermix, there is no past, present, or future when music draws its tentacles through our audiophonic brains. Why should we not, in this tranquil Cambodian village where there is only one radio set so far, mine (and I shall give it away, as I said), be as articulate as you are amidst the cacophonies you create? Really, my friend, you suffer from the closed mind of the cultivated person, just as they do in Paris.'

'Because,' said Jacques, 'I had not expected it.'

'Now,' said Philippe, 'listen.'

Voices:

Jacques: Now will you say something, anything? Don't be afraid, it's just a game.

Philippe, laughing: Oh, leave her, Jacques. She is still hypnotized by machines. Look at her eyes, like two great lakes the sky has fallen into . . .

Voice of girl, Sylvie, at which Maté's face suddenly lights up: But *what* shall I say?'

Jacques: The first word that crosses your mind. The very first.

Voice of girl, Sylvie: And what will it *mean*?

Philippe: Our dear Jacques will read your mind then, Sylvie, like an open book.

Sylvie, a little afraid: Oh, I don't want to be read.

Both men laugh.

Jacques: Come, come, dear little Sylvie, it won't hurt you one bit. Just try. Try. Ready, Philippe?

Philippe: Ready. You'll see how amusing it is, my darling, especially when you play it over. One's voice sounds quite different . . .

Jacques: I begin: city.

Sylvie: People.

Jacques: Red.

Sylvie: Blood.

Philippe, interrupting: How strange, Sylvie. I would have answered: blue.

Jacques: That is because you have a trivial mind, Philippe. Isn't it so, Sylvie? Your brother is so conventional.

Sylvie, simply: Oh, I don't think so. I think he is wonderfully clever.

Jacques: We continue: fruit.

Sylvie: Mouth.

Philippe, again: How charming. Sylvie, you are lovely.

Jacques: Quiet, please. Love.

Sylvie: What?

Jacques: Love. The first word that comes to you.

Sylvie: Nothing.

Philippe: How, nothing?

Sylvie: I can't think of anything. There is no word.

Philippe: How, no word? I can think of so many. Beauty. The sea. Sylvie . . .

Jacques: Oh, for heaven's sake, Philippe . . .

Sylvie: Well, then: brother. Love. Brother. Philippe.

Voice of woman: Philippe, are you there? I want to speak to you . . .

The tape-recorder stops.

Maté: 'Is that all?'

Philippe: 'Yes.'

Maté astonished: 'All? Nothing but that? Is that what you have been feeding on? What a vicious man you are!'

Philippe angry: 'Vicious? I do not think so. Say, possibly, too sensitive, unable to let time deface and dilute my feelings . . . yes.'

The astrologer: 'That woman's voice at the end, your wife? Yes?'

Philippe: 'My wife, yes.'

The astrologer, conversationally: 'But it is your friend, my friend now, the doctor, who sleeps with her, yes?'

Philippe, more angry: 'Yes. By God, yes, yes!'

Jacques: 'I protest. This is ignoble.'

The astrologer: 'Ignoble? How can the truth be ignoble? Facts are ignoble, but stating facts is not ignoble. In the dimension in which we have now propelled ourselves truth is possible, as you may have realized. Possible I mean, although falsehoods are occasionally permitted, as the Buddha permitted the snake to hiss in order to establish his nature as a snake, but they are to be labelled falsehoods.'

Jacques: 'You mean to say that we have all been telling the truth, all this time? This is astonishing.'

The astrologer: 'No. I mean that we have occasionally told falsehoods, but that they will be disclosed as such when we go on talking.'

Philippe: 'I am only beginning to appreciate it. All this time I thought I was the one who was a little mad, who needed what my friend, my *dear* Jacques, called psychological treatment. It was I who clung to the past. But now I see that Dr Rouvier also needs treatment. I want to stay in this dimension of truth, for it is domiciled at the confines of the normal, on the edge of extravagance and myth, and I feel that my Truth is Sylvie and my love for her. To that I shall cling with my last breath.'

Jacques: 'You always knew. About Anne and me.'

Philippe: 'And you dared to look at Sylvie. You dared. Sylvie, who was Purity and Innocence incarnate. My sister. That is why I wanted her to leave with me. I had bought the tickets. We were going to Europe, Sylvie and I. Back to France. I would have shown her everything, opened her mind, her spirit . . . away from this dirty village, stinking of fish and manure; away from you, Jacques, your lecherous, middle-aged man panting after her youth, away from Anne, with her bickering jealousy, her silliness, her need to prove herself female –'

Jacques: 'Stop, Philippe, stop. Don't say any more.'

Maté, simply, to the astrologer: 'How Moen must have suffered, among these people. See what they are. No wonder she came back to me.'

The astrologer: 'Only the going and the goer make the road real, Maté. You were the tangled tree in the flood for her, the saviour wood; you too would not let her go.'

Maté: 'You are wrong. I would have saved her again, I would have given her –'

The astrologer: 'Rahit? *Your* son? What is love, Maté?'

Philippe: 'What do I care what you do with Anne, Jacques? She is stupid, a thoroughly second-rate woman. I was relieved, my dear Jacques, when I knew it was you, and not that bastard Moniveau whom I had suspected, but his partiality for Asian cabaret girls made him impotent with European women. The reason why Solange Moniveau, his wife, was also available to you, I imagine. Hence the hunting party, to which you dragged me, hence the murder of my sister Sylvie. I am beginning to think you wanted to kill her.'

Jacques: 'Philippe, you are mad. Yes, I am Anne's lover. A nice woman, thoroughly neglected. A simple woman, and I am soft-hearted, the cry of a human being for help moves me. She needed reassurance, as a woman. You neglected her, were cruel, in your reticent, detached way. As for Madame Moniveau, that is nonsense. She was angling for you all the time. And you knew it. That is why, pretending to look for Sylvie, we all went out on safari with Solange Moniveau.'

The astrologer: 'May I remind you, gentlemen, that time is money, even in our village? Is there anything else you wish to know about your sister's past?'

'Anything else?' cried Philippe. 'But you have not told me anything, not anything. She, so alive, so smiling, so real, you are now making her escape me with your lucubrations, as if she too were but a watery reflection of my mind.'

'That is always so, when one talks about things,' said the astrologer comfortingly, 'they evanesce into description.'

'It is not so,' cried Philippe, brandishing his tape. 'This, this is real. And as you pointed out before, thanks to our machines, voices have now become eternal and universal, prolonged to the ends of time and space, reverberating echoes in the outermost nebulae. They are as tangible as star-dust. And this is what I want of you. I want to make Sylvie immortal, not only in me, but through me, to every-one –'

'Ah,' cried the astrologer, turning with laughter to Maté, 'he wants to do knowingly what Rahit does all unknowing.'

'What else does the man want?' Maté complained. 'Have I not told him all? That we loved her, that she was happy, that all was well until the police came and took her away from us? And now

I have to spend my love on other things, other people. I cannot sit and mourn, mourn for my daughter taken away and my son lost, for have I not a sum of blessing in me to render to life which goes on for ever? To dwell in a pleasant land, right desires in the heart, not weary in well-doing – the monks taught me this when, after Moen the beloved was gone, I shaved my head, forsook the world and wanted to bury myself into sorrow. But this was not Right Action or Right Intention, for I burnt with fires of anger and ignorance, unworthy of refuge in the Wisdom that knows not Good or Evil. What else does this Frenchman want? Look around you. For all this is part of Moen too: the new wells, the road our village women built, and this electric light you deride, to you no miracle but to us night-blindness abolished. You who do not know what it means to a child to be unable to read in the evening, after the fields have furled their colours and the work is laid down, look at this and see Moen in this too. All this would have come, certainly, but I helped it to come, I and many others, and I only did it because I had life and to spare, left-over life after Moen went away. Is not this echo and star-dust enough, endless germination in others of what once was Moen?'

'How selfish she is,' said Jacques, smooth with joy.

'You call me selfish because I have no merit in all this but the merit of having been bereft,' said Maté. 'The lotus grows impeccable out of mud. Rice, the body-nourisher, needs the body's dung to grow wholesome. Which is wiser, you or the wind which sows tomorrow's flowers? Yet you call me selfish?'

'Quiet, quiet,' said the astrologer. 'Remember, both of you, that the Lord of Justice said: "Neither the flesh of fish, nor fasting, nor nakedness, nor tonsure, nor matted hair, nor dirt, nor fire, nor the many immoral penances that men do, nor hymns nor oblations nor sacrifice, purify a man so long as he doubts." '

Jacques said: 'Doubts what? God?'

'There is no God,' replied the star-wise man. 'An old pine-tree preaches wisdom, and a wild bird is crying out truth. Within the mystery provided for the purpose of living, there can be no doubt. Maté is right, soldering the abyss of grief with the air of action.'

At that moment Jacques turned as if called, shading his eyes, blinking at light beyond their long-fringed lids. 'My God, there is Anne. What is she doing here? How did she find us?'

'I think you must have called her, both or one of you,' said the astrologer, as Philippe turned also, in surprise and some apprehension.

'Yes, it is Anne. I didn't hear a car.'

Anne comes up the stairs with tapping medium heels, a palely blonde woman whose face creases easily. In the morning waking up she is at her best, and her face deteriorates visibly during the day. She appears to have the chronic tiredness of blondes in the tropics, an exudation of ennui, malice, and fatigue. But this is not true, for Anne is actually a Valkyrie, a Fury, a Gorgon, when aroused. And the creases that grow on her are not due to age, they are a product of her thoughts and her temperament, and both during the waking hours beat relentlessly at the truth and the trivia which tear her life between them. With a little more of either she could have been an actress, or a doctor in philosophy, or a revolutionary; but her environment has bred out of her persistency, and her education has done nothing except to canalize her energies in the most useless occupations a woman of her class could assume. All this is written on her face, more deeply etched as day erodes itself around her, most startling at night when, with make-up hiding nothing, she fulfils the duties to which her position assigns her, well dressed, brittle-voiced, and desperate, the successful hostess of the dinner parties of the season.

Anne: 'We are a little late, Rahit and I. Because of the flood on the way.'

Maté exclaimed: 'Rahit? Rahit is with you?'

Philippe, irritably: '*What* flood, Anne? There is no flood. The road is intensely dry. Look at the dust on my clothes.'

Anne: 'You were never observant, Philippe. Water covers the rice fields on each side of the road. At one spot it spills over it. And there is an accident, a bad smash-up. They are heaving away the debris. I thought for a moment it was your car. Same make and colour. But your car is here, intact. You too.'

'Of all the coincidences,' said Jacques.

Maté: 'Rahit? You say Rahit is with you?'

Anne: 'Yes. He gave me a lift on his bicycle. He stopped to chat with his uncle, the headman.'

'I must see him,' said Maté. 'Rahit may be hungry. I must cook rice.' She ran down the steps, agile as a girl.

The astrologer said: 'We were discussing Sylvie, madame.'

44

'Of course,' replied Anne, looking round and electing one of the two armchairs for show, so that she appeared regal, the men at her feet. 'Always Sylvie. No one else has ever existed for Philippe, except Sylvie. He married me because I looked like Sylvie, although at that time he said "a blonde Modigliani". So trite, don't you think? But then he never was very original, Philippe, although he fancies himself a poet, especially after an excellent business deal. Do not protest, *mon cher*, it is so. You wanted to marry your souvenir, unfortunately you married a woman.'

'I left you free to be a woman, Anne, in your own way.'

'Except,' said Anne, 'that a mortal blow is dealt to a woman when she finds her husband relieved that she should take a lover. She does not recover from such complaisance. I married you, Philippe, because I loved you. At first I did not know I was fighting against that most potent, undying shadow, your sister. That impalpable, molesting, damask scent of someone else was ever between us. I learnt it the first afternoon, when the Vice-Consul and the police brought her back, brought her into our house, and you were in the hall, waiting for her, and you said: "Yes, yes, that is Sylvie, my Sylvie, my sister, at last." And I was on the stairs, a little above you all, looking at the scene stamping me an intruder in my own house. Later, the hours, the days, you spent acclimatizing her, you called it. The hours in the living room, on the veranda, in the garden, in her own room, talking at her, talking to her, to make her remember, you told me. You came away from these duologues repulsive, repulsive, hands shaking, face sweaty and illumined, as if you had had a stroke. You smelt of rut, though nothing happened, as you would put it, as I knew.'

'Anne,' said Philippe, 'how base you are.'

'Base?' said Anne. 'Because I tell the truth?'

'Do not worry, monsieur,' said the astrologer, 'you are safe with truth at this level.'

'She cannot hurt me,' said Philippe. 'My love for Sylvie is the purest, the most beautiful, and the most sincere thing in my life. She cannot hurt me with her lies.'

Anne laughed. Her laughter was remarkable. She laughed like a seal barking, with expletions, inhalations, raucosities, spasms, stoppages, a rampage of sound in no wise connected with gaiety, which made people at cocktail parties turn round and smile and whisper, or with raised eyebrows indicate that it was Anne Bergerat laughing.

Her laughter was the first thing that had become odious to Philippe, and later he always used it to justify his disgust of her, as a man hooks his overcoat on the strongest hanger. In him it inspired a counter-rhythm of fastidious, elegant diction, and restrained gesture, as inevitable as the traffic-roar of great cities creates sound-proof rooms. The astrologer stared at the willowy woman who should have been all undulation, susurration, equivocation, allusion, and had become all angles, even in mirth.

Anne continued, imposing, almost grandiose, in the grotesque baying laughing from her throat. 'Pure,' she hiccupped, a sea-lion vocalization, 'pure. You do not know the facts of life, my dear. You've spent all your time obfuscating their lineaments. As if *every* brother did not desire his sister, as if every man's dream had not dwelt for a while on a sister, with more pertinacity perhaps on a cousin, sister at one remove, before sallying forth to the unknown, strange freedoms of other women. Show me the man who has not dreamt of sleeping with his sister. It'll be a eunuch born.'

The astrologer nodded. 'In that respect the Egyptians were wise, and some of our old traditions maintain that tale. But you did not speak, madame, in apt time. If you had told your husband about this interfering shadow, he might have understood himself, accepted the normal divarication of his desires, and slept with you again.'

'Impossible. Philippe would never step out from the profile he had invented of himself. I knew why he had married me when I saw her, and it was more than I could bear to put in words. So I hovered about them, in my turn a hampering shadow, fruitful with ripeness of my hatred. To talk would have been charity, simplicity, Christianity, and you know, Mr Astrologer, that we women are never Christian, never.'

'What fury,' said Jacques. 'What passion of loathing I did not know, Anne . . .'

'Did I not play well, Jacques, did I not?' replied Anne, suddenly radiant. 'I even used you. Most successfully. Soon you three were inseparable. You three. Always in each other's way. And me, malicious, irritable, to be shrugged away: "Anne has one of her headaches." But always watching.' Again she heaved the air with multiple joyful barks.

'You take too much upon yourself, Anne,' said Jacques. 'I am not a player in this perverted game, however much you put me in. I loved Sylvie because she was so intelligent. So unusual. A French girl of good family, losing her parents in tragic circumstances, brought up by a Cambodian village woman, at fifteen taken away from an Asian village, restored to her brother, to a French environment. I watched her mind develop, make adaptations so startlingly quickly. I understood her first surly reluctance. Philippe did what he could to make her remember the past. I too tried to help. I understood her so much better, if I may say so. After all, I was trained for this work. Sylvie did not want to remember, for when her brother spoke to her of their childhood she was brought face to face only with terror, the terror of the Japanese attack, the face of the Japanese soldier, the horrible spurt of the motor-cycle; and then the forest, savage, sinister, haunting, the mud, the loneliness, until Maté. It was of Maté she thought when he spoke of mother, it was the village she saw when he spoke of home, and when we talked of love she was silent, because she spoke the truth, she did not really know love, except that her feeling for Rahit was shameful, unmentionable in *our* company, *our* environment. She knew that to pronounce the word Rahit was dangerous, because of Philippe. So she turned to me, came to the hospital where I worked. Anne, you brought her there deliberately, stayed deliberately with her. The solicitous sister-in-law, seeking to amuse, to interest, to instruct the savage little girl plucked out of her hut on stilts and brought to the benefits of civilization. Also the woman of the world, coming to see her lover in irreproachable friendship, Sylvie your chaperon. Also, at other levels, all your other schemes I did not know. I did what I could to abolish this ignoble hide-and-seek, though I was not aware of it. I sought to turn Sylvie from the past, where Philippe held her, turn her to the future. I fell in love with her. She became the one real love of my life, though I do not spread it out in dazzling adjectives, as Philippe does. And she, I think, would have learnt to love me, if Philippe, sensing that she was escaping him, had not deliberately destroyed my image in her eyes, emphasizing the father and teacher side of me rather than the virile male. He castrated me in her mind with his "dear old fellow" and "the wise doctor has pronounced himself", made her feel that any feeling for Dr Rouvier other than esteem would be incest. And all the time –'

'All the time,' interrupted Anne, 'she was protected by another image, the image of Love itself, become potent by absence. For even if she did not love Rahit as a man when she was taken from the village, she began to love him in her room when Philippe left her alone. Rahit became the God of Love in a mirror, and when he appeared in the flesh she did not look twice to recognize the countenance she had created.'

Philippe said: 'I would like to see this Rahit, this village hero. I do not believe my sister would love a rustic. As Anne says, she was in love with love, with the image of a boy she had grown up with. But very soon the natural differences (for, after all, they were not of the same class or breed, or even, to use a malefactory word, the same race) would have become obvious. She was too young and pure to know love.'

Anne said: 'No one living in a village hut, crowded in a space ten feet by twelve, is pure in the sense you mean.'

'I said pure, not ignorant.'

'We should ask Maté about that,' replied Anne. 'But, of course, Rahit will be able to tell us when he comes.' And she looked at Philippe with deadly fury, all the more oppressive for her sudden silence.

The astrologer, feeling the leaden colossus of her rage raping the air about him, murmured: 'There is no shark like hatred, no flood like greed. The Lord Buddha said: "Take a ploughman from the plough, and he rules a kingdom."'

'I have learnt so far,' said Philippe, cutting in, 'that only I knew how to love Sylvie, and I do not fear Rahit. Let him come. Let him confront me. If it had not been for the treachery of Jacques and Anne, Sylvie would be with me, happy, in Europe.'

'Monsieur,' said the astrologer, 'I am supposed to read in the planets events which orbit out of the range of my own perceptions, and I have seen this in the stars: a sea, sand, your sister stretched, the first woman-child of world, and you by her side, knowing, knowing, *knowing* her in love with someone not-you.'

'Philippe,' said Jacques, 'the day we went to the sea. You knew.'

'What do you mean?'

'He means the bangles,' said Anne. 'Those two poor little glass bangles, so cheap-looking, she wore round her wrist. You took them from Sylvie, Philippe. She kept looking for them. While she was swimming, laughing with the water lapping her, a child for the first time acquainted with sea's swaddle, you took them from her bag, broke and buried them in the sand. I was not asleep, my eyes were open under the sun-glasses.'

The astrologer: 'Rahit will make a song of all this, because he is a poet, and poets make songs out of everything, even the murder of their mothers.'

'A village poet,' said Philippe. 'How diverting. Tell him this story, if you wish. I did not like the look of those bangles on my sister's slim arm. So cheap. It was time I took them away, bought her a Cartier wrist-watch instead. And she never mentioned them afterwards. They did not mean anything to her.'

'Liar,' said Jacques. 'I knew her better. She never mentioned the bangles because she knew that you had made them disappear.'

'I will tell you one thing more,' said Anne. 'It is not because you want only Sylvie's past that you came. You are dying to see Rahit, her lover. Dying to see the one who took Sylvie away from you. Jacques too. Both *voyeurs*, impotent themselves, dying to see others make love. Am I not like that myself? I would have liked to see all three of you making love, in front of me, on the beach. And the horror, the disgust, the regret afterwards ... that would have been pleasure for me. And the comedy you played between you, it fed my fury to see you play at playing it, at laughing, at teaching Sylvie, while all the time you wanted to murder each other.'

Jacques said: 'Anne, stop, stop. Philippe is bad enough, don't try to outdo him.'

'Here is Rahit,' said the astrologer. 'I see he has not changed. Welcome, Rahit. Maté your mother went to look for you.'

Rahit places his bicycle, of Cambodian make, neatly against the side of the house, and strokes the muzzle of the bullock once as his hand leaves the handle-bar and as if it were part of the same gesture; his legs move, and he comes up the stairs, his actions following one another in the continuous, flowing movement of a wind-bent flame moving along the wood it burns.

He looks like Maté in the face, mouth, high cheekbones, golden skin, brown eyes, smile. His body is slim like all Khmers', but with strong legs, and large shoulders with the pectoral muscles emphasized, their lower edge going almost horizontally to the arm-bone. He is naked to the navel, with a loin cloth, has tied his shoes by their shoe-laces and dangles them in his hand; his bare feet have mobile toes, each one full of its own independence,

49

so that at any moment one feels he will climb a palm tree with these feet much like hands; and it is his feet which make Philippe mutter, loud enough to be heard: 'Almost simian.'

There is not a hair on Rahit's body, his skin is smooth; only his dark hair waves, springs from his head with a life of its own, as if it could wing itself away. It is a casque of hair that Rahit has on his round skull.

And so it is with all of him. Every separate part is separately beautiful and has come together by willingness. He moves, completely unconscious, never bumping into anything, because all things round him are also come together by willingness. He does not seem to know anything about himself at all.

And Anne's eyes go up and down Rahit, up and down. Her nostrils smell him. But it is not lust, it is a recurrent surprise. Anne becomes likeable, though her frustration does not permit her to be amiable.

'Tell these men,' said Anne, with imperious coquetry, 'you are a poet, Rahit.'

'How can men speak of what happens to them otherwise than in words that adorn? How can bullocks pull willingly if not rewarded with necklaces?' replied Rahit.

'I have heard this before,' said Jacques. 'Poetry, not an art object, but spontaneous, of the people. Very social-realist. Asia today. Poets not special, poetry a natural function of the human spirit.'

Rahit, a little defensively: 'I sing words as they come to me, and don't think before or after.'

The astrologer: 'Sing to us then, Rahit, now that you are, like us, delivered into the dimension of absence of fear, the dimension called Nearly Truth, sing to us of Moen the beloved.

For they have come, these three, giving themselves astute and complicated reasons for their journey;
And you and I know how the journey ended, then began again.
But they do not know, yet, what has happened to them.
They are hungry, these meagre ghosts, for words,
To explain their games to themselves, to tell them once again that they are clever;
All their lives they have lived by words to prove themselves clever,
Consumed words at their mothers' laps, to tell them right from wrong.
Used words to deceive words, to cheat themselves at cheating.

Until the universe was non-existent if not put into words for them,
Their own emotions, strange, unknown to them if unworded.
That is how they have lived, until today.
Today, O poet, you must tell them words again,
To release them for the time before them,
Release them from what they call the past, which is only words already
    elaborated,
To feed them for the passage which they shirk, beyond the flood,
Word to come.'

Rahit said: 'Give me a cigarette first. I can never make up poems without smoking now. The song of my thoughts needs this exhalation to carry it out of my mouth. I need it, as a young bird needs pushing out of nest, its wings hardening and drying, the stronger the farther it flies. It was not so before I went to the city, but now the city has made me need smoke to forget that I stand between my word and its mouth. Then my melody will soar into a sky of its making, the child's kite, needing to sustain it but the nourishing wind of heaven.'

Philippe said: 'Sylvie left you, did she not? In the forest?'

Anne said: 'Rahit, I want to see them in pain. I suffered too much. Sing and let me see them wither in the blast of your song.'

The astrologer: 'Rahit, it is said that the word of the poet alone flouts destiny, revives the past, gives the lie to death. These three have been talking of love, but they are not poets and love has eluded them. Rahit, sing of love.'

Rahit said: 'There is no happy or unhappy love, no pure or impure love, no love that is useless. There is only love, to be lived in all its forms, love in whose shadow we all live. All loves are valid, and all loves are imperfect. As the trees of the forest eat away the stone face, gouge its eyes and twist its lips, so encroaching time eats the face of love, blinds its sight and seals its singing mouth. As the field is left to forgetfulness when the village goes, plague-possessed, crossing water to a new clean land, so do our bodies of love waste after its passage, and in this forgetting we grow new again towards the same word, the same yearning, in another time, another place. For even the Lord of Compassion loved man so much that he comes back, again and yet again, taking upon himself the face that is to be eaten by worms, the body that is to fester in putrescence, so that love can be manifest and live, from death to death.'

Anne said: 'Rahit, stop being religious about love. Tell these men they don't know what it is.'

Rahit said: 'It is difficult for an intellectual to love. I do not wish to offend, but the Lord of Justice, the Buddha, said that speech must be bold as a lion, gentle as a hare, pointed as an arrow, evenly balanced as a waist held by its middle, and deadly as the serpent: intellectuals have the conceit of their ignorance, and the ignorance of their conceit. These are the worms that gouge the eyes of love for them.'

Jacques replied, somewhat impatiently: 'I do not dispute that for an intellectual, as you put it in your Asian fashion (and Asians use the word with a mixture of reverence and scorn, derision and respect, which points only to the disruption of their own traditions which they have suffered at our hands), it is difficult to "love", as you say with such whole-hearted candour.

'Intellectuals are too much aware of themselves. Their obsessions with their own perplexity occupy them fully, for in their problems they see a reflection of the world's ills. They hear with exultation their own heartbeat. All for them is pretext to masturbate their souls, in order to produce an orgasmic flow of phrases. Apt phrases, elliptical enough to give the sensation of a prodigious skilful leap, an electric carbon arc flashing across a gap, a coded message unde-cipherable to the non-initiate. All is turned to feed their unquiet and delicate attentive self, for the universe revolves within their stomach.

'But this is not only our doom; to you, Rahit, this will also come. You are still exploring the unknown, superbly unconscious, like a baby you need no other presence to urge your piercing curiosity. You still have what we have lost, spontaneity, non-awareness. An elemental tranquillity permits your poetry to flow like breath. But already awareness is coming, already you need a cigarette to set you off, where once the mechanism worked without urging. Soon you will need the Other One, the presence of the palpable, valid inter-locutor, to talk to; a public-faceted mirror-image, what the Others want. And that will be the end of you. You will be split in two, to survive becoming the bodiless voice, trailing its body behind it at safe distance. You will become the watcher, the actor, the director, and producer of your own film, and this film will be you, and you will be wondering how to utilize it to get most applause, and you will die, self-consumed, or become mad and cannibalistic like my friend. You will never love again, but make a show of love, with the hope of making it serve for a poem to move more people to the ghost image of love-that-is-not.'

'In the paradise of intellectuals,' said Anne, sneering, 'there is no place for the un-motivation-conscious. All must be made explicit in syllables.'

Rahit said: 'I live in the shadow of a love that was waiting for life and its own renewal every day. I count myself fortunate that it darkened my existence before I needed smoke like green water at the heart of summer to commemorate its passing.'

Anne turned to Jacques, and she was speckled with the gold in her hair, suddenly untired, alive like golden snakes stretching after sleep: 'I told you, he is a poet.'

Jacques: 'Women are always partial to the word poet.'

'I too,' said the astrologer, 'am a poet stargazer. When I look at their astral leer, wondering what to say next, I sometimes lose control of myself, navigate beyond my body poised beside the chequer-board, forget the client bow-arched in expectancy, into the impossible blueness of the word love, all the more poet for the stellar definitions I coin of that word.'

'I begin to believe, with Rahit, in beauty and truth and even, yes, even a purity, far from the acid derision of Philippe's,' said Anne. 'Rahit's brain is not atomized with the fissions of explicativeness, his heart is not creaking at the joints with the rheumatics of chalk-filled literatures. With Philippe I had to become of the lecherous, careless species that fills the drawing-rooms and tans its skins on the beaches of fashion. Now Philippe has nothing left except his sister's purity to chew over. But I have Rahit, and my life steps straight. I shall learn to live well now.'

Philippe said: 'You are boring us, Anne, with your latest enthusiasm.'

'Anne,' said the stargazer kindly, 'the less of yourself you put into a thing, the nearer to the truth will it be. Poetry has feet of marvellous alabaster, and her eyes are the rainbow, and in the deepest mine and on the highest tower sings in the same clear voice. There is no need for you to worry whether beauty, truth, and purity exist. We intercept the planets with our wills, and live in their penumbra, as Rahit dwells in the shadow of his love, however perfect or hideous it might be. Does it matter? What need of further probing? Learn silence, which will teach you to listen for the thunder in a bee's wing. Is that not enough?'

'Is there nothing real, then?' asked Anne. 'Nothing more solid than words? Nothing sure? Are we all prancing on the quicksands of our own apprehensions? I cannot live like that. I must have something to cling to. And revenge did well, until Rahit. Now Rahit is, and must prove me alive. Do you know, Rahit, that it is these two who killed your Moen, your love? That it was I who drove them to it? Not directly ... the Furies who led men never goaded them directly. But I brought this about, none the less.'

Rahit said, without listening to Anne: 'The songs I make of love remember themselves, do not need debate or battle with carved stone or blank paper. Our children sing them, is not that enough? My songs are safe with Death, the only apparition exempt from change, because they do not strive for immortality. My love is safe with its murderers.'

Anne said, disappointed: 'I don't understand you, Rahit.'

The astrologer, a little annoyed, explained: 'We Buddhists look upon ourselves scientifically. We know that all matter is an affair of wave-length, like the metre, whose definitive length is equal to $1,656,763 \cdot 83$ wave-lengths, in vacuo, of the radiation corresponding to the transition between the levels $2P10$ and $5D3$ of an atom of Knypton 86.

'So is individual man but one of an onward movement in the poured cornucopia, the endless stream of Existing. So is Rahit but a singing filament in the great shroud which wraps all towards the renewal in extinction. He, as you and I, dwells in Possibility, roofed by Becoming, resurgent in the dateless dynasties of the millions to follow. And we exist by witness, completed only in others; as assembled in this house, we become defendants and judges and guardians to each other, sharing nearly all in this domain of Near Truth. Do you understand?'

'What I want to understand,' said Philippe, 'is not your Buddhist jargon –'

'But it's scientific,' protested the astrologer. 'Ask your nuclear physicists, they are all becoming neo-Buddhists –'

'– but what Rahit has to say for himself. What he did to my sister, which brought on her death. For as I look at him I can perceive nothing that would have attracted a girl like her. And since I am paying for the truth, let him tell the truth.'

'I remember,' said Rahit, 'the lemon savour of that morning when Maté, my mother in this life, carrying within her body Chok my brother, took me to the forest pond, where the lotus raised their lucid monarchies above their slime-bred stems, and the cicadas tyrannized the air in senseless praise of heat. The mud squelched between our toes, sucked at the soles of our feet, water and earth breeding their populous myriads. And then a cry, of the born, not ghost, not demon. Maté went forward, and found Moen.

'Moen was with us, and became everything that marvels, glories, dreams; eyes, ears, tongue, and skin in prodigious sun investing my being and making it sing in cicada joy. The whole earth was a lotus, and Moen its heart. Her eyes the Great Lakes with no horizon, her hair stirred the winds of Will, and her hands the moon's volcanoes. I sang then, words poured from me easily as the river rises after the monsoon. I became a poet without knowing the category, only that in our village at night we sat, dancing and clapping hands, and someone would call: "Rahit, Rahit, sing the new." And newness would come, because Moen was, and I never knew anyone's face, for each day I discovered their face for the first time.'

'Words,' said Anne. 'Words too, Rahit, from you. Newness. Discovery. My God! You should have seen the newspapers this morning. A crowd in Oran stamping to death a small twelve-year-old because he is Arab. Rape and murder and horror everywhere, and no distinction now between ourselves and what we called the non-evolved, all labouring the same manure pit of brutality. And in the Congo the tribesmen go to war wearing dinner-jackets and ties and black dancing pumps, their best clothes now, replacing their tribal outfits of masks and magic tattoos; they engage in single combat still, as they have always done, not knowing the refinements of push-button massacres, and the victor eats the vanquished, as we do by gorging an impersonal death with cadavers. Then you talk of ecstasy and newness. It's obscene.'

Jacques said: 'There have always been horrors. That doesn't mean that beauty, purity, ecstasy, don't exist, as well for a Cambodian peasant as for me.'

'No,' Anne said, 'they don't really exist for you, or for me, Jacques. The words remain, the reality that stung us like a steel blade, upset us with its quiet earthquake, has ceased to function. Only for Rahit I believe it exists. But he also begins to disgust me.'

'Continue, Rahit,' said the astrologer. 'Though time waits for us, it will not wait for ever. Maté is cooking rice for you.'

Rahit said: 'I give you my memories, word and feeling faithful to each other as substance and shadow, uncautious birds singing in trees, a myriad suns twinkling in puddles after rain, all the leaves of the forest shaken like green bats. Moen loved to look at herself in the water, watching her moving face in the inconstant glass, and I watched her reflection in my eyes, loving substance and image, and one afternoon drank the water that held her face imprisoned for a while, and she laughed at me and called me silly and danced away.

'One night, when the drums beat and the men played flutes or sang, we festooned the smoke of our fires with weaving hands and feet, not touching, following each other in the willowing procession of the dance. Sometimes she danced far, sometimes next to me, the distance between us making closeness true, keeping us together with filigree certainty.

'I bought her two bangles, blue as her eyes, green as her eyes, peacock eyes when she opened them wide upon me, saying: "Nothing. I have nothing to say." I thought her unfathomable and satisfactory, as the great sky, seeing everything in this nothing ... She had nothing to say, all she wanted was happiness, and in this she was true as the sunflower to the sun. She ran after happiness all the time. Sometimes she hid, playing a game with herself, pretending herself lost, only to find herself again, and to be found, to resurrect the happiness of being found. "You love to be loved," I said to her one day, a little sad, for she had laughed at me and I loved her so much. I gave her the bracelets, thinking I was giving her love. "They are pretty, I like them," she said. She never said a word that was untrue.'

'Your bangles,' said Philippe coldly, 'are in the sea. I threw them in the water.'

'I know,' said Rahit. 'When she had returned to me, she returned without them, and that is also why she died.'

'I would have you know,' said Anne, 'that Rahit spent a night under our roof, with your sister Sylvie, in her room. *I* arranged it, Philippe. Part of my revenge. I never spent a happier night with you than that night, thinking of what was happening in the next room while you turned your back on me and went to sleep.'

'Have I said that you were vicious, Anne? You are vicious and dirty.'

Jacques said: 'Like all women, Anne likes to play Providence.'

'Continue, Rahit,' said the astrologer.

'So we grew up. And I did not know the shame of love convicted of itself, withheld from self-knowledge which kills. Through the flood, and the years afterwards, I had to be the man in my mother's house, do all that men do except make love, grown up while still a child. I knew the quickening of all I did because of the bloom of the lotus, Moen, beloved of the moon, a constant tropic, ruby of the noon. And how tall and strong one grows in the enamoured day! Love was the spanning air and the refreshing breeze, and the tall, approachable sun thrust an easy grace among us. We grew up.

'After the flood, I built my mother-in-this-life Maté's house again. With Maté and Moen helping, we chopped the limbs of trees, praying that the sap forgive us, and pared the wood with love, though our axes stirred with harshness to mutilate a thing of life. Thus our stilts were put up and the house made. The fields dried and we planted rice again. We had no buffalo left to plough the mud, but I drove the plough, with Maté and Moen pulling, in place of the buffalo, and all we did with hands of love, though gruelling and harsh, and so we did not die, but lived to eat again, to sleep, to laugh.

'In two years we had robbed back from the thieving waters what they had taken. All of us in the village built a school, and Moen went to school in the day and taught me at night when the work was done. Maté wove baskets and sold them to buy the oil for the small earth-lamp I needed to clear the night in front of the letters I read.

'We grew up. And I remember, like pools of green water in summer thirst, trifles bricked together as tiles of roof, solid against the doubting weather. Watching the sky's peacock's eyes mimic Moen's, with clouds as flecks parading both, with other children flying kites in the flying month of dexterous strings. With food grew many children, and they became to us the brothers that had died in the flood, and there was another Chok, not of Maté my mother, but that did not matter, and he came with us for he loved Moen, and she played with him as she had with her doll Chok, my brother. We ranged the childhood we were leaving behind us, exploring the world without and within us, and never expounded to or having to expound, ripening out of sight and speech. And I remember Moen one day flying the kite of this Chok, when I saw the high-stepping wind stoop to eat in her hand, beckoned by her string, obedient to the wrestling suspense of that great eye of paper she stretched to mount heaven itself, as if seeking the Lord of Life in its see-saw ascent of air.

'I remember her laughter at the grinning over-horror of the stone demons when one day we lost ourselves by the stone that remembers, which our ancestors carved, Angkor the wonderful, the lost, to commemorate immortality, from which they died. And all the forest round began to laugh with her. Then I understood the stone that speaks, the stone that dances, until now but profile of the excellence of death, become to me a song beyond the grave, proof against dissolution. Her laughter had compelled a total resurrection. I knew myself a fragment of these great stones, handled, carved, by my ancestors, bearing upon me the same testimony that man makes Divinity, and dowers the world with the shapes of his dreams. Thus the laughter of Moen was my Illumination.

'Then the day came when I was away at the lakes, shifting the net-heavy waters solid with fish. By now we had purchased a young bullock, still wild in the eye and frightened in his youth, but Moen had tamed his heart with croons as to a child, and hung round his neck the necklace that is both servitude and adornment, reward for his labour, my servant, my brother. And coming back in the bullock cart, with others from the village, with us the vast fish rescued from the water, twisting rainbows in their agonized release from watery solicitude, I saw a crowd standing in front of the house we had built.

'And there was Maté my mother weeping, and Moen in her arms weeping, and the village headman my uncle, and many others, looking on, a needless show of stares.

'"Uncle," said I to the headman, "what is it?"

'He pointed to the strange men, strangely wooden, smelling different from us because of the city, their faces uneasy, protesting. Then he told me that Devi's family had returned, the war over, and she was not of our village, but belonged to another race, another people, and now must return to them.

'And then all of us shouted: "No, no, no! Devi belongs to our village. She is the daughter of Maté, and the sister of Rahit, and of Chok who is dead, and Maté has no other daughter."

'And some of the men my brothers picked up stones and others ran home to find their knives and axes; although we do not like bloodshed, and never kill to eat meat, but merely catch the fish in the lakes to save them from the water, as the Buddha allowed us to do, yet at that moment we were doomed to the howl of battle and the pawn of slaughter, and I among them most violent of all.

'That day the demons of night and lust entered, a raping flood, into my soul, sucking all at once the marrow of my joy and dealing death to Rahit-who-sang, and in his place, structured like him, stockaded with murder, stood Rahit-who-wanted-to-kill.

'That night they took Moen away, in spite of us, and we threw stones and shouted, but the headman kept us from murder. Maté clung to Moen and would not let go, and a policeman pulled her off. As for me, I went amok and struck to kill the men taking her away, but they were stronger and I fell, and knew nothing until after she was gone, the car that took her leaving only the grit of dust behind it. It was dust first hit my nostrils as I woke again, I knew that I would follow its cloud, follow to the ends of the world. That night I left the village, leaving Maté with no man in the house.'

Jacques said: 'Yet your mother seems to have done well. A very capable woman. She is the village representative, I hear.'

'Yes,' said Rahit, 'and perhaps it had to be so, even as for the poet, who, making his song of the past, is delivered of memory's parasite. Maté is free of the past; not altogether, but in good measure.'

Philippe said: 'And so are you, callow young man, who thought for a while that my sister, *My* sister, would stoop to you. Yet I am happy that you hold her memory slight. I do not wish to free myself. It is you who have to give me your memories. I am buying them, through this astrologer who somehow has summoned you, by some Asiatic telepathy. I will take them, possess all, own Sylvie entire, for the rest of my days.'

The astrologer said: 'He despises you, Rahit, for telling your love. How little he knows of the poet who wrought his pangs in syllables, whose soul is a door ajar that all may inquire within.'

Rahit: 'You said he had come to be healed at the fluent spring of words.'

Jacques said: 'So you left your village? You went to the city? You found Sylvie?'

'I left and went to the city, many days' journey.'

'All journeys are the same,' said the astrologer. 'Steps, the day and night chess-board, food, and sleep. I who have travelled much know.'

'One day I met a clown,' said Rahit. 'Working on a road, pouring the pungent tar on to the stones, pitchforking gravel, earning enough for the next twenty miles to the next small town, I saw the clown come somersaulting to make us laugh, telling stories of guerrilla wars and the fight for independence to make our hearts swell with pride. Do you remember, stargazer?'

'Yes, I do. I was that clown.'

Philippe said: 'I thought you were a wise man, and a priest.'

'A wise man and a priest is also a mountebank on occasion. I cannot remember all I have done, for unlike Rahit, I made no songs to remember. When the drop of water knows itself also the sea, true humility is attained. But,' said the astrologer, 'there is no doubt that I am wise.'

'Suddenly I had no power over the world,' continued Rahit. 'The trees were strangers of manifold arms to bar my way, I walked in my own night, leeches of anger sucked my blood. As after death the soul goes seeking a new abode, I was going to the city. But the clown made all this absurd with somersaulting, and healed me, talking of guerrilla war.'

'I suffered more than you. I remember her better than you. My love is stronger than yours, for I cling to it harder,' said Philippe. 'And no clown can cure me with a few pirouettes.'

The astrologer said: 'This is your Christian background, which places value on things only if pleasure is paid for with pain. You never separate the two, in time or in place, must have both together. That is why you are at the moment enduring exquisite joy listening to Rahit, exalting yourself at Rahit's lack of suffering.'

'Ah,' said Anne, 'the Christian canticles of suffering, titillation of verbal vermiforms, pregnant with malign piety, the loaves and fish of charity breeding hatred, how useful these pinions to a perfidious holiness. I have these obsessions too, riding pillion on Rahit's bicycle to come here, myself a mirage of slaves dragged in his pagan triumph. And Rahit does it too, offering his memories to Philippe, a sacrifice to the eternal guilt of mankind, east or west. For shame, Rahit no longer Orpheus. My faith is leaving me.'

'There speaks a woman frustrated,' said Jacques, 'a woman deprived of child-bearing. "I desire a child, any child, Jacques, or I shall go mad." And now you seek a pagan hymn of Rahit, whose heart-ache was healed by a clown.'

'Riding pillion on Rahit's bicycle?' said Philippe. 'And you used to be so proper, making me go to those cocktails of Madame Moniveau.'

'That was another dimension, as our friend the astrologer-clown-priest-guerrilla told you,' retorted Anne. 'Sylvie played her role of child, I can play the roles of woman, lover, Providence, eloping gipsy, wincing Christian conscience or Fury betrayed. You cast me as the proper, conscientious Madame Bergerat, the frigid wife, because this suited you. Riding with Rahit through the flood on his bicycle, the bicycle he had yearned for since his boyhood and only been able to buy recently after Sylvie's demise, the past and its conscience blew itself out of me with the wind we raised, and I thought: why not Rahit, if I am good enough for him?'

'There was the accident, of course,' said the astrologer.

'But we did not see any corpses,' said Anne. 'Such a wild entanglement of machinery spilling silent guts, the only suffering one could feel was of that complicated assemblage of wires and cogs, screws and wheels, agonizing in strenuous silence.'

'Poor disembowelled created beings,' said the astrologer sadly. 'Their screams, pitched higher than the cicada's so that your ears could not reach them, are not lost however. Somewhere in the cosmos their complaint has been recorded in electro-magnetic indelibility.'

'I threw tar on the road, black shining tar, and met the clown,' said Rahit, 'and those two things shocked me back into myself. That night I made a song, to rest myself and those who worked with me.

> What colours have the blind in the brightest hour?
> When the sun hides beyond the melting hill
> Even lake water becomes dense night.
>
> I made a kite for my brother,
> To bring the wind to nuzzle in his hand,
> To bring my love back from the horizon's loss.
>
> Who hears the funeral music? Not the man in the coffin,
> When earth leans against him,
> Only the worm his brother listens, plush with gorging.

I made a cart for my mother,
To bring the worry-coloured fish to her harsh mercy.
My love did not return from the precise distance.

What stings the singer's tongue? Not the billowed words,
Sundered by breath,
Only the quickening sand raised by the dancer's feet.

I made a song of glow-worm sorrow
To light my steps along the road I take,
To bring my loved one back even from beyond death.

'The clown heard me sing, and said –'

The astrologer hitched himself up so that his chin rested on his knees, as if he had a hump on his back; he arched his eyebrows into circumflex bows, as do clowns, and spoke in the high voice of a clown: 'Now tell me, young man, for I can read faces, human, animal, and planetary, who is the girl you love, and where is she?'

'When I had told him, he looked at me entranced, as if I were a young white elephant captured by his praying hands, shook his head, and said –'

The astrologer, in the same piping clown voice: 'Do you know how many blonde young French girls there are in the city? Do you know how many people there are in the big city? O poor fool from a small village, how will you find her?'

'I said I did not know, but would walk about the streets until I saw her; and surely, one day, I would see her. And then the clown said –'

The astrologer: 'I will help you. By the Lord Buddha, I will, for now I see that distance is until you have found her, and number an intercepting chill of heads till the golden head of Devi-the-lotus shines upon us.'

'We had no money, but went on together, through the villages. Clown told stories, I sang songs, and in tired bitterness one night made a new one:

They took away the one he loved,
A bird in a golden cage she is,
But if she thinks of the one she loved,
He will find her and bring her release.

> A cool wind from the world at morning
> Whispers to her of a lover's guile.
> O lover by the river gazing,
> Look once again to see her smile.'

'A pretty song,' said Anne, disdainfully. 'Troubadour. We've lost all this now. Trivial.'

'It went over well,' said the astrologer, keeping his clown stance. 'Children sang it everywhere. It went over great, precisely because it was as common as a leaf.'

'What I find extraordinary,' said Jacques, 'is the way you parrot trite idioms of our commercial advertising: "It went over great." You bewilder me with your changes of personality. I too, like Anne, am losing faith, she in Rahit, I in you.'

'No more than you bewilder us,' said the clown-astrologer tartly. '*You* have lost the right to preach consistency, for you are past masters at sabotaging yourselves. Why should I not at one moment recite the Holy Words of the Lord of Compassion, and at the same time be delighted that a bad song was best loved by the children of this world? There is room for both in my spirit.'

> 'On this new and every morning of the living dead,' sang Rahit,
> 'I send you my face, O love, that changes hour by hour;
> The clown's mask laughs itself away,
> The solemn priest carves features that do not let me sleep,
> And all is lost in the night hole of a gun's mouth.'

'Oh,' said Philippe, 'that I cannot endure. Sylvie, O Sylvie!'

'I told you, Sylvie must be reincarnated elsewhere,' said the astrologer, 'otherwise she too would have come, summoned by her name.'

'How can she? She is dead,' said Jacques.

'But the stars are propitious,' said the astrologer piously, yet still with a linger of clown in his tone, as if this sentence explained everything.

Rahit sang:

> 'In this dawn of the world's end, O love, I make our shadows meet,
> So that we may all joyful wish each other our narrow sudden death.
> The flood has taken all, that we may rejoice,
> No longer solitary, sharing all we have.
> The river carries its storm of leaves to the sea, our memories run
>   together,
> A storied past, influential with the nothingness of tomorrow.'

'You must hear to the end now,' said the astrologer. 'Trust me, the time will come when you will stop clutching this tape, and the worm that eats within your skull will cease its mumbled gnawing, for the inundation of understanding sweeps away the forests but leaves the water whole.'

'I will never give up, never give up what I have,' said Philippe. 'I despise you, Rahit, for sitting there, meek, so submissive, singing of love so freely, displaying your indifference. I see that Sylvie was not sacred to you, since it means nothing to you to sing about her. That consoles me. But I despise you.'

The astrologer: 'You are still under the delusion that you are acquiring, wresting from us, something that can be counted, a mathematical sum of introspective legacies, and that you will be the richer by it. Well, let us go on. We sang songs, Rahit and I, up and down the streets of Pnomh Penh, at night. For at last we reached the city. At the doors of the cinemas, in the odd corners of the cafés, at the gates of the French houses, and in the tenements, we sang and turned somersaults. But singing songs in a hard, big city does not earn much. Rahit worked in the day-time, delivering groceries, I went round telling fortunes, until I met His Excellency Prem, Prem of the lofty mien and noble mind, whom I had known in my time as a monk. And Prem saw Rahit, and like all holy men a born fisherman, sought to capture him, and to turn him into a monk, of course. Prem himself was on the way to non-attachment, and wanted others to walk this excellent highway with him, not knowing that this desire was the great sin of his life. I had known Prem full of the sweats of passions, exuding the human groaning vices as a light bulb pours incandescence, but that was many years ago. When Rahit and I came to Pnomh Penh, His Excellency Prem had half-turned to living stone, entombed within the excellence of his meditation. You have such cardinals in your Christian Church, who put on the garb for predatory purposes, and then it grew upon them, and sanctified them; capsulated in its growth, they were saved in spite of themselves. Thus Prem, when one day we sang outside the market, came by, tall, strong, lofty, and noble of demeanour, and recognized me at once. At once he captured my spirit once more, for I am accessible to greatness. But it was not me he wanted, it was Rahit. And then began the struggle between Prem and myself, for the spirit of Rahit: I to keep him as he was, Prem to turn him to sanctity.'

'High, and still, was Prem's gaze,' said Rahit. 'Black water spaces empty as thought. "What is the song you sing?" he asked. And I had to reply: "I am seeking Moen of the golden hair, whom some call Devi, a forbidden name, and whom the French have taken away from me. My mother Maté found her under the lotus, and she lived with us until the day she was taken back to her people. She is here in the city, and I have come to seek her and to take her back, for I love her and without her my life is living death."'

'And Prem,' continued the astrologer, 'suddenly grew a face twice the size it had been, with dark water pools of eyes, a voice tremendous with quietness. "And when you have found her, will she follow you, now that she has known another life?"

'"Of course."

'"And you love her?"

'"Of course."

'Then Prem said: "Rahit does not know what love is." And left us. That was the first time.'

'Well done,' said Philippe happily. 'I agree with this Prem. You do not know what love is.'

'For Prem, love was renunciation,' said the clown. 'You did not renounce her. None of you did.'

'I did,' said Philippe. 'I have let you talk, Rahit, play the hero, with naïve ardour flinging yourself in your romantic role behind the dust of the car which took Sylvie back where she belonged, *with me*; leaving your village, on what I presume you thought was the Great Quest, a crusade, an epic . . . tarring roads, singing songs, to pay your way to the city. All this is valorous, worthy of praise, rococo, romantic, and a little burlesque. Allow me to say that in all this you received your own reward. You felt important, a triumph straining towards its goal, an ample meaning in all you did. But you never once stopped to think that perhaps it would have been kinder to leave Sylvie alone, to let her make a new life for herself, not to interfere.'

'Human beings do not stop changing with regard to themselves, yet what we carry within us is a fixed memory, a graven image entombed in time,' said Jacques. 'All of us have a different image of Sylvie, and none of them is the real Sylvie. It was as valid for Rahit to pursue his image of Sylvie, as it is for you to clutch her voice on tape. Had he not pursued –'

'She would have lived,' said Philippe. 'With me, she would have gone to France.'

Anne: 'I feel Philippe's graven image is eroding. Are you not afraid that you will find yourself suddenly empty of Sylvie? Her solidity melted by the drip-drop of words like water upon stone? You should not have started on this search *à rebours*, for you may lose all.'

'No,' said Philippe, 'nothing can alter what we were together, Sylvie and I. All of you will change, but not I. I will carry her eternally within me, all the more precious, all the more venerated, for the many facets of her that I am learning – even if it hurts unbearably.'

'The truth of night is larger than the truth of day,' said the astrologer, 'but since you wish it, be it so.'

'It was my song that found Moen for me,' said Rahit. 'The song travelled when I stayed immobile; restless, it roamed the streets, house by house; it lingered in the market; the children took it up and sang it at school; the barbers, lathering faces, told their clients the tale of Rahit and Moen; the housewives gossiped of it; the song spun itself a great web throughout the city; only the French knew it not. One day a child came to me, and said: "We have found Moen for you. She lives there, on that street, in a big house." I was then helping a potter to make clay figures of the Lord of Compassion, the Lord of Justice. I washed my hands, and left the clay. The master potter cried:

'"You have found?"

'"Yes."

'He said: "I shall make for the festival new images, paint them the most dazzling colours, and call them Rahit and Moen; I will show you apart, and then together, and all the world will love the new lovers that redeem the spring." And he set to work there and then, abandoning Compassion and Justice. But I did not look back.

'When I got to the house, the large white French house, there was the shut gate. I could see the gardener sweeping leaves off the grass. He said: "There is no one. All have gone, to the seaside. They will be back in a few days." And Prem appeared a few paces from me, looking at me. He had followed me.

'"I have found her house," I said. I was angry with Prem.

'And Prem said: "You have found . . . the habitation. When you have found Moen, look for her soul." '

'Aaaaaah!' cried Philippe, jubilant. 'I knew it. I knew that I had won. Her soul. It was with me. The ties of blood. How could she ever be anything else but French? Heredity, blood. It was a fugue, running away with you, Rahit, but she would have returned. To me.

'At the beginning I sat for hours with her, trying to stimulate her memory. "Do you recall," I said to her, "our mother sitting embroidering with you on her knees, me by your side? Do you remember the smell, the feel of her silk dress? I remember playing with the bottles, the powder-puff and the pincushion on mother's dressing table, sniffing . . . and when she took you on her lap, keeping one hand running through my hair, I was divinely happy. I wanted to enfold you both in a heart vast and magnificent, like a palace full of golden light, surround you with golden walls topped with great pearls for battlements . . . our mother had a pearl necklace with pearls that became bigger and bigger till the last, biggest pearl of all, and she wore it with a pale blue satin dress sometimes; and you and I, Sylvie, would be kissed goodnight, and I would run my hands round her pearls, warm with her warmth . . . all night long it seemed to me that these pearls were tingling in my palms.

'"And then there was your doll, Little Sylvie, with green eyes and fair hair, who you always thought was yourself. I remember when two years old, Sylvie my darling, you used to touch Little Sylvie's nose, then your own nose. I thought it a wonderful sight."

'It was through my sister, her doll, and our mother, that I was lodged in a feminine universe, scented, empyrean, prolonged into the landscape, the blue hills, the forest, the river; a perfect, warm, feminine world, a world brutally lost, which Anne never gave me, for Anne proclaimed a female right which had nothing to do with this delight, this melting, cloying, enveloping sweetness all mine.

'Remember . . . remember! For weeks I strove to make her remember. She sat on the floor of her room, obstinately refusing the chairs, the bed, the dresses: mute, surly, locked within herself. And I, as obstinate as she, endlessly talking, remembering for her.

'Did you have such patience? Rahit, did you lick her spirit with your incessant tongue, like the water for ever rubbing itself against the refusing shore, eroding grain by grain the contour of her refusal, until at last, at last, one day, I remember, she put on her first French dress, green as her eyes, silken as her skin, and looked at herself in the mirror, smiled, then became thoughtful again. And it was then, for the first time, that in her eyes the doors of memory shut upon you and your little village, the reflection superseded, obscured by her own clear image in the mirror looking at herself, become the whole world of herself unto herself. Woman contemplating her only self and succumbing to it, accepting thenceforth the idolatry of her own idol body, face, being. And then again you were there, you and Maté, an infant paradise of security, a hide-and-seek with happiness. You came back, silent shadows flocked back into the mirror, refusing to leave her alone . . . but for an instant abashed, they had been shut out.

'I now learnt the way to make her forget.

'I had gone the wrong way about it. What I would do was to make her accept the gestures, the speech, the dress of the world to which she belonged, to make her *see* herself as that world, and no other, through every motion of her body. The more I tried to make her change by recalling childhood, the less she wanted to remember, because between my talk and it rose the undying terror of her saviour, the Japanese soldier, who had picked her up in a whirlwind of screams and blood and boots, thrown her on his motor-cycle and left her in the forest to live.'

'And the flood,' muttered the astrologer. 'You forget the flood. Maté saved her twice.'

'I would have won,' said Philippe. 'After the first dress came another, then another. Then the hairdresser, the shoemaker, the stockings, the perfume, the dressing table. I bought her an inlaid silver comb and brush. She let me brush her hair in front of the mirror; I brushed and she combed her beautiful hair, her eyes larger and larger, until I felt once again that delicious drowning in a world fragile, enclosed . . . I recaptured the past, so vividly that I began to sing with joy. And she looked at me then, as I sang, Sylvie of the sea-faun eyes, mermaid combing her hair, and all the legends of beauty were in the dry electric spark which her comb drew from the golden wave. And Jacques looked on, desperate with anger, the wax of his *bonhomie* soft with anger.

'Flowers next. Her room, the balcony, always full of flowers. Not the scentless, tropical kind. Roses flown from Dalat, orchids from Malaya, and from Bali a friend of mine, a painter, sent white dove-blossoms that only open in night coolness, and from the Chinese banker whom my father had known as a hawker and who had prospered in the years, who recognized me and came to the ship to meet me (for his son in Paris had kept track of me), I got the *ken-hwa*, the wondrous flower that opens only once and for a night only, whose heart is a multitude of pistils vibrating like moths' wings as the flower petals unfold, white splendour thrilling with life, to fold again a few hours later. People come from miles around to see its beauty.'

'The only thing you forgot,' said Anne, in heavy irony, 'was a couple of love-birds. Budgerigars, pecking at each other's gaudy plumage in a thin-barred cage. And perhaps a fawn poodle, adorably barbered. That would have been the perfectly trite establishment for the cherished mistress of a wealthy degenerate.'

Philippe: 'I discovered in Sylvie great understanding of beauty, a wide-eyed muteness before the shock of beauty. I began to form her taste. I knew that I must take her to Europe, that reliquary of centuries of loveliness. Once she had known the orderly beauty of Europe, she would no longer be able to endure the poverties of Asia, the hodge-podge of her markets full of what is cheap and gaudy, the mass-produced gadgets we fling to Asians avid for machines, for they prefer everything they have not had, and their good taste has gone, their handicrafts are for tourists, they seldom appreciate their own art of the past. I would take her away from tawdriness, want, mediocrity. She would find it impossible to return to Asia. She would be herself, a total Sylvie, as if the village had never existed. Together we would have roamed the world, searching for beauty, knowing only what was good and artistic, ignoring the sordid . . . We would have been happy.'

'What a programme,' said Anne. 'I was out of it.'

'For you, Anne, for your mordant spirit, this was not possible. You argued with life, you wrenched your rights as a female. You could not be all savour, iridescence, moon-prospect, essential attar, as Sylvie could. She was all spirit, purity, flame, music. With her I knew I could have done so many things. My cinders would have sprung to living fire, I too would have become poet. You, Anne, smothered me with your rancid clamour, the grinding of your bones.'

Anne said: 'Sylvie played the child of miracle to you. But it was to Jacques she went, in despair, broken by your aesthetic dictatorship, that imperious hardship of diamonds, the crown of thorns with which you diademed her captive forehead. She went to him because he had a continent of misery to give her at the hospital, that poverty, that squalor, that sordidness, that lack of taste, that Asia from which you were trying to save her. And this, too, she kept from you. I went with her, and I know.'

'True, Philippe,' said Jacques, 'she came to me. When she could endure no longer the strain you imposed, when the high peaks of artistic beauty you imparted to her as revelation had iced her flesh, she rushed to my clinic, and there half-crying she played another role, the nurse. Many an afternoon has she plunged her hands into wounds, rubbed her clean skin with ulcers, fingered rags with ravishment, bathed purulent eyes, her nostrils dilated to receive the smell of festering flesh. "Here I feel alive again, near to the people, my people," she said. It was no use, Philippe. Even if you had taken her away to Europe, she would have come back, returned to the warm, dirty, fertile mud of Asia; because she was no longer wholly French, she belonged here too. Heredity is only half the story, much the smaller half. And that is why she would, in time, have loved me and been happy with me. Because I alone could give her all that she wanted, both worlds, with both their needs of each other: our need to rehabilitate ourselves, to find an inner core and a meaning to our spoilt, senseless, and affluent lives, and *their* need to accomplish some measure of relief from poverty, a misery which our despoliation in the past and our niggardliness of the present continues to impoverish. With me she could find that, and neither with Rahit nor with you, because with either of you she had to choose one world, and no other.'

'Not true,' said the astrologer angrily. 'With Rahit, she could have grown with him, with the village, with all of us. You underestimate us. You think that we cannot reach to your level, as you call it. But, my friend, look at us. Look at Maté. Four years ago she was still an ignorant village woman. Then came Independence, and now she knows a good many things, and can organize as well as any of your women deputies, if you have any. Look at me. I can manipulate a transistor and repair a car; I speak three languages, which is more than you or your friend can do. With Rahit, Devi could have fulfilled herself totally, in tune together they would have reached out to become a light for others, to raise other people from darkness, as the Lord Buddha lifted our souls into the sun of understanding. For whoever teaches and helps others is a carrier of the Great Illumination, which is the world of reality.'

'Oh,' said Philippe, 'are we going to have eternally from these Asians boring lectures on social context? I did not know astrologers were also Marxist nowadays.'

'Boring to you, because you have enough to eat, enough to dress, and you can afford the luxury of introspective, fictitious agonies. A well-filled stomach allows you to elaborate fantastic realms of sensitivity,' retorted the astrologer. 'We have been pirated, robbed, and reduced to a level where the necessity to survive comes before anything else. And it is a wonder that, pauperized as we are, we have yet kept so much of good manners. And we have not become, as yet, as callous as you are. We would hesitate to commit some of the horrors which your art-loving businessmen inflict, because they do not have to witness directly the graceless monstrosities they produce. Your ancestors used to crow with delight at hangings and quarterings. You do it by proxy, on a much vaster scale, and because you wash your hands before dinner you think your soul is clean. We bore you when we say that we are hungry, that we want equality, independence, human dignity, but you bore us when you talk of your sensibilities, and your good taste in art. You can call it Marxism if you will. Lord Buddha too was a Marxist, or would be one certainly today. In fact, I am not at all sure that Marx was not a reincarnation of the Great Compassion. Both opened our eyes to the human condition; with different words, at different levels, both sought the salvation of mankind, both had utter belief in Man fulfilling his destiny within the context of change, of man transmitting life, non-attached to greed, envy, and hatred. Yes, there is much in common between Buddha and Marx, for neither believed in God.'

'Goodness of God,' said Anne. 'The kingdom of heaven has changed indeed.'

'My friend,' said Rahit, 'do not get so angry.'

Philippe said: 'What a tempestuous wise man when nettled!'

'I, too, was unworthy,' continued Rahit, 'because of the bangles. Oh, the curse of man, who observes and remembers himself, for nothing else will observe or remember or mourn for him; can never stop himself by prescience from the precise sin which will become the subject of his mourning, his agony of remembering. I forgot that I loved her, because she no longer had the bangles I gave her. I too betrayed.

'We had fled together, Moen and I, issuing from the grey morning into the bus and too much sun, accomplices all the strangers my brothers round us, helping by their indifference, their inattention to the sight of a man and a woman together, a couple; Moen muffling her hair, but her eyes visible, and quickly our unknown accomplices looked away, resolved not to know, not to observe, not to remember. Perhaps they had heard the song. We were safe in their knowing unknowingness.

'Oh, the lovely-to-remember hunted days, across the rice-fields, in farms, one night in a boat crossing the lake; Moen and I knew the happiness of being hunted beasts together, a footless harrying keeping us taut, obviating fear because we fled together. And on the boat we took to cross the lake, a moon of course, mildly swollen, with a polished, sleepy face, and we two nearly falling asleep, our happiness watching us like a night-watchman. And in this harrowing bliss of love, Moen said: "How I wish that Philippe could be as happy as we are now."'

Philippe: 'She said that? She remembered me? Even then, she remembered?'

'She said it, because at that moment she felt safe enough to say it,' said Anne, tartly. 'You were not valuable enough to become sequestered in her silence.'

'But I betrayed then,' said Rahit. 'Once again I lay eating dust behind a vanished car. I was felled to the abyss by the wound of a spectre, boat wrecked by an emergent rock, kite torn limp in unsuspected tree. At first there was no pain, only an averted instant, during which the moon and the water withered, and Moen, a soft and cunning stranger, falling asleep, winked, slobbered, and lolled about in a dullness without horizon, fully satisfied after this deathblow dealt to me, her lover, her enemy. I rose and left her in the wicker-round small shelter, and sat on the boat's keel and sweated copiously, knowing the death hour.'

'Go on, go on,' cried Philippe. 'Go on.'

Anne said: 'Are you not ashamed, Philippe?'

'Of course not,' cried Philippe. 'What is this melodrama compared to what I felt? When I went into her room that morning, singing and saying: "Sylvie, my dearest, arise, for the sun is up and our plane leaves at ten" – and found her suitcases fully packed, everything neat and prepared, yet the room was empty, drained of her, and no word, no message. And you, you, Anne, when I ran to you – "Where is she? Where is Sylvie?" – turning round with mad joy and saying: "Where is who? What do you mean?" A bayonet could not hurt more. You knew.'

'Of course I knew,' said Anne. 'When we returned from the seaside he was there, this Rahit, standing by the closed iron gates, their scrollwork his jail bars. I perceived him again, some hours later, when I looked through the bedroom window, and he was still standing, watching from the imprisoning street. The next evening you were out with Sylvie and Jacques, a night-club jollity under the excuse of initiating Sylvie into European life and teaching her to dance, and I had my usual headache. I saw Rahit pacing slowly the street, a leopard braked to a bobby's stroll. I went for a walk, and purposely left the gates open on my return. I looked again through the window, and the street was deserted. Then I knew he had crept into the garden, would sidle into the house, wait there, crouching in some dark corner, probably below the stairs, waiting for the return of Sylvie . . . melodrama, pre-arranged by me.

'A woman who owns a house makes it her outer skin. Asleep, she knows the stairs creak, the dog sighs a dream, she itches with the dust on a table-top, the raw edge of a curtain hem sears a charted wrinkle in her watchful cheek. When Sylvie came, a foreign object, my thoughts encircled, pawed round her door, trying to digest this disorder of my meticulous ownership. I knew how she came back at night, walked barefooted, throwing the high-heeled shoes, part of her new self, on the rug, opening the window, turning off the air-conditioner Philippe had fitted up and which she found too cold. That night the window did not open, the air-conditioner remained turned on to cover their whispers. You slept. You, her brother, slept, your instincts fooled in the coma of sleep. I rejoiced. How I rejoiced! I felt mighty as God who holds the sun in His hands. And the next morning you said to your sister, not noticing her eyes, lids half down, and the fine down of love upon them: "Tomorrow, Sylvie, we shall be leaving. It will be spring in Europe. Perhaps you'll even find it cold, you so used to the tropics that you never perspire." You went on thus, and I, watching, saw her mouth a new mouth, and

73

had to leave the table to burst into laughter. "Where is she?" Ha ha, where is she? Your Sylvie, in Rahit's arms in your own house, and you snoring.

'How she and you used to return at night, full of laughter, saying "Hush" as you tiptoed upstairs not to wake me, and at the door she turned to whisper "Good night, Philippe"; until one night Jacques came up with you, and put his arms round both of you, *bonhomie*, that *bonhomie* hypocrisy of his, the good doctor, blessing all, sheathing you in the purification of his role as seer, only so that he could put his arms round Sylvie too, in fatherly-brotherly lust. And then he sat in her room while you showed your sister how to use her new brush and comb, and watched you caress her with the stroking brush ... Oh, I knew, I knew, and Jacques had spent the five to seven with me as usual, but thinking of Sylvie even as he sweated and heaved over me, and I watched him while making the usual noises to indicate to his activity the stages of performance I was supposed to have reached, right up to the simulacrum of a final satisfaction ... Oh yes, I watched you, Jacques, for you too were part of my household. I saw your ooze of desire for Sylvie, while utilizing me.'

'You are exhausting yourself and us, madame,' said the astrologer. 'I pray you cease this pale carnage of a scene, for melodrama as you say is the greatest of sins against artistic sophistication. Let Rahit sing.'

'Rahit,' said Anne bitterly, 'is the possessor of his own melodrama in which he took himself seriously. To him love-o-love was named Moen, or Devi, a patchy composition of lotus and lute music and love, pastel-boring to me, inviolate because, a pantheist without a God, he mingled with the elements everywhere, valid as a poem, untruthful as all poems once written down. Rahit loved a stream and a shadow and his own songs welling out of him, entering life; and lost his love because of a pair of bangles which were not there, and the name of a man who was her brother and kissed her forehead. Yet he has everything, I have nothing, and Philippe is now robbing him, because Philippe is tragic and Rahit is not, though both are laughable. Yet it was I, I, who brought it about, and yet you all deny me this triumphal bitterness which alone rescues me from triviality.'

'Anne,' said Jacques, 'it is truly a mania with you to believe yourself Providence and Fate itself. I have already told you that even without you, sooner or later, certain things would have come to pass.'

'"Yes, doctor . . . no, doctor." How well Sylvie played it with you, Jacques. "I want to learn something, I want to be useful. I know Philippe means well, but I want to be someone, not only to receive, but also to do." Oh, these parrot emotions, parrot words, the deceitful child-woman, Sylvie-Moen, an orthography of haze, insulting the exact logic of sunlight, which I brought in to dry the sentimental moss.'

Rahit sang:

'I came out in the loveless night,
The world dry as a dry dead leaf,
Parched the moon.
The boat lifted and sank, plop, plop
The slippery snakes of water mocked me with hooded wave-eyes.

'I shall never forget that walk, with Moen behind me, walking, and I hardening against her at every step, filled with agony, anger, desire, as we left the boat in the early dawn, going away together. Between our touching bodies all thirty-six hells were roaring their damnation in my ears.'

Jacques: 'You mean jealousy. Ordinary jealousy. Sexual jealousy. Like any man. And for two bangles.'

Anne: 'Sylvie was never anything but a weak character.'

Jacques: 'Shut up, Anne. You don't know what you are talking about. A weak character? After all that had happened to her? She was a being torn between two of everything, two men, two civilizations as well . . . how can you reduce this to a simple explanation of jealousy? She was a host to savage turnabouts, from one life to the other instantaneously transported, and like Cinderella on the stroke of midnight, a midnight not of her choosing, struck in the middle of the ball, the dance, the happy pickaback, every time . . . can't you see it? Can't you see that she was never given a chance to be herself?

'Every time something happened, a flood, a war, a kidnapping, a tearing away . . . she was picked up and whisked away, picked up and thrown. How could you expect her to make a decision? And not only Sylvie, but all of us, all of us on this earth, have become the prey of events that go too fast, happen too suddenly . . . can we do anything else but acquiesce, always acquiesce? Sylvie became the shadow of what wrecked her, docile in the whirlpool, surviving the wasting change, the thud of the engulfing victor. All she wanted was to be loved. Every time she found love, a different kind of love, but still love; but these loves were mutually exclusive, where she wanted them to complete each other. You, Philippe, could not abide the memory of Rahit; tried to wipe out all that would remind her of the village. You, Rahit, could not bear to hear the name of Philippe; it sent you mad. Only myself, Jacques, only I understood her. She needed someone who would bring all her worlds together. I could have done this, making her share my work, giving her a love wise and patient, that would have directed her enthusiasm, her youth, to something worthwhile, the service of her fellow men, her compatriots here. Thus the Asian side of her, hungering for a social context, away from the perpetual preoccupation with her own ego of the West, would have been satisfied; and the European side too, for she would have been performer as well as receiver, become a wholeness restored.'

'Yet you,' said Anne, 'pulled the trigger, seeing something move in the bush, remember? You killed whatever was of her in hiding behind that bush.'

Rahit sang:

> 'Plop plop, I heard the water. Philippe, Philippe, it said.
> Slowly the madness rose
> An overflowing river belting corpses
> Whispering brother . . . brother . . .

'I crawled back to her side, her sleeping, faithless head, and took her wrist, feeling, hoping, hoping for the clink of glass bangles. But she woke, and I said: "Moen, where are the glass bangles I gave you?"

'I could feel her cringe, frightened, frightened of something that she did not wish to know.

'"I lost them . . . at the sea-side."

'"You lost them? How?"

'And she wailed: "I don't know. I couldn't find them, I looked . . ."

'And I said: "Moen, that man, he is not your brother."

'"Oh, he is, he is. I swear he is."

'But I would not listen. Or rather, what she said went far away, and now I know what Prem the monk meant when he said: "You will find her, but will it be herself, will it be Moen?"

'Night the accuser sidled into my soul, smudging the sky out of my eyes, swallowing Moen, nudging what I had been out of the way, and cackling: "Brother, brother." I stared at Moen, a stranger, an unknown girl with large horrified eyes. I could not touch her. We lay all night, near each other, feigning sleep, in the boat cradled on the mother-swing of the lake.

'Alone,
Hearing ourselves breathe,
Afraid to betray
By a quicker inspiration
The accuser, the curse
Delighted, sucking me into nothing,
An aching dullness of nothing.
The night death grew and devoured me,
Devoured Moen.
We lay,
Bereft of ourselves.
I wanted to scream: 'Say a word, something.
Just a word. Release me. For I die.'
My breath, in and out, ticked the silence away like a clock.

Brought to death in the bride-bed of love,
Laid to rest in the whirlpool at the wanting centre,
Untouching, alone together,
While the voice of water never faltered outside
And the sun insisted on coming, harsh, to thrust our faces at each
    other.

The boat stepped ashore,
Bumping the edge of earth.
I rose. Moen rose,
Spectres of ourselves walking ourselves away.'

'All for a pair of missing bangles,' said Philippe. 'Who was Providence, who Master of Destiny?'

'All of us,' said Jacques suddenly. 'You exasperate me, both of you, with your claims to a hand in the administration of Sylvie's life. All of us, or none. One might as well invoke the stars, as our friend here does.'

The astrologer said: 'I concur with my colleague, the Western medicine man. I have never heard so many claims to what is usually regarded as a divine prerogative, the caprice of deity. It was the stars, those sensitive mystics pullulating their rays, electromagnetic equilibrium a single prayer disturbs –'

'Oh, nonsense,' said Anne. 'It was a pair of absent bangles. The stars have never done anything for me that I know of. It was Will. Human Will. All our conflicting wills did Sylvie to death. But mine was the stronger, for strangely I feel more fulfilled than I have done before.'

'And what is Will, may I ask,' said the astrologer, 'but impulse to a course, whether reason or emotion have swayed you to it? And why this sudden brainstorm of will, like patches on the sun, electric cyclones which influence our weather and even the rise and fall of massacres on earth? You have not looked for primal cause enough. Or, shall I say, you have used your intellect as a desiccating instrument, to cut you off from the great currents *qui font frémir l'univers*. All of us are microscopic stars on our own, emitting signals, as they do; from all your pores exude, not only the sweats of emotion (and emotions too are electro-chemical, recognizable artifacts of the great cosmic pulsations which bring the universe into perpetual labour), but the components of an eternal energy, merging with myriads of others, transmitters all. And our words, our words which strike the ear, batter the universe as continual bells, set up waves, fluxes, tides, violate the interstellar spaces with inanities, live on for ever. They too, emanation from us, have their root in the heartbeat of the universe, and return to it, completing the cycle. To me astrology is the most modern of sciences, for it is the science of cosmic awareness, awareness that every single act of man, thought, motion, is a modulation of the Infinite, never lost, ever returning to its source. This is what the Lord Buddha knew in his great Illumination, and what we rediscover. Only thus can all life have a meaning, for even the meaningless then have function, like nebulae yet to be formed, beyond our grasp. But none of this is free, nor is it our Will, not as you define Will. It is all a matter of interaction, arranged aeons ago without any plan except its own Being.'

'Not a sparrow . . .' said Jacques, '. . . without His knowing it.'

'Buddha said: "Even the blind pheasant is fed,"' replied the astrologer. 'There is no God, as I said, for there is no apartness from

Existence which can be individualized as God. Your anthropomorphic gods are valueless, archaic father-figures with no place in our twentieth century. Only Buddhism, the atheist religion of scientific change, can compete today, keep pace with the science and knowledge of the comos.'

Philippe: 'I am like Anne, a Westerner, and I believe in free will, in the voluntary conscious exercise of one's personality, in choice. I *chose* to come here. Sylvie was *my* sister. All the time I could feel *my* will upon her, willing her to become herself, Sylvie Bergerat, my sister.'

'And how do you know that your will is your will, is not due to the influences round you, your choice being so limited, so hemmed in by your very knowledge, your childhood impressions, the state of your body – all these things which make up You, and give you the illusion of freedom? Believe me,' said the astrologer, 'you are using words that you know not the burden of. When I say predestination, I use it in the Marxist sense, in the Einsteinian sense. It was as aberrant or miraculous for Einstein to predict an eclipse, as for Marx to foretell some of the laws governing man's society, as for me to tell you the future . . . we're all in the same boat, insane or not. Once you presuppose a free will, you must presuppose a God, and a God with a Will, and then the whole cosmos becomes illogical. Man has always required a guarantee against the accidental; he has sensed, obscurely, that there were laws of what you call Nature, and these laws are the laws of his own thinking. Predetermination, under various guises, ever recurs to him, for he cannot abide the unexpected, mistaking it for the unconnected. If he but knew enough about himself and the universe, he could take out an insurance policy against the unpredictable, which is only what he has not yet been able to imagine. Prophecy is his dearest passion, the desire to encompass time part of his fear that he cannot be dissociated from all that surrounds him, that he is helpless beyond a certain moderate limit he calls freedom. He is himself, only in function of all that is not himself. He cannot choose, except by choosing to be himself, which means choosing also not-himself. It is this Awareness which the Buddha recognized as the fountain-head of living; the perpetual no-future, annihilating distance and time and self in others. Do you not think this philosophy much more adapted to the twentieth century than your meagre concept of individual free will?'

'But then,' cried Anne, 'if there is no Will, no God, no purpose, no beginning, no end, nothing except change and more change and the changelessness of change, what proof do we humans have against the terror of becoming nothing?'

Jacques: 'I agree with Anne. Otherwise there is only despair.'

The astrologer sighed: 'Man has always required a guarantee to launch him into space on a mission that had to be from the beginning.'

> 'Three spirits came to me and drew me apart,' sang Rahit.
> 'The wind moved about the rice
> With a silver glitter.
>
> They sang to me songs of great mistrust,
> And I saw the moon's disk melt
> In a sky abashed.
>
> How many will come after me singing,
> And be drawn among the growing rice
> Sprinkled with pollen of stars?
>
> Seeds of the stars for ever asking, yet no answer comes,
> Save the shadow of a man, etched out of darkness,
> Stump immense in the small lantern of the sun.

'Truly,' said Rahit, 'no answer comes, either to star's asking or woman's cry or child's wail. Yet the answer is there, and here, and now, in the instant absence of for ever. Now alone.'

'I will not be captured by these phantasms,' said Philippe. 'My logical mind cannot abide this word-spinning, though it may sound convincing in a moment of exaltation. I say that man still has a right to his free will, his private event, his mental property of something sacred, untouched, belonging to him, and to no one else at all, no single particle of it to be desecrated by another's breath, sight, touch.

'So Sylvie to me, a shrine apart, an echo . . .'

'A crying in the cell, a heaving in the sepulchre, a grovel of worms, your Sylvie, now and always,' cried Anne, laughing horribly, 'now and for ever, Philippe, to the day of your death. And such a small, ridiculous matter of no moment, in a world of death, the death of one little girl who never knew her mind, who was cork, flotsam, fallen leaf. Sweet as a razor, I hope, will be your memories, for as long as you live.'

'O Anne,' said the astrologer, 'see your words, like the winging bats crowding in the darkness of the vaults, muster an evil reek that will hound you for aeons to come. What can I do to abolish them inside this universe and this dimension? For you have called death of many names, death with all the names of delusion that man gives her in fear of her mystery.'

'Let me be,' said Anne, 'let me be. It is Sylvie who was killed, but it is I who died. And you know it well. When the charge exploded in her chest, there was I wrecked, and all of you are my murderers too. So I will go now, if Rahit has done.'

'Rahit has not done,' said the astrologer, 'but I will be Rahit, and he can take you wherever you want to go.'

'On a bicycle,' said Jacques, 'where can you go, Anne?'

'I will know when I get there where I want to go. Why not a bicycle, when nothing else will cross the flood?'

'She is mad,' said Jacques, eyeing Anne descending with pelvis painful, stiff with dissatisfaction, the pelvis he knew, the loins he had used, insipid, a measurement of hands anonymous and confused among others, no known likeness to desire, not even his own excitement remembered. But the nape of her neck held still a lingering pity and he felt a mild elation at sight of those untidy, timid hairs, because they were truth; he had seen them first, been moved towards her one night when her strident laughter compelled him to observe her. All the rest was gone, an argosy of flashbacks to be scattered, to be used by others perhaps, in other stars perhaps, but no longer his own, for he was no longer moved by them.

'That bicycle,' said Philippe. 'But really, it is absurd. My wife running away with that coward on a bicycle. Don't say he is not a coward: he cannot face what he has done, and therefore pedals his way off, his story abracadabra half chanted. He never loved Sylvie, he as much as owned it. It will all be obliterated in no time. I am glad. He did not mean anything to her, nor she to him. It was as I said. If he had not come, if Sylvie had not felt she had to go with him, she would have stayed with me. God knows what he made her suffer in those days they were together.'

Said the astrologer: 'Rahit suffered in the same smallness as you, shrunk to your stature by his jealousy. But he does not hanker after a private eternity of longing. Funerals in our country are most perfunctory affairs. The effort to Eternity demands enormous pride, and Rahit does not have pride. He knows it meaningless to hold Moen back, a mild ghost with a face laid in her hair. Moen is his share of universe scattered among repetitive ticks of days. And the bicycle you scorn is also Moen, for he looked at a bicycle with her when they were children, desired its possession ardently; bought it after her death, rides it and is pleased with the scuffle of wind through his hair.'

'That,' said Jacques, 'is lucky for him. But it is not very admirable.'

'Now,' said the astrologer, 'your turn, is it not, doctor?'

Jacques said: 'I can only repeat what I said. About Anne I feel no compunction. About Sylvie . . . yes, I did love her, who would not? She came to me in despair, two days before Philippe had arranged to take her to Europe. "What shall I do? I do not want to go," she said. "I want to stay here. To work in this hospital. This is my country." I told her that I would find a way to bring her back. I myself would go to France soon. I thought: I shall see her there, marry her, and bring her back with me. I told her: "If I come to fetch you in France, will you return with me here?" And she said: "Yes, I will."'

'That,' said Philippe, 'shows your treachery, Jacques. You took advantage of her distraught condition, exactly as Rahit. Both of you. I tell you, she did not know, when she said yes, what she was saying yes to. I alone could protect this childhood innocence which all of you conspired to betray.'

The astrologer said: 'Philippe, you too wanted her otherwise than as she was to be. You could not bear the thought that she would grow up, go away, marry a man not your kind, not you. Her childhood having failed you, you were creating for her a deep-freeze world removed from what you call vulgarity.'

'What should I have done?' demanded Philippe. 'Left things as they were? Left my sister here? Not try to educate her, to take her away from ugliness? Non-action, non-interference, let the dogs rot, the cows die, the babies perish of smallpox – that is your philosophy, is it? You are all the same in Asia: do nothing, yet you want all that we have. I am a European, I do interfere, of my own free will. I *make* destiny, for myself and others.'

'Don't be stupid, Philippe,' said Jacques. 'You know you are twisting things.'

'Destiny cannot be made by you or me, directly,' said the astrologer. 'What you should have done was to interrogate yourself as to Right Action, Right Motive, Right Thought, Right Intention. You talk of purity, but you used means to reach *your* end which were not pure. And that is why your sister could not speak to you of Rahit, nor tell you of her visits to Jacques. You did wrong towards Sylvie, your sister. Rahit also did wrong, and so did Jacques. But Rahit, in the end, delivered her to herself, and restored the harmony that was to be. It was all to be, even what was done in evil.'

'You say that because you are his friend, of his race. You are against us because we are white,' said Philippe.

'There you go again,' said the astrologer. 'Immediately playing the game of war, one side against another. When will you free yourselves of this barbarous weed? When will you stop considering the mind as a castle entrenched, with moat to cross, battlements to conquer, women to violate and treasure to loot? When will you stop considering your own memories as pillage to be defended? My friend, you have a long way to go before you begin to understand the Buddha, whose ideal is loving unity with all, however imperfect. There is no individual salvation which can be perfected, as long as there remain others who hunger or thirst or need. You can no longer choose yourself alone, only the kind of humanity you wish to belong to.'

'That idea is far from the Marxism you preached us a while ago,' said Jacques.

'No one who teaches salvation for mankind is far from the Buddha,' retorted the astrologer, 'no matter which level he starts from. However strenuously Marx denied metaphysics, yet he himself owned a transcendental belief in Mankind with a big M, in a constant upward evolution of the brain to make his own work worthwhile. The compassion of Marx for man, the emotional discipline which guided his work, is akin to our Buddhist thinking, and the studies of Marx in the British Museum remind me of the seven years spent by the Master under the *Boddhi* tree, thinking out the mystery of life. I see no contradictions,' said the astrologer, 'or if there are any, then they are made up by words, by the verbiage we use, the levels at which we reflect a comparative lack of knowledge due to the centuries' lapse. Nirvana, the Beatitude of the Buddha, is nothing but complete and exact knowledge. Just as for Marx, once the laws of the material world were grasped, humanity would move forward, bettering itself, into a socialist Beatitude which would establish justice to all men upon earth.'

'Let us go back to Sylvie,' said Philippe. 'I have had enough of this philosophy, yet we for ever fall back into it.'

But the astrologer was vexed, as wise men in disputation brook no carping comment. 'Rahit liberated Sylvie, gave her back to herself, for the first time, perhaps. She began her walking on the road to herself; in the wrong direction materially, to her death, in the right direction spiritually, towards herself. And this private event is a salvation, a redeeming as meaningful as that elevated to the realm of mystery and dogma for all mankind in your religion with its flavour of ritual murder.

'When Rahit and Devi-Sylvie left the boat that morning, dragging their souls with dust-sifting feet, they walked for hours, Rahit walking first, fast, and brutally, not turning back, knowing Moen had to follow. And Evil assailed him, as he has told you. He hated you then, Philippe, and unable to reach you made Moen suffer, himself enduring torment, for that is what men call love. Dragging Moen by his presence, never turning his head to look, he wanted to weary her until she should fall on her knees. And so she did, unable to endure the silence of his back. "Rahit, I am so tired." He turned, sinister-faced, said: "We must reach the forest." They rested a while, then went on, mute, and his back was still his face to her.

'When they had reached the forest the trees were each an enemy, disfiguring the day. She sank under one, called, tired and frightened, Rahit's name. He did not look, but took out his knife, and toyed with it. Then she knew terror, closed her eyes to ward off the disaster, searched in her mind for something to say, to do, turning to trivia as women do, as Maté does, escaping by cooking rice for her son, finding the common useless gesture of the normal routine day to shield her from the avalanche disaster. "I am hungry, Rahit. Is there nothing to eat?" "No," he said, "there is nothing." For they had taken nothing from the boatman who had rowed them across the lake, Rahit had forgotten to make provision of fish and rice; he had crossed the villages in an ecstasy of pain and violence, without buying or begging, dragging Moen behind his blind shoulders to the forest.

"'I am hungry," she repeated, and it made him more angry and he cut air with his knife, eyes fixed upon it; and she too felt her eyes drawn to the blade's glint, now clear like glass, now bland as skin, in its shifting glaze a promise of inflexible menace to hurl her into the perils and rendings of her childhood. She wept, looking at Rahit's knife, and nearly asked: Is this going to kill me? But instead, once more holding up like praying hands her words, moaned: "O, I am hungry and so tired."

'Rahit said, weighing the words with terrible deliberation, and never looking at her: "That man never was your brother. He was in love with you. He threw your bangles in the sea, and took your soul away."

"'It is not true, Rahit, not true."

"'It is. If I had not come, you would have gone away with him. You were not waiting for me. You lied when you said you were waiting for me. I saw the suitcases. That night, in your room."

'And how could Devi explain to him that it was true and yet not true; that she did not choose, and never could have chosen, to stay or to go, because all her life had been thrust upon her? How could she speak about Jacques, the middle way out of both perils? She was not sure of anything, except that she could not love any other shoulders but Rahit's, skin but his, voice but his; yet she was also attached to Philippe, she also needed Philippe . . . How could she say it all, not knowing it herself, knowing only the impulse to hide to be sought for, to be wanted; this perpetual hide-and-seek within herself that was her life?

'She said: "I was hoping you would come. I love only you, I came away with you, Rahit. You are my love."

'He replied: "I saw the suitcases." For he wanted her whole seeing the world only through him, needing no other, a foolish and entire desire, as foolish and demanding as yours. There was no pity and no understanding in him: only the armies of greed marshalled to trample her down. "You are mine," he shouted, "but he has taken your soul away. You are no longer Moen."

'And he heard the devils howl, the forest a malevolent swamp their abode. A leaf spiralled its slow downfall, like a dooming finger. Rahit was also of the village, nourished upon dreams of tree-bodies come walking in panoply to stifle wrongdoers with tentacle branches, of spirits with wrinkled wings, that cackle among leaves and drink men's blood. This returned to haunt him, as the pickaback you gave your little sister haunted you. So immured was he in this self-made horror that he sprang, shouting, knife in hand, giving great gashes to the air, crying: "I shall kill him, and you too," and Death laughed and danced to see him tearing holes in the air.

'"Rahit, Rahit, I am Moen, your Moen."

'Yet even in his ferocity Rahit knew he must not hurt Moen, must not hurt the little girl clinging to his neck in the sweeping waters of the flood, must not let go of that one helplessness, even though they were once again closing on him, slimy, sucking, screaming waters of the river's bottom, peeling off him his life. He must bear her to the end.

'So he turned, writhing, screaming: "Run, Moen. Go, go, or I shall hurt you," and ran himself, away from her, wrenching his body, and slobbered with an effort as strong as birth, while demons clutched at him: "Look, Rahit, see her lying thus, helpless in her lair, and be relieved, for this is the body of a possessed devil, a soulless body possessed by another man. Moen will come back to you, out of this bloody birth, herself restored, if you strike."

'He heard, believed, at the same time knew it not entirely so. He ran away not to hurt her, lunatic among the trees. And on his shouting, crashing way, came upon a small fawn lost by its mother, and fell upon it as an army upon a taken town falls and slakes its blood-lust, and gashed it many times. The blood spurted upon him, he looked as if he had stabbed his own limbs. The fawn died very quickly, and with its tremor wrecked the man's fury. And Rahit was left with the small corpse, half drowned in its own blood.

'He heard Moen's cry, and: "Oh, what have I done?" he whispered, stroking the fawn's wet nuzzle, suddenly filled with horror. We Khmers do not take life, except that of fish, with the excuse that they leap into our nets of their own accord; for Man is compact of compromises, as the Buddha knew.

'Rahit now knew himself criminal, and when he heard feet rustle the fallen leaves, and it was Moen, he wept aloud; but Moen, her weariness forgotten, had followed him in his delirium, in spite of her terror, in spite of his wildness. And this was love.

'He turned to her then as men will turn to their first hiding-place, the mother, woman, in desolation, and she for the first time knew another's need, knew her anguish outgrown in her need to give.

And this was the miracle of Compassion, which is Love. She alone could give him that most difficult thing of all to give, the small private miracle of millions by which we live, consolation by presence, wholeness by being another, Mercy, dark and wordless like a womb. She alone could insulate him from the blood that bespattered him. And this could only be done by her, Moen, becoming herself, someone she had not been; for no one else could do or be this to Rahit.

'She stood by him, and with her skirt she wiped his face and hands, sharing the murder, his guilt. And Rahit said to her: "Oh, Moen. It was in place of you. I am not fit to touch you now."

'She replied: "It is because of this killing that I understand at last."

'Thus Awareness was granted to both, that in all that is dear and beloved is the perversity of separation, alteration, and pain, for all that is born is compounded with dissolution. And Rahit knew that what he had willed was wrong, for he had willed possession, a Moen that was not, a love of his own devising, not the Love that waited for his understanding. Illusion dropped from him, like a mustard seed from the point of a needle.

'"Oh, Moen, I see now that no one has ever asked you: what do you want? And what I called loving you was our reflection in the water, shadow troubled by the wind."

'So he knew the desolation in her too, and how she needed protection, and care, more even than in the night flood of their childhood. But she would not ask for it. Now she had learnt to give as easily as the wind of summer, and precisely now that he understood her he would have to let her go from him entirely. He could no more retain her in the mirror of his eyes than poured water can hold the shape of its cup.

'And so, exorcized, knowing the hours precious and short, they rested, and made love, found forest fruit to eat, and burnt the fawn with piety to speed his rebirth; and knew in the hour of parting the fullness of Love. The trees were guardians of the long summer day, and at night the darkness wrapped its silk tents about their sleep.

'The next morning he took her a long way through the forest, nearly to its edge, and set her feet towards the village. For Moen said: "I will go back and see Maté first. Then I shall decide what to do." And Rahit said: "Do not let her make up your mind for you, do not let her speak for her son Rahit." And so, afraid his mother might weaken him, he turned back alone among the trees.

'That is when Prem caught up with them. It is easy for a monk to follow those who run away, none will withhold an answer from a holy man. You and Jacques went searching, searching for Moen, everywhere asking questions, but no one had seen the two, no one knew. But Prem caught up with them. Again he sought to take Rahit away, to make him renounce this life and its sorrows for the perfect peace of non-attachment. But Rahit said to him: "Prem, you are wrong as I was, for how can I decide to renounce or not to renounce? I shall be there when and if Moen needs me. This is the true Middle Way, more difficult than that absolute gesture you demand." Prem then lost the swell of confidence, and knew that he too had been self-willed, demanding possession of a soul to his own greater glory, wanting a better, holier life for Rahit, and thus doing evil.

'"Rahit," Prem said, "I see I too have much to learn, and chiefly abstemiousness in my desire to convert others."

'Meanwhile, benighted with search, both of you had joined Madame Moniveau in a hunting party. Solange Moniveau is a keen sportswoman, nosing the wind and killing pitilessly in those safaris she organizes with so much success. She too is a giver, dealing out death, releasing for so many the deaths that hang in us, green like unripened fruit, until the time they redden and overhang us in the required explosion. And it was Solange Moniveau who provoked the required explosion, all unknown to her.

'Perhaps your stars went out of joint at that premeditated yet unplanned moment, for you were all gathered together within a space where your contrary destinies met to produce the necessary disarray. It flung Moen into rebirth, and all of us, including myself, into this dimension where, remnants rather than whole beings, we were to be made whole again in this confrontation.'

'How do you know all this?' interrupted Philippe, still defending, in a last sortie, the citadel of his world of words and images. 'How can you know all this? Astrologer, guerrilla, monk, who are you?'

Said the astrologer: 'Have I not told you that I am the indispensable witness, essential as the surrounding, impassive, all-feeling air, and that without me there would be no meeting? Of course I was there. Not as myself, but as Rahit, as Prem, as the homeless wind itself. Rahit is not a renouncer, but a maker of words and songs, and it was wrong of Prem to attempt for him a monk's vocation. Prem too had his use, for it was he who warned Rahit that Moen was changed, and perhaps because Rahit was warned understanding came more swiftly to him when the fawn died – and that too was necessary. And all this I know, having picked up this knowledge as a squirrel gathers nuts, until today, when you come to me for my store, my story.

'I know too how at the end of the forest Rahit turned away from Moen, wrenching the light out of his eyes, accepting night and the dustgrit of her absence, and in doing so accomplished what the woman disciple of the Buddha did, and obtained Awareness: she was of great beauty, and a man, enamoured of her eyes, told her they had fired his soul; she wrenched one out of its socket and amiably gave it to him: "Here is what you say you want," and he fled. In the same way Rahit went back to the forest, turning away from Moen, saying: "I shall wait for you, for ever. If not in this life, then in the next. But always shall I wait, and waiting, find you everywhere, in everything, and you shall be all my singing." He delivered Moen of all promise, exaction, or care, and himself accomplished his own knowledge. So that when Prem came to tempt him, he was not misled.

'And when he had gone, Moen-Devi-Sylvie stood where the trees grow sparse, only a few miles to go to the village, to Maté. This was nearly where Maté had found her, many years before. And then, suddenly, Moen went back into the forest, back the way she had come. And Moen met your hunting party, and fearful of the noise hid in a bush. And thus came to an end.'

'Yes,' said Philippe. 'Jacques shot her.'

'Your turn,' said the astrologer. 'You must complete this story, Dr Rouvier.'

'Have I not suffered too? I have said less about it than you . . . but I shall never forgive myself. Philippe and I went in search of her. Many days we searched, in many places. We drove to the village, but Maté hid from us. We were told that Sylvie had not yet returned.

'And then, I don't know why, we became convinced that Sylvie and whoever was with her (for we did not know about Rahit, not until Anne told us) were hiding in the city, and that we must go back to the city, hire a private detective agency (Philippe wanted to avoid publicity), and find her, in the maze of the tenements perhaps.

'It was afternoon, we were both tired. But, perhaps because we were tired, a little euphoric. "She can't leave the country. She's not in the villages, we've done nearly all of them. No one has seen them anywhere. They *must* be in the city." I don't know why it made us feel that it would be easy to find her in the city, easier than in the expanse of the fields. "She might come home at any time, of her own accord," Philippe said.

'And it was then, by the edge of the woods which begin the forest, that we saw the pitched tents, and slowed down. Solange Moniveau waved her bright bandanna at us and hailed us gaily.

'We stopped. I knew all about Solange and her itch for Philippe. Solange was not alone. Her latest beau was with her, a herculean Brazilian who spent his time going from country to country to hunt. Solange thought this superb, for she too had the frenzy of the body, the brutality which goes with hedonism. But in spite of the Brazilian, it was Philippe she wanted. She found him seductive because of his haughty, distant look and voice, his blue eyes fixed on an inner land-scape, unperceptive of her charms.

'"But you must stay the night with us," she cried. "Return to Pnomh Penh tomorrow in the early morning. It will be time enough."

'Of course Solange knew about Sylvie, but did not mention it. Her eyes sparkled with malicious happiness. This was a splendid occasion to seduce Philippe. She proposed an evening walk, "to kill something for our supper". The Brazilian and I took guns. I am a sportsman too, and I like hunting occasionally.

'We went for a walk in the forest, the Brazilian and I in front, Solange following with Philippe, her voice cooing, confiding, caress-ing, with just the right note of subdued grief. And walking, with the long sunset stabbing in and out between the leaves, I suddenly thought of Sylvie's hair, and Philippe brushing it in front of me . . . It was like a hand clutching my heart, so that I had to stop, and everything went a little dim. The Brazilian stopped too, or perhaps he had stopped first, for he said: "There, in the bush, there's some-thing." And raised his gun.

'And then I distinctly saw, distinctly as I see you, behind the bush, the head of a young deer. A fawn. Its eyes looked at me. My gun came up to my shoulder.

'"Oh." Solange Moniveau made a small round O with caught breath, and I fired as if her O pulled the trigger for me.

'I saw the fawn, I tell you. I saw it. When we heard the scream I still thought it was a beast.

'And then the Brazilian had leapt forward, run to the bush, and he screamed, a funny high-pitched cry for a man who usually emitted low, r-rolling tones.'

'It was Sylvie, my sister,' said Philippe. 'Jacques killed her. I nearly killed him then, I know. But I fainted. I was unconscious for two days. Solange took us back. And then Anne told us. About Rahit.'

'Why did she hide?' asked Jacques. 'Why did she not come out of the bush? She must have heard us. She must have seen us. Why?'

'She was afraid,' said the astrologer.

'Afraid of us? Afraid of being found? Why did Rahit leave her alone in the forest?'

'He did not,' said the astrologer. 'He left her at the end of the woods. She turned back.'

'Why?'

'I do not know,' said the astrologer. 'On this point not only the stars are silent, but even I must stop explaining. I really do not know. Because where you killed her was not on the way to Maté, it was not on the way to Rahit. I might as well ask you, Jacques, why you thought you saw a deer. It had to be.

'And now that there is no more to say, do you feel that you know more than you did? Do you feel you know enough about your sister, the whole of her, to keep to yourself the rest of your days? Because if so our seance is at an end, and I shall draw up your account.'

*

As always, Philippe Bergerat drove with vicious speed. He liked to *prendre corps* with the machine. Velocity obliterated separateness. He felt his own muscles, nerves, sinews, penetrate the steel, the car body an extension of his brain, the wheels a loping swiftness denied to bone, but which could be exacted from an engine driven at a hundred miles an hour. Conquest, possession, power, in easy sweeps of wind, were his when he drove.

Over his shoulder he threw words at Jacques. 'Well, are you satisfied now? Now you realize who's mad. All of you. Not me. And that weakling, Rahit, so slippery, fluidly vanishing on his child's bicycle.'

Jacques shrugged his shoulders: 'You must get cured of this obsession, Philippe.'

'And Anne,' said Philippe, 'Anne going off on that bicycle with him. Utterly ridiculous. We should catch them up any moment now. They can't have gone far.'

The road swerved to the right, beyond a clump of kapok trees. The car screamed round the bend, and then, with an exclamation, Philippe theatrically clamped on his brakes and stopped. 'My God, look at this!'

Jacques said: 'The flood.'

Water was everywhere. A sea emerged, over the fields, the trees, lapping over the road, rolling fat billows like listless elephants. Farther on it covered the road entirely, as if the water had thickened, and went on thickening the farther it was from them. Here and there a few tree-tops emerged, a scribble of topmost small branches, silvered with water; and all this water was deep blue, with silver lappings, a quiet, deep, deadly nonchalance of water, as solid and deep as can be.

Erect at the edge of the flood, with the water nearly reaching their feet, still as children, with heads raised looking at a television set, Anne and a monk in a yellow silk robe, with ample smooth skull and imperious face massive on a strong body, stood side by side. The set was tied midway up a tree still on dry land, one of the clump which had hidden the flood from view round the bend.

Philippe jumped out from the car, not forgetting, as he got down, the tape, safe in his hand. The tape-recorder, packed neatly in its case, sat on the back seat, an unperturbed machine-being, a master, waiting calmly while the driver went to inquire about an obstacle on their course.

'Anne, what is the meaning of this?'

Anne turned her head. The television set was alive with noises and movement. Anne said: 'I told you. The flood.'

'I can see there's a lot of water. How do we cross?'

'I don't know,' replied Anne. 'It is impossible. At least, it was impossible for me. They told me so.'

'Who are they?'

'The people who take you across, of course. The boatmen. They took Rahit. He could pass, but he had to leave his bicycle behind him. It is there, you see, leaning against that tree.'

The monk turned, looked at Philippe and Jacques with benign interest. Anne said, as if introducing people at dinner: 'This is His Excellency Prem. This is my husband. And Dr Jacques Rouvier, my lover.'

The monk folded his hands in salutation. He turned back to the television set, and twiddled with the knobs.

'But what do we do?' cried Philippe. 'How do we call the boatmen?'

'I couldn't pass,' repeated Anne. 'Only Rahit, I tell you. Oh yes, I forgot. Maté too. But she had to leave her rice behind. It hurt her very much. She wanted to take it, but they said no, the rice was too heavy. She was so angry that she threw it in the water with the rice pot.' And Anne emitted her personal seal-bark chuckle.

'Rahit is lucky,' said Prem, still twiddling and fumbling, while the grey screen blitzed with zigzag static. 'He always has a song to carry him across. He could pass the Deadly Floods, my friend, having given up all but his singing . . . lucky Rahit. All people are lucky who can thus sing their love for things away, and be left light, light, light enough to cross any ocean.'

'But this is extraordinary,' said Jacques. 'There was no flood when we came, only a few hours ago.'

'Oh, there was when Rahit and I came, but it was quite small. There was the accident, but the flood waters seem to have covered it up,' said Anne, squinting into the waters. 'A pity. I would have liked to see those ripped and disembowelled machines again. I really do dislike machines so much.'

'There was no accident,' shouted Philippe. 'No accident, no flood. This is crazy.'

At that moment the television screen burst into life and agonizing screams. On it appeared some men, busy round one tied to a table. They were cutting pieces out of him. Attentive, concentrated, their knives sliced his flesh and drew thongs of flesh and skin, which they held in their hands like small leaping snakes, and threw at a crowd of men, women, and children who held their hands out as beggars do for coins, and roared each time a piece was thrown.

'That's the third one they're eating,' said Prem. 'I understand there are thirteen of them.' The television blurred, and he adjusted it.

'Oh God,' cried Anne, 'what was it?'

'A play,' said Prem, frowning as he worked, 'somebody being eaten up.'

'But it's terrible. I wonder they dare to show these things on television nowadays,' said Anne, indignantly.

'But where is this happening?' said Jacques. 'Where?'

'I don't know,' said Prem. 'Somewhere or other in the world. What does it matter where? All places are the same.'

'I didn't see,' said Anne, with trembling voice. 'Were these . . . Africans? It's more understandable if they are . . . but I couldn't make sure . . .'

'I'm trying to get it back,' said Prem. The machine crackled, the shadows steadied, solidified their outlines. Now the men were chopping up the hands. Deftly they chopped with two shining choppers, holding the fingers down, then gathered handfuls of neatly chopped squares and threw them in the air. With much laughter the children caught them, and started sucking them like sweets.

'I can't make out,' said Philippe, straining his eyes, 'what people they are . . . And the children . . . it's perfectly horrible, I don't think I can stand it.' But he looked on. There was so much gaiety and laughter in the scene, and though the victim screamed he did not move, and the screams sounded far away now, fainter.

'Oh, but you can, you can,' said Prem. 'We've all become so accustomed to atrocities, cruelties, massacres, really our sense of horror is quite blunted, I am sure. You can stand this quite well. I sometimes wonder if it isn't the effect of seeing too much of reality as shadows on a TV screen, moving images empty of emotion, lacking a dimension of feeling, that has made us all as callous as the Romans became after decades of the amphitheatre. We have no fund of horror, pity, or indignation left, except for our own selves. And of that too much. We end up without any awareness outside our own emotions, emptiness turned inwards wholly, never admitting its own consequence to others. All of us, all of us, can easily stand looking on. Other people's sufferings are so easy to bear nowadays.'

Now the hands had gone, and it was the turn of the feet.

Jacques said: 'I wonder who took these photographs.'

Philippe: 'I still can't make out whether these people are . . . like us, or not.'

Anne said: 'What does it matter? Hasn't Prem told you that it's all the same? We're all at that table, eating this flesh, sucking these bones. The communion of the saints,' she cried, 'that's it. That's it. Oh God, when will the boat come back?'

'Why wouldn't they take you, Anne?' asked Jacques.

'Didn't I tell you?' shrieked Anne. 'Because I couldn't, I couldn't get rid of him.' And her finger jabbed forward, jabbing close to Philippe's face. 'It's him, it's because of him. I couldn't give him up.'

'Give him up? You've never had me,' sneered Philippe.

'Do I not know it? Yet I couldn't give you up. They asked me: "Are you prepared to give up Philippe, your husband?" I said I could not. They said: "Sorry, then you cannot pass." I argued with them. I said: "But surely I can't throw Philippe in the water, like Maté's rice. How *can* I give him up?" They nodded without speaking, and went away. You may think me mad, but I still love you, Philippe. And I will not relinquish you. Because it's the best thing I have, the noblest, my love for you. I won't give it up, even if I have to wait here for all eternity.'

'Ah,' said Prem, sighing, 'never does one have to wait for all eternity, you know. Not if you are a Buddhist. The Lord of Compassion is not ruthless and absolute, damning for ever, as your God is. The only trouble is that in this dimension there is no convenient scapegoat, as you have in yours. The invention of the scapegoat was an excellent way of evading responsibility. Once you had laid your sins upon one, you felt exonerated. But here it's different. Here it's quite different. No one can bear your sins for you. On the contrary. We are collectively responsible for all misdeeds, and the innocent pay for the guilty, but the guilty are still guilty, all of them together. It's somehow more fair, isn't it, than the other way round? But it takes longer, it's not so neat and packaged as your formulae.'

'I never thought of it like that,' said Jacques. 'Do you mean to say that we all have to wait here because Anne is guilty of something, or you? And of what? What is this dimension you speak of, and the astrologer spoke of? What has happened to us?'

'The dimension of Nearly Truth?' said Prem. 'I really don't know. I only know that as we become callous because reality becomes too easily shadow in our midst, so shadow and word become flesh and reality in this dimension. Look at this flood. A perfect example of Word made Real.'

'Word made Real?'

'I forget,' said Prem, smiling, and Anne noticed the beautiful mouth, so much like Maté's mouth. 'You are Christians, not Buddhists, so you would not know that the Lord of Compassion spoke, figuratively, of course, of the Deadly Floods, three in number: the waters of death which are ignorance, lust, and desire of becoming, of never ceasing to be. Only those who have forsaken lust of becoming, who do not care whether they will live on or not, and who have been made aware, can cross the flood. I am afraid we are lacking in some respect or other, and must wait until Awareness comes, or until we give up whatever holds us back and makes us too heavy for the boat.' He turned back to the set, which instantly emitted loud music, upon which Prem put his hands to his ears, muttering: 'My Order forbids me to hear music, but you may listen if you wish,' and went and sat down at the edge of the flood, so that the water was just an inch away from his bare feet.

'This is preposterous,' cried Philippe. 'I don't believe a word of it.'

'You'll have to give up that tape,' cried Anne. 'And the recording machine. You'll have to throw them into the water, as Maté threw her rice.'

Jacques approached Prem, and squatted next to him. 'Tell me, Prem, tell me. Is there rebirth, on the other side? Or are we damned for ever?'

'Damned?' cried Prem, with surprise. 'There is no eternal damnation. How could the Compassion which is life itself condemn for all eternity? Such a barbaric and silly notion. As for rebirth, that is a question which was also asked of the Buddha after he attained Enlightenment, but he did not give any answer, for the simple reason that it would not serve any useful purpose. Men, however, have gone on clinging to the hope, because it comforts them. But the subject is undeterminable. That is all we Buddhists know.'

'Then the Wheel of Rebirth, the continuous link of life?'

'True and not true, real and unreal, shadow of words masking reality . . . how do I know?' said Prem. 'I only know that there is no God. Only Life, and the Awareness of Life, and that goes on for ever, each one of us but one facet of the continuum which we together are. . . .'

They waited for the boat, and their shadows were cast upon each other.

Winter Love

Winter Love

It was nine in the morning, on the centre courtyard at the Horsham Science College. I was a second-year student. September 20th, 1944. London September, young, not stark cold, but flabby, shiver-making, viscous, yellow-grey chill sticking to the stones and pillars of the courtyard. All the girls were there, our year and the third year, and the new first-years huddling together embarrassed and dumb. High-voiced, self-consciously laughing groups reformed, much the same twosomes as last year moving about together again. It was a duffel-coat and macintosh year; everyone seemed to wear one. I can't see any other colour about except Mara's. To me she glowed in green and blue tweeds, standing all by herself on high heels, while colourless fawn-greys eddied round.

'Hallo, Red. Had a nice vac?'

'Yes, thanks.'

It was Louise, blue eyes looking at me, fawn camel coat. I'd protected her in First; we'd gone around together. She'd spent the short summer vac in Ireland with her people, and we'd written to each other quite a lot.

'I've bagged the best locker, Red. Came early and got it from the Frump. Told her I'd share it with you.'

'That's fine.' I stared at Mara's heels, with the nylon stockings above them. Nylons I hadn't seen except in magazines. Strictly black-market in 1944.

Louise followed my eyes. 'Who's the new bod?'

'Don't know.'

'Good gracious, just *look* at those nails.'

Pink varnish. Her toes might have pink varnish on, too. Her feet must be beautiful in their smooth suède navy shoes. She had black hair, longish, smooth as a blackbird's wing but the ends tipped upwards.

'Italian or French,' said Louise. 'Oh, lord, one of those married bods again. She's got a ring.'

On her left-hand ring-finger was a plain band, which I thought silver.

'It's the war,' said Louise. 'Married bods everywhere these days. Platinum ring. Bod with dough. Dog with bough.' Louise tried to talk as I did, to please. And I talked the way I did because it rather showed up the snooty ones, like Louise. I'd picked up the lingo from Rhoda, and lots of girls now thought it smart.

Daphne came up to me. 'Hallo, Red, had a good vac? You look spiffing, darling. Who's the new item?'

'Lenora Stanton Number Two,' said Louise. 'Another of those married students. What's the Horsham coming to?'

'I say, Red, will you dissect with me,' said Daphne, 'you and Louise, I mean?'

Louise looked stony and said, 'Thanks for nothing, Duffer.'

There I stood with Daphne Meredith and Louise Wells, my chums. I'd known them both since school-days, and Louise said she was in love with me. But I walked away and stood by Mara, only of course I didn't know her name. She turned her head, her forehead came up to my mouth. She had a pointed, cat's face, dark eyes, pale skin. 'I say,' I said. 'Good morning. This your first day?'

'Yes, but I'm going straight into second year. Miss Eggleston said I could.' Eggie was our Zoology Demonstrations teacher.

'Got a partner? To dissect with, I mean?'

She shook her head.

'In that case, would you like to dissect with me? I mean, if you don't mind?'

She said: 'I'd like to, of course.'

'I'll see you in the lab then,' I said. 'We're meeting there to share the bods; I mean, you know, the specimens. By the way, my name's Bettina Jones, but everybody calls me Red. . . . My hair' – I pointed – 'true mouse, hence Red.'

She laughed. She looked at me. I had my leather jacket on and my grey flannel skirt. I hid my hands in my pockets.

'And my name is Mara Daniels. I'll see you, Red, in the lab, as you say.'

I went back, whistling under my breath, to where Louise and Daphne stood. Louise gave me that widening of her eyelids at the outer corner of her eyes, pupils dilating then narrowing suddenly, a trick that someone, not I, must have told her made her eyes more seductive. She did that quite often. At first it had attracted me, now I suddenly didn't like it any more.

'Who's *she*?' Her lower lip tried to snake up at the word 'she'.

'Nice kid,' I said. 'I've asked her to dissect with us.'

'You've asked her . . . Another Stanton married bod? You're slipping, Red. Never knew you fall for that kind before.'

Daphne just looked far-away.

'I suppose,' Louise went on, 'she'll be sharing your locker next, the one I got for us?'

'Hadn't thought of that. But I suppose I'd better get cracking finding one for her,' I said.

'Wow,' said Daphne, 'we've all had it, chum.' She stepped smartly away, her face quivering a bit.

Louise could blaze up, but she wouldn't start a scene now. She had dignity. Next thing, she was chatting and laughing with a group; that was her way of getting even with me, but I didn't care any more, and I didn't say anything as she turned her back to me.

I watched Mara. She stood against a pillar. Girls looked at her, furtively, curiously. She was going straight into second year. My year. She was to dissect with me. She stood there, not looking at anyone, not even me, a far-away composure upon her face. I knew it was the most beautiful face I had ever seen.

★

The Zoology Lab at the Horsham was as dismal as the rest of its mid twenties four-storeyed structure, though more recently built and full of glass windows. Just before the war some dear old Horsham girl, bursting with zeal for female emancipation, had left enough money to modernize that bit of the College. As she put it in her will: recalling the awful hours she had spent trying to get herself an education, she wanted us to be more comfortable than she'd been. Some crumbling walls had been replaced. All one end and right down one side we had plate glass staring at the sky and the serried thousands of chimney-pots of London. In 1944 with those buzz-bombs it didn't make one feel too happy. Nothing had happened as yet – the blitz had spared us – but one did feel unprotected when the V1s droned overhead.

Our cement post-mortem table, upon which lay the formalin-injected animals (we'd graduated to vertebrates and were doing cat), was in the left-hand corner, just where the glass ceiling began; and looking up from the specimens stretched out, dripping congealed grease and spreading acid chemical stench in the cold lab air, I could see a grey balloon, behind it another, and yet others, quite a lot of watching balloons, suspended in the still, grey sky.

Mara and I worked on one half of the cat. Louise with Daphne did the other half. The formalin made our eyes water, the smell made us cough. Coughing was not liked by Miss Eggleston.

'Now, now, ladies.' She would come in, tapping upon the slabs the thin wand she kept in her hand and with which she pointed at organs and exposed nerves and tendons, like a maestro at the Proms picking out the musicians with his baton. She went tap-tapping, tut-tutting, from slab to slab. Some of us she liked, others she didn't, and she never bothered to hide her feelings.

At first Eggie disliked Mara, and it wasn't difficult to know why. Mara was so different; first there were her looks, her clothes, the way she spoke. Then, about a week after we had begun on the cat, Mara went skipping down the lab to the cloakroom. Why she skipped instead of just walking I wouldn't know. She was like that at times, like a child who'd never grow up. The next day Eggie wrote in red chalk on the blackboard: 'Ladies will *walk quietly* and refrain from skipping through the Zoology Laboratories.'

Mara could not understand why, and said so.

Louise, scalpel scratching, said: 'I agree with Eggie. It's bad form, skipping.'

'Disrespect to the cats,' I explained. 'We may be cutting them up, but we've still got to show respect or something. I mean not laugh or sing or talk too loud, and all that.'

In those early days Eggie quivered with suppressed irritation whenever she saw Mara: the varnished nails, the make-up, the nylons, and the heels; the over-long hair with a sheen on it. Everything about Mara meant money, care, glamour, and I suppose it offended Eggie's puritan delight in ugliness. Mara had an absent-minded, far-away ease, which often looked like impudence when it was only detach-ment; she didn't care what she said or did, and Eggie wasn't used to that. Most of us played up a bit to Eggie, even Lenora Stanton.

Mara's looks did things to Eggie; that was obvious. A lot of us during the war rather wallowed in frowziness, didn't keep our nails or hair too clean; things were hard to come by, and somehow it was good to let oneself go. Just as it was good to talk lower-middle-class talk, it made one feel somehow more 'in' with everybody else, less class-feeling about, more chummy and sturdy; it reflected the 'I-can-look-after-myself' feeling of some of us; it was an attitude, and we grew to our own attitude.

Mara wasn't like Lenora Stanton, who insisted on telling everybody about her husband's demise, about her infants, encouraged the girls to think of free love and sex as a beautiful ecstasy, and shouted gaily at the canteen: 'What all of you need is a *man*!' when men were so damned hard to meet in those days. Mara didn't talk, but it was obvious that she had another, secret life, besides this life among the dead cats in the lab with those glacial, sky-staring windows. That bandbox look suggested care, a man who looked after her, the assurance of wealth behind her, and yet there was something slightly off key. One couldn't imagine her *not* having everything she wanted, in spite of the war. But then why was she here? Of course Eggie disapproved. The lab was Eggie's life. She was bound to it. For her, I thought, there couldn't be much else. Year after year after year she'd go on teaching zoology. We knew only that part of Eggie's life which existed in bleak day. We knew that with winter coming Eggie's nose got redder and redder, the only bright thing about her. Beyond the lab we knew nothing of her, could not imagine anything exciting happening to her. One could not visualize her doing anything other than tapping her stick and asking for the name of a bone or the comparative phylogeny of the jaw. Whereas Mara suggested . . . oh, so many many things, envy-making things: warm beaches and cosmetics and music, and lots of clothes and no coupons, and eggs and tins from America, and French wines, and oh, so many things we were forgetting in the war or had never had.

After I knew Mara I began to wonder about other people. I mean, about what they really were inside. Far more than I'd ever done. It was Mara who brought these thoughts to me. At the Horsham she was for ever saying and doing the wrong things, or so it seemed; always someone or other there was speculating about her, talking about this or that she'd said or done. But they kept quiet if they noticed I was about. But it didn't matter to me: I was already in love with her. I didn't like it when people said things. And as for Eggie's dislike, well, that hurt me too, but somehow it made me see Eggie differently, made her more human. I knew why she disliked Mara. But Mara's worst enemy was Louise, who made remarks whenever she could. Louise hated Mara, and I think it wasn't so much because of *me* as because Mara was so beautiful.

Because we were all girls together it was cosy, even with the malice. I mean, we felt at ease, shouting gaily to our partners after lab, striding away by twos, semi-permanent duos formed quickly or slowly, sometimes (though rarely) changed after a few months, every change bringing with it a 'situation', quarrels or tight-lipped scenes which we all pretended weren't. I'd had my situations, so far, outside the Horsham. Some of these friendships went on for years, on through life, complete and whole in themselves, requiring no one else; but they were few. The names of these became to us semi-legendary, perpetuated by generations of Horsham girls. Many more broke up. When they broke up because of another girl there was drama, or farce, or both together, but things all settled back. Sometimes a man came in and broke it up, and then we all felt it much more. And occasionally there was a tragedy, but not often at the Horsham.

Few of the girls there were permanently like that. Most of us knew we'd grow out of it one day, get married as soon as we'd left, have kids. With the war we also had married women like Lenora Stanton, who took a course in science in order to do war work later, or so she said. Lenora was a Pain, and I did my best to avoid her. I disliked her on sight. But she had her own little court, girls who hung on her lips and went round talking of Life as it ought to be lived, as a Grand, Glorious Experience, and of Woman's Role, and the Love-Life. Lenora had been an actress for a short while; her actor husband had died trying to vacuum the carpet. 'Electro-cuted,' she Tallulah'd in ringing, stage tones, 'he was electrocuted. I came home to find him dead, holding the vacuum cleaner.' No one in her coterie seemed to think it funny.

Lenora was now getting married again, and hinted she would soon be doing a hush-hush war job with her new husband. Meanwhile she wanted all of us girls to understand Life and Love, and we were spared nothing of her grand, glorious clinches with her husband-to-be. Lenora had travelled a bit, and after the war she and her husband intended to settle down in Australia. He was part-Australian, which she didn't seem to mind at all, though it made Louise snigger: 'The great wide open spaces.'

'Of course,' Lenora used to scream gaily, 'they're *terribly* conventional over there. I mean, at parties all the women sit together and all the men sit together, and they never *talk* to each other. And if a girl crosses over to talk to the men, all the other women gang up against her and say she's *Fast*.' Her eyes shone happily; she was looking forward to preaching the Love-Life in Australia.

Lenora, in that same ringing voice, told me one day about Eggie. It seems that she'd gone to tea with Eggie once, for, incredibly enough, Eggie *liked* Lenora Stanton. 'Lives with her friend in a small flat down the Bayswater Road. Friend's a biologist, female of course. Poky little place, lace curtains, fringed lampshades, crochet rugs, and all that sort of thing, and of course a tom-cat . . . neutered,' she added.

Apart from Lenora and Mara, the married ones in our year, our landscape was female, spinster: young, eager, and boisterous, or greying, middle-aged, and abrupt. The young men were away at war, and many of us had come up from school without meeting them as we ought to have done. There were lots of Eggies everywhere doing wonderful work, aftermath of the First World War.

To begin with, Mara looked like a hopeless student. How they ever took her straight into second year I couldn't guess. How they ever took her anyway I never knew. They must have had a vacancy, and she got it. At the first three quizzes, whenever Eggie asked a question she did not even try to answer, but said: 'I don't know,' and Eggie kept on at her.

'That's not good enough, Mrs Daniels. I *know* you may have many other more interesting avocations, but we take our work seriously here.'

'Yes,' said Mara. And looked remote, away.

I sat with my hands in my pockets. I couldn't do anything – not even talk about it afterwards with Mara. I was ashamed for her, and unhappy that she made such a poor show. But she would smile at me as if it was nothing at all. Now I know it wasn't, but then I was still at school and I had the reflexes of a schoolgirl. I wanted her to be brilliant and popular, to protect her and shield her from Eggie, shield her from the taunts of the other girls, especially from Louise with all the answers. Everybody knew that Louise would get a Distinction. She always got top marks, always worked hard filling notebook after notebook with that even, smooth writing of hers, and now when Mara said, 'I don't know,' Louise sniggered and Eggie tapped her wand to bring back order.

'Don't think our friend will linger with us very long,' said Louise airily one lunch-time as I waited for Mara in the canteen. Mara and I had 'our' seats in the lecture room, 'our' table in the canteen.

'None of your business,' I replied.

'Of course not, Red, my poppet,' said Louise delicately. 'Let nature take its course. She shouldn't have come to the Horsham. She should hang on to whatever man she's got hold of and stay at home. She's only keeping someone else out of a career by coming here.'

I didn't reply, and then Mara arrived, and after lunch we went for a walk in the park. There was going to be a mid-term quiz in a week. I felt unhappy about it, and I said, 'Look, Mara, I've got some notes. They're not much, but you won't have to plough through the whole book. Think it might help?'

'Oh, thank you,' she said, 'but I enjoy reading zoology.'

'Look here,' I said, 'you're supposed to know your bit, especially the mammal you're dissecting I mean, otherwise Eggie won't let you go on. I mean, it's quite stiff, the competition.'

'Too bad,' said Mara.

We went in St James's Park, but it was dark when we got there and so I walked home with her. She lived in Maybury Street. We'd been dissecting four weeks. A week ago I had walked home with her for the first time. She had turned at the corner and said, 'Good night, Red.' I knew she didn't want me where she lived. And I didn't want her to know where I lived, because I was afraid she'd find it too dingy. I could picture her going back to a beautiful place – glamorous, warm, exciting – with rugs and satin-smooth curtains, not at all like Eggie's poky flat, not at all like my bed-sit in Camden Town with the dining room in the basement, the smell of frying everywhere, the cat's hair in the tea, and Andy and his pals – the medical students from St Thomas's – smelling of formalin as I did after a dissection (only they didn't seem to wash), and sweat and dirty clothes. And Nancy, who ran the boarding-house, with her blonde dyed hair, and her boy-friend Edward, the travelling salesman who did Swedish exercises in the bathroom, and her dentures she left lying about, and the stomach ulcers which gave her halitosis . . .

I went home and prayed hard that Mara would get through the

first quiz, and me too, of course, but I didn't believe she could do it. I'd never worried over anyone else getting through quiz before.

*

'Well,' I kept on saying, 'well, well.'

We walked along the Embankment. I heard Mara's footsteps and mine sounding together, and those of a bobby on his beat ahead of us. There seemed no other sound on that Sunday afternoon: a cold and silent river, a languid flow of hours about us. London was all beautiful pictures, grey and silver: delicate airy buildings traced against silver sky, the balloons anchored puffs swaying in a sprightly wind. Even the sunlight was silvery. Mara's footsteps tuned with mine; her heels tapped the stones, my flat soles an accompaniment to their neat tap. I can still hear us and the bobby, and me saying, 'Well, well.'

'Well, well,' she parodied, laughing at me.

'Mara,' I repeated, 'you've done it.'

I'd said it at least ten times, elated by her triumph as if it were mine. I went over it again. I kept on thinking of it, thrusting my hands in the pockets of my macintosh, breathing in the cold air. It was wonderful walking on a Sunday afternoon on the Embankment with Mara, recalling the way Eggie had sat at the head of a long, narrow table, we girls grouped round bones, and bits of formalin-soaked cat, fish, frog, scattered around. Eggie held the bits up, or pointed at them with her wand, precise, ironical if one didn't know, full of impatient knowledge which made us stammer and become unsure. Her eyes darted from girl to girl, her stick pointed. This was the test which I thought Mara would fail.

Louise had asked her as we settled for the practical test: 'Do you know any zoology, Mrs D.?'

'Do you?' Mara had countered.

Louise had tinkled a laugh, amused, superior.

When it came to Mara's turn everyone, it seemed to me, leaned towards her in cruel, glittering expectancy of error. But Mara knew. The stick went from piece to piece, prodding, insisting, and the answers came easily, so pat that at one point she seemed to be ahead of the question, to harry Eggie on. It was a wonderful show. Even Louise couldn't have done better. And then Eggie, rigid yet game, said, 'Congratulations, Mrs Daniels.'

There was a cold silence as Eggie walked away, and then I began whistling. I always whistle when I'm happy.

One or two girls came up to Mara and said, 'Good show,' and 'I say, you *have* kept your light under a bushel.'

'Well, well,' I said, 'you're a dark horse, Mara.'

'Oh no,' said Mara, 'I just learned it up quickly.'

'After this,' I said, 'I'll be asking *you* to coach me. If you're as good in physiology and organic, I'll be taking lessons from you.'

We leaned over the parapet on the Embankment and looked at the muscular river silently swinging its brown barges. I still remember upon her face that day the reflected sheen of water, light from sky into river and back into her face. Thus with my happiness; it came from her, through her achieved, made whole.

We had tea in a sweaty, smoky little café, where taxi-men and the like ate fish and chips, a roaring, smoky throng of men, alien to us, altogether cut off from us. Then I saw her home to Maybury Street in Mayfair, stood with her at the corner; she walked back with me to Oxford Circus; I walked back with her. I could not bear to leave her. For ever, it seemed, we would be walking enchanted, untiring, back and forth, footsteps together in the cold night streets.

*

Each morning now, getting up earlier by half an hour than before I knew her, I gulped breakfast, hurried to catch the trolley, then changed buses twice to get to the corner of her street, there to wait for her. Every morning recurred the anxiety that I might be late, that she might have been waiting and, not seeing me, gone ahead, and I wouldn't know whether she'd gone or not and I would wait and be late at the Horsham. But it did not happen. Always I was there first, and after a short while saw her come walking down the street towards me.

It was a very cold November. I heard myself saying it as I stamped my feet, as we caught our bus to the Horsham. But I did not mind it as much as I had always minded winter, for I'm a naturally cold person; the doctor told me my circulation was poor, and I get chilblains. But this winter there was an eagerness in me which made me forget the painful smart of my customary chilblains, the frowstiness of Nancy's bed-sit. Perhaps because I spent shillings more carelessly, keeping the gas-fire on, sitting for hours in front of it, dreaming.

In the afternoon I walked with Mara back from the Horsham. Sometimes we'd stop for tea at an A.B.C., and then suddenly she would say: 'Oh, it's late, I must get back,' with a little anxiety in her voice. Off we would go then, and yet, in spite of her saying how late she would be, we would linger at the corner of her street. It was so dark with the blackout I could only guess her face as we said good night; sometimes I thought I could see it, pale, nearly luminous, like a pearl in the darkness. She would say: 'Well, Red, see you to-morrow.'

'Tomorrow. I'll be here.' I would turn and walk away. She always waited until I turned. I felt her eyes on my back.

At other times she wouldn't mind what time it was, and would walk part of the way to Camden Town with me, and I'd walk with her back to the corner of her street, Maybury Street, again. We must have tramped miles every day.

One day, at the A.B.C. where we were having tea, she said: 'Would you like to see where I live?'

I knew the house she lived in: 34 Maybury Street, it said on the register at the College. Mara Daniels. I had walked up the street early one Sunday morning (Sundays we never saw each other), hoping she might accidentally come out of the house. Number 34 was a fair-sized brick house, good-looking, rich-looking; hers the flat on the third floor, the name was under the bell-button. She must be very well-off, living in such a place: expensive flats, a good address.

When Mara said: 'Would you like to?' I was happy, yet frightened. We walked up Maybury Street, meeting two pros, scarcely in ambush yet, still slacking, talking to each other. We entered the hallway. There was a chap in uniform in a kind of booth there, who said: 'Good evening, madam.' We walked to the lift, all polished wood, with seats of red leather. Everything smelt of polish and warmth, not nose-plugging grime and cold. The house enveloped one with a warm, tranquil, rich kind of smell, good polish and regular dusting and fires kept going.

'You do live in a posh place, Mara.'

She said: 'We've got a char who comes in twice a week, and the porter downstairs is awfully good at keeping the place warm.' She opened the door of the flat with a Yale key; then we were inside.

'We took it furnished,' she said, shutting the door on us.

It was good furniture, and well kept. But it didn't seem to mean much to her, one way or the other. She moved about easily, but she wasn't showing it as her own.

'Want a bath?' she asked.

'Do I look dirty?'

She looked at me, my duffel-coat, my grey wool skirt. 'Oh, Red, you told me yourself your pipes had burst.'

That was true. It had been freezing and there was no water at Nancy's boarding-house. Nancy had announced it at breakfast in her disaster voice, the one she reserved for the cat's misdeeds and pregnancies, or a particularly bad bout of her gastric ulcers.

'I'd *love* a bath, chum.'

She opened a door upon the bright glaze of tiled walls; a tap turned, I heard the clink of glass, she came back. 'The water's boiling hot.'

I went into the bathroom and she shut the door on me. The bathroom was full of fragrant steam; there was a large glass jar full of bath salts, and I could see from the yellow-green tinge of the foaming water that Mara had poured some into the tub.

When I came out of the tub there was the towel, large, pink; and putting on my clothes I felt them sour-smelling, stiff with cold dirt. I had not noticed the collar of my shirt before. I didn't like my clothes one bit.

I came out. Mara was sitting on the bed. It was a big bed, or rather two beds made up as one. It had a wonderful bedspread, something beige and shining which made one think of smooth skin. I sat on it next to her. I was at ease now, a dreamy softness about me, looking at the bedspread, suddenly helpless in a sea of memories, transported back to a similar moment of childhood, not recollected until now. Like a wave it swept me up: memory of a warm night, a scene of lilac, the soft arms of my mother. She wore a satin dress, something the colour of the bedspread, her bare arms glowed. She'd smelt so nice. I had nuzzled into her dress, hard.

'Verbena,' said Mara. 'Did you like it?'

'What is?' For a moment I was confused. Was it the perfume of many years back, enclosed memory of warmth and fragrance dwelling deep within my frosted childhood, that she meant? How did she know its name?

'The bath salts, Red. You were sniffing, just now. I thought you'd like to know they're verbena. They're from Switzerland.'

I smelt the back of my hand, smiled at her. She was smiling at me.

'Oh Mara,' I said, 'it's nice to be here, with you.'

'It's nice with you, Red.'

I put out my hand, and there was hers, underneath mine. It was small, compared with mine. I was glad it was so. Glad of the silk under me. Glad. I could have fallen asleep.

'Come,' said Mara, 'I'll show you something.'

Another door, locked. She took a key from her pocket, turned it, found the light-switch. A small, bare room, an easel, canvases with colour on them, one on the easel, others turned against the wall.

'I didn't know you were an artist,' I said.

I walked up to the easel, but she pulled me back.

'Don't look,' she said. 'I do it for fun.'

'So long as you know it's just fun,' I said lightly. There were lots of bright colours. I didn't know whether it was good or not, but it was Mara, so I said: 'It's awfully nice, chum.'

'Oh, I know I'm no good,' she said.

We went back to the bedroom.

I heard the lock turn, knew the outside door had opened. Mara rose quickly, crossed to the living room. I followed her.

It was a man, coming in and taking off his hat, and Mara saying: 'Oh, Karl,' and to me: 'Red, this is my husband, Karl.'

I wanted to look at Karl, but first I stared at Mara because her voice had changed so much. It was different now, small and stiff. There was nothing to be scared of, but I was scared. The man stood there, rubbing his hands against each other. He wasn't tall; he had long blond hair, a little too long at the back; he was handsome, with eyes appearing hazel-green through his horn-rimmed glasses; his eyes were careful.

'Karl,' said Mara, 'this is Bettina Jones. She came to have a bath, as the pipes have burst in her digs.'

'I wish,' he said, with a slight foreign accent, 'that my wife wouldn't use these slang words, Mara.'

We shook hands, then he withdrew his hand from mine and started rubbing his hands one against the other as if soaping them. Nice, revolting hands, shapely, manicured nails. I could hear the rubbing sound as he said: 'It's on the thaw now, but I expect it'll turn cold again.'

Mara said: 'I'll make some tea,' and disappeared.

We sat in the living room, and he asked me how long I had been at the Horsham and what I intended to do after the war, and I knew Mara hadn't spoken to him about me; he hadn't known I existed until now. He kept looking at me in a careful way, all over, then his eyes dropped as if I wasn't worth looking at much, and he turned his head as if listening for Mara in the kitchen; and she came in with a tray, and then he started baiting her. Baiting is the only word for the way he spoke to her, as we drank the cups of tea Mara produced.

'How was your cat today?' he said heavily, expecting us to giggle, I bet. And he sniffed at the air: 'I don't think pretty women should take up ill-smelling studies, like zoology,' he said. And then: 'Don't you think I'm a model husband, Miss Jones, allowing my wife to spend her days cutting up dead cats? But so long as they are dead, and she is my loving wife when I am at home . . .' And he laughed.

I stood between them, although I had only just come in on the scene and he hadn't known of me. I didn't like Mara any more while Karl was there. She was so brittle, talking on a false, high note I had not heard, trying to head him off by elaborating about my bath and that there was no water where I lived, that the pipes had burst with the frost.

'Oh dear me,' he said with a smirk, turning to me, 'why don't you choose a decent place to live in? But then it is so difficult in London, such a dirty place, London. I am longing to get back to the Continent,' he said. And talked about how badly built the houses were in England.

And I said with some heat: 'Well, we're being bombed, you know.' And then I found myself saying yes, I'd love a flat like his – Mara gave me a tortured look – and how kind Mara was, asking me to have a bath, how grateful I was to *both* of them, what a lovely flat they had, and how wonderful it must be always to have hot water, wish I'd got something like that. But I could feel my heart going thump thump all the time I spoke, as if I'd done something wrong. And Karl rubbed his hands and said he was glad that I had come, and he hoped that I would look after Mara and not let her work too hard.

'I don't understand why she wants to study zoology. She does not *need* to do any work. She has a good husband to provide for her. What can a woman who is so pretty want to study for?'

Mara said, all brittle: 'But you're so often away, and I get bored doing nothing.'

It sounded coy and silly, and I felt ashamed for her, so I heaved myself off the chair and said: 'Well, I must be toddling along.' Everything we three said was all wrong; toddling sounded as if I'd said a dirty word. 'Good night, Mara,' I said. I always added: 'See you tomorrow,' when I left her after saying good night, but this time I didn't.

And she said: 'Good night, see you at the Horsham tomorrow.'

Did that mean I wasn't to wait for her at the corner the next morning? Her eyes were wide and dark as she followed me to the door, only to shut it on me. Click, it went, and I was in the lift, going down, down, and my heart seemed to go down with it; then in the street, with the smell of the slush freezing up again, a smell drawn right into me as I took a big breath.

So, I thought, that's her husband, Mr Daniels. Karl. They lived together in that flat. I saw the big bed again, and the beautiful cover on it. They slept in it, together. Mara and that man. That awful man.

I could visualize Karl clearly as I walked back. Good-looking, blond, nice eyes, nice hands. Nice husband Mara had. Just a trace of accent; he wasn't English. Trying so hard to sound English. And brutal all the way through – I was sure he was brutal. I'd behaved like a fool, blushing and stammering. After all, what was wrong in Mara and me being friends?

Then I was back at Nancy's and going up the stairs. Andy was coming down them with his striped hospital scarf round his neck; he had bought it second-hand from his brother, now in the R.A.F. Corduroy trousers, a duffel-coat, a hospital scarf, and a small stiff moustache above it all. He was trying to copy Big Brother George.

'Sniff . . . um . . .' He stopped. 'Where'd you get that? On the black market? Smells like Fifi.'

(Fifi was, possibly, an invention of Andy's, a Free French woman, enamoured of his virile charms. I had never bothered to find out.)

'Let go of me, Andy. Hands off.'

'My, aren't we high and mighty tonight? Come on, just going on a pub-crawl. Fun.' He winked.

'No, thank you.'

'Oh, come on.' He squeezed himself against me, moustache searching. 'C'mon.' He drooled a bit.

'No, no.'

'Aw, now, old thing, be a good sport, like you were last time, remember? You need it, you know.'

'You –' I said. I pushed him hard against the wall so that the back of his head hit it. He let go, astonished at my violence.

I ran up to my room, slammed the door; locked it though I knew Andy wouldn't come. I wasn't really frightened of him. A silly medical student boasting of his affairs with French girls. I'd let him, a couple of times, out of curiosity and because he said, 'Aw, be a good sport,' and swore he'd be careful, and I wanted to be a good sport and broad-minded, not silly and old-fashioned. Also I wanted to know what it was like. I mean, one does want to find out what it's all about. But I hadn't felt anything, not one way or the other.

It's so strange to think back to Andy then, when he's so respectable now, a different person, getting fat, and fussy about his clothes. He's my husband and I'm used to him. We don't talk about the past. Why should we? Andy has never guessed about Mara. That's one more reason I can't love him; he'll never know how I *can* feel, *can* love . . . He just hasn't a clue. And though he keeps me safe, I know I'll leave him one day, walk out of this safety which is a mess.

*

I expected Mara to look different the next morning. Yet why should she? Because I had seen Karl? He came home every day, didn't he? That flat was their home. That bed.

I was uneasy as I strolled in the locker-room, talking to the Frump who cleaned the lavs, waiting for Mara. There was a weight in my chest; I wanted to see Mara, her smile; I also wanted to have a fight with her, to say harsh, hurting things.

I was all clenched and raw when her perfume reached me. (Louise was always catty about Mara's perfume. It heralded her, filled the locker-room, we all sniffed it, deliberately or unconsciously. 'God, that awful *scent*,' Louise would say, tossing her hair and rolling her eyes. Even in the lab, with the throat-scratching smell of the specimens, we caught Mara's perfume. Eggie must have hated it, but it wasn't a thing she could stop by writing on the blackboard about it.)

Mara stood near, glowing as if bathed in sunlight, little gold earrings in her ears.

'Where you going, chum? Lunch with the Duchess again?' That was a joke of mine, when she appeared all dressed-up.

She had a thinness of gaiety laid like make-up upon her face, already that smile line at one corner of her mouth etched an ambiguous droop, joy using the same line as sorrow. And I thought this face held all I meant of happiness . . . until I lost it, and the loss would burn in me slowly, like a cigarette-burn spreading, sloven-sure. Oh God, to think that for years I may go on like this, wanting to see that face, till the unholy time when all things blunt, and hurt or joy are no more, when all is as if it never had been . . .

'Not a Duchess. Friends. Nice people for a change; we're taking them out to lunch at the Hungaria.'

We. That meant Karl. Mara's married. Got a husband. It would burst the bubble of whatever friendship Mara and I had for each other if I became obsessed with Karl. I don't like Karl, but I'm sure Mara does. It's natural that she'd be happy going out with friends and her husband. Leaving me alone during the lunch hour.

'That's fine,' I said. 'By the way, I've got a date tonight, too. Won't be able to walk home with you.'

'Oh Red, too bad,' she said. But she didn't look unhappy, and I only hurt myself.

We changed into our white coats. It hurt all over to be with her, because there was something newly inaccessible to me which I hadn't been aware of, and I wanted to break it. I wanted to be with her, not shut out, like that, by a couple of friends and lunch; by her husband, her other life, friends she would go out with, all dressed-up. She never dressed up for me. How would it look if I took her to lunch at the Hungaria? Odd, two women together.

I looked at her ear-rings, and went soft inside, soft and shaky. I wanted to put out my hand and touch them, and I had to shove my hands deep in my pockets because suddenly I also wanted to tear them off her ears. She'd cry then. I wanted to see her cry, badly.

Mara would be going out to lunch, she wouldn't sit with me at our table in the canteen, she wouldn't be back until the lecture at three that afternoon, and three o'clock was a terribly long time away.

She was cheerful. We weren't dissecting any more, but looking at slides and bones. She was far from me, and then gone.

All through lunch I hated her and Karl. Last night I had thought that she was scared of Karl, but I was damn wrong, she wasn't a bit scared. She loved him. She'd no use for me except as a convenience. He was her husband, and they lived together in that warm, expensive flat. She waited for him, and they went out to meet exciting people, and he came back and made love to her; and for him Mara put little gold ear-rings in her ears.

*

I sat with Louise in the lecture theatre at three that afternoon, and there was no place for Mara in our row when she came in a few minutes after Eggie had begun. Louise sniggered. She was happy to be back with me, I told her I'd walk home with her that evening. Mara saw us, I think, but her face didn't change and she walked along the steps at the side to a higher row. Eggie stopped lecturing. We could hear Mara's heels clicking up the steps.

We all stopped writing, looked at Mara walking the steps on high heels, waiting for some scathing remark from Eggie, something we could rehearse and comment on later. Faces grinned, bodies settled back. 'She'll catch it.' All of us waited for Eggie's words slung at Mara like arrows, for the blood-letting. We weren't beastly, just girls out of school; cruel only in a group, foretasting a pack relish at someone's pain, or just welcoming a relief from boredom, from the drone of Eggie's voice.

Still Eggie didn't speak, only her face got slowly more purple as she looked at Mara.

'Oh boy, now wait for it.' Louise glowed, her lips moving.

I lowered my head and pretended to read my notes. I felt beastly, yet glad too, in a way. That would teach Mara to go out with gold rings in her ears.

And still there was nothing. I had to look up again to see why there was nothing. Mara was sitting there on the top row alone, fountain-pen in hand, looking at Eggie with a reflective, nearly tender smile. Her eyes didn't leave Eggie, and Eggie was staring at her as if she were trying not to choke. Then Eggie sighed, her eyes dropped, and she went on lecturing.

Our pens scratched assiduously, following Eggie's voice, precise and dry. Louise's pen ran her impeccable handwriting along, she squeezed the holder a little too hard.

I couldn't do anything but wait for Mara afterwards, wait for her by our locker, acquiescent, waiting, in acknowledgement of her strength: for in all of us there is this submission to someone who has earned our respect; the way the others made room for Mara, a scarcely perceptible hush in their voices even if they pretended to be unaware of her, proclaimed it too. She was somebody now. She had beaten us all, beaten back into us the ever-present, smug, pin-prick sadism towards someone different. She was different, but she was strong, and I was proud of her, even more than after the quiz.

'May I see you home?' I said.

'What about your date?'

'It's off,' I lied.

'All right,' she said. But there was no victory in her voice. She looked tired, she had the face of a beaten child. She did not say anything about Eggie or arriving late, though later I was to find out that she'd apologized to Eggie. Somehow it wasn't surprising to me that after that Eggie began to like Mara; stopped to talk to her about zoology, always zoology, and smiled at her a rapid, quickly with-drawn smile.

*

The London winter deepened. It was bitterly cold all the time; and dark, the sun never there, round-the-clock glumness, dim to dark and back again. Yet this was my enthralled time, such as I had never had, such as would not recur. O halcyon winter, solstice of my days . . . a magic ring of hours, rounding itself within the undiscern-ing dark. I have stepped out of this charmed circle, gone on living, not wanting anything strongly. Should I be asked now what I wanted of life, I would say, 'Happiness, I suppose,' then add quickly: 'But I'm *quite* happy, you know. A good husband, a child . . .' If I were to tell the truth, that their existence, my family's being in my proximity, remains vague to me as tombstones of strangers in a common cemetery, that only a certain winter exists for me, vivid and clear, surging with life, and that all else is neutral, formless, indifferent, people would think me queer. Only when my mind goes back to that London winter do I feel alive, instead of merely knowing as a fact that I live. In that closed memory do I count my heartbeats by the spirited blood's surge, there once again I walk with Mara through the evening that is night, holding an electric torch in my hand, the blacked-out glass letting through a faint yellow ring at our feet, and I know what it is to love, to want to die for love. This is still so, and I'm a married woman with a child.

We talked a lot, Mara and I, at first not about us but of books, people, places, ideas . . . then later of ourselves, more and more. I could talk and talk and talk, and it was like being a child again, comforted, full-fed, and never tired. But I don't remember our words well, in fact I can scarcely recall one thing she said of all the things which at that time seemed so important and vivid. I remember our walking together best, the pacing, the streets, the cold, beneath invisible balloons of a haunted sky, forgetting the winter and the cold. Now it becomes in my day-dreams a walk through sunlit spaces, under windless trees, amid quiet grass. At the time our surroundings would on occasion break into our consciousness: a screech of buses, the rumble of the Underground, the tremor of the stone underfoot; hurrying passers-by, shoulders hunched, pounding with feet eager to run into tea-shops, to catch buses, away from the cold. But we were close held in mutual enchantment, and lingered on in the cold streets, pacing a lovely spring, unheeding, oblivious except by fits and starts of all that went on round us.

Of other winters I remember chiefly the unpleasantness, how ugly and painful to get up, to shiver, to catch overcrowded buses; the Underground smell of feet and breaths and rancid smoke; my hands rough with chilblains, clothes cold and stiff with grime. But about this winter, Mara's winter, I continue to feel its substance, the wrench of its happiness like a pain, an ecstasy which flares up, despite what we did to each other; even when I was trying to kill it.

Whatever has happened, there is always that magic winter haunting and hurting me with its marvellous echoes. The shortest days of the year, when nothing had begun and nothing had ended, all the roads of life were alive, and time beat round me like a heart.

I remember small, precious winter fragments, snatched out of darkness and oblivion. Mara saying to me one day as we left the Horsham: 'Do you always wear slacks or skirt and that leather jacket?' I said: 'Always in winter. Can't keep warm otherwise.' I remember the way I showed her, the first day, where to hang her coat: 'If you want to use a peg in the cloakroom, write your name on it and tell the Frump.' 'Why my name?' she asked. 'Because otherwise someone else will bag it,' I said. Our locker, I remember that locker so well, the locker Louise had found for me and which I gave to Mara to share with me. I got a good strong padlock for it, and we each had a key, Mara and I. And soon everything in the locker smelled of her perfume. One day Mara wanted to go home earlier, Karl had a party or something, and of course she'd left her own key at home. I let her have mine, and instead of bringing it back to me she went off with it. Next morning she appeared without either her key or mine, and I spent a long time unscrewing the latch of the steel locker, while she stood by and alternately looked rueful or laughed as if it were very funny. I was angry and yet all the time I loved her more, and now my fingers ache with unused love as they rehearse the unscrewing, the lifting of the latch, my ears rehearse her laughter: 'Oh Red, you're so clever!'

Our first lunch at the canteen together. The hubbub of voices, beef stew, then pudding with custard. The first day of term the food was generally good. I watched her eat. I was already in love with her. Right from the first moment.

Yet at times I felt that Mara was a bad spell cast upon me, something I must break away from. I was enchanted, but also terrified. She had dominion over me, and I resented it. Writing this now, the old exaltation is back, and also the old hatred and desire to hurt. There is nothing to break away from, yet I still am not delivered of this love and hate, vampire memories of the past which suck meaning out of every hour of my existence; memory of love sharp and sweet and nothing like it ever to be. Sometimes I want to be made free of that winter; and yet, and yet, I'd give everything to see Mara again.

One afternoon out walking I said to her abruptly: 'Sometimes I feel tied to you, I feel you're dragging me behind your heels, as a puppy dragged by a lead.'

As I spoke there came along a little peke, gloriously free, with a lead trailing behind its flag of a tail. We both dissolved in laughter. 'Red,' she said, 'I'm not dragging you. Perhaps you're dragging me, but I don't mind.'

We went to the pictures sometimes. War pictures, filled with the shriek and rent of airplane engines and the bark and boom of guns. There was a particular one in which at a certain moment an English Commando bayoneted a German soldier. The blade went in with a sound, and a lot of people in the audience heaved a sigh, something between feeling sick and pleasure, and Mara got up and left.

'I can't stand it,' she said, 'it's beastly.'

'But Mara, you know we've got to fight this war. It's the Germans who are beastly. Hitler's a monster.'

'I know,' she said, 'but I still don't like it. All this killing, it's insane. There's no need of war. Or if there must be, let the politicians go and fight duels, it would be cleaner.'

It sounded childish and awfully romantic, and a bit unpatriotic, but even that didn't matter. Mara was different.

One day I asked Mara what I had wanted to ask her for a long time. 'Mara, why isn't your husband fighting? Is he a V.I.P. or something?'

'Karl? Oh, he's ...' Her voice flattened. 'Karl's got a Swiss passport. He's neutral.' And then she added: 'Don't let's talk about him.'

But I persisted, to wrest from her something about herself and Karl. 'Well, all I can say is, you're lucky having your husband with you these days.'

'Oh, Karl isn't always here,' she said. 'Besides, I don't like men.'

That day I felt much happier, freer, as at a boundary crossed. I wasn't afraid of Karl any more. Mara didn't really like him. I wanted to sit in the flat and look him over carefully, as he had looked at me. I wouldn't be shy and stutter this time. Mara said she didn't like men. That included Karl. But if she didn't, why had she married him?

I did see Karl again. About a fortnight after that first time Mara suggested my coming again to her flat. I said: 'No, don't bother,' but of course I wanted to come. But then Daphne also came with us, and had a bath. Mara had heard her complaining of the pipes at the place where she lived, and had asked her too.

'You're awfully awfully generous,' I told Mara. I was cross because Daphne was with us, I didn't want her. I was angry with Mara for asking her too, so casually. But lots of the girls now liked Mara. Daphne positively grovelled in front of her, though she was cautious not to monopolize her and ask her out or make a bid for her, she knew how I would react.

After baths we sat in the comfortable living room, and had coffee and hot buttered toast, and that was the second time I saw Karl. He came in, just as Daphne was going through one of her interminable stories about her aunt, who was a *terror* as well as a *character*. Karl displayed excellent manners. Again he tried to say all the right things but they sounded all wrong, though Daphne giggled and said: 'Oh, Mr Daniels!' He poured some brown sherry for Daphne, saying her eyes were brown like the sherry. Daphne looked up at him adoringly, and I thought they looked like a cow's. After that Daphne adored Karl as well as Mara, spoke of them as such a lovely, intellectual couple. Daphne is now in Africa, running a school.

Some time after, Mara said: 'Coming home with me?' and I followed her. Karl was already there, and I thought Mara didn't expect him. She was stiff, a strained smile pinned on to her mouth, eyes looking nowhere, not at me. Karl made awful conversation, about books and art and music. He showed me that I didn't know much, and then rubbed his hands together and looked at Mara and made a joke about her studying zoology: 'I think she'd like to cut *me* up too, like a frog.' It went on and on, and I knew he did not want me there, he wanted to be alone with Mara, but I also knew she did not want me to leave. And I did not want to go, I wanted to stay on being with Mara, just to annoy him . . .

Finally there was a silence, and he said: 'It is getting late, shall I see you home?' Which was rude of him.

And so I said, starting as if I was surprised: 'Goodness, I hadn't realized it was so late. I must toddle off.' This time Karl saw me to the door, down the lift. In the lift he didn't speak to me, kept looking at the floor. Then he said: 'Good night,' shook hands, the lift gate clanked shut, and I heard him open the door of his – their – flat, then slam it.

And I felt unwanted, shut out. Jealousy like a clamp round me, an intercostal jabbing hurt, squeezing my breath out. It grew less or more, but it was there, it went on and on. Karl and Mara, Mara and Karl. I couldn't get those hands of his out of my mind. I woke up that night, hot and cold all over, having had a dream where Karl and Mara and I were hiding and hunting, but who was hunting whom I didn't know. It was all mixed up. And there in the dark bed at night, as always happens, all the past began to come back, hateful, acrid like something vomited, and I tried to sleep again and could not.

Two days later we had a quarrel, violent, but made up quickly. I don't remember how it began, but then I passed a remark about how nice it was to be provided for. She didn't answer, she looked at me and then away. I then said lots of things, horrible things which I can't remember. She just kept looking away.

I stopped. 'Well, I must get back. Can't dawdle today I'm afraid, got something else to do,' and tried to leave her, she so silent; to run away from her, but that was not possible. So I stood, immobile, in the cold street, wanting to go away, wanting to remain. And then I said, 'Oh, Mara, I'm a bloody idiot.'

And she said: 'Oh, Red, why d'you always want to hit out at things and people?'

I said: 'I don't know.'

And so we made it up.

Then Andy began making passes again. He was swotting for his finals, and that kept him more in his room at Nancy's. At about midnight he'd scratch on my door. I locked myself in every night. And the next morning he would make remarks about spinsters.

One day Mara said: 'Karl's gone to the Continent for a week, come to my place.'

That evening I went back to her flat with her, and we had coffee and toast and eggs, and laughed and were happy, wonderfully happy.

'Have you done more painting?' I asked.

She said yes, but didn't offer to show me. And I didn't ask to see. 'I'll paint you, one day, Red,' she said.

'Thanks,' I said, 'that'll be a laugh.'

She sat opposite me and started sketching, but when I wanted to look she didn't show me. 'Some other time,' she said.

But I never saw it.

While Karl was away Mara began to speak about him to me. And it was obvious she did not like him. 'He's really a kind of black marketeer, except that he's a respectable one. Travels in liberated Europe, making business connexions.' She smiled briefly. 'The democratic reconstruction of Europe. France is full of businessmen, American mostly, dressed up as colonels and generals, with ladders of medals climbing up and down their chests. And people like Karl do business with them. They call it putting things back on their feet. It keeps Karl very busy.'

During the days Karl was away I went every evening to Mara's flat, and stayed later and later. There was a nice kitchen, and things to eat like Jerusalem artichokes and tinned peaches and tins from Fortnum's which cost the earth, and new-laid eggs from a friend of Karl's in the country.

'Lovely grub,' I said to Mara.

Mara laughed and laughed. It always made her laugh when I talked like that, as lots of us did at the Horsham now, in keeping with the times. Mara didn't talk like that, she didn't even listen to *Itma* on the radio, but she laughed when I did it and that made me feel good.

Mara was quite extravagant; when a tin was half used she'd throw the rest away. Once I rescued some anchovies which she'd discarded.

'You're so thrifty, Red,' Mara laughed. 'I just don't like left-overs.'

'We're at war,' I said pointedly.

And Mara said: 'Oh, yes,' guiltily, and after that she was more careful.

But the word thrifty hurt because I'd been called something like that before, by my stepmother; yet, God knows, with Mara I wasn't, I didn't want to be.

But apart from expensive things, there wasn't much solid food around. 'We eat out a lot, Karl and I,' she said.

Mara did not bother to cook much, but when she did it was like a banquet. One day we bought a goose, as geese came on sale just before Christmas. It cost the earth, and Mara roasted it in the oven, and we ate as much of it as we could; but there was far too much, and after two days she gave the rest to the char.

I was horrified. 'A family could have eaten for a week.'

'Her family will,' she replied.

Walking back from Mara's flat to Nancy's boarding-house was going from one world to another, but I wasn't jealous of Mara's comfort, I was pleased and proud to have a friend so well-off. Not that I myself wouldn't be well-off one day: my father had left some money in trust for me, I'd get it when I was twenty-one. Meanwhile I had an allowance. Then there was Aunt Muriel. Aunt Muriel always said that everything she had would come to me. And I had a great-aunt up north; she was a bit queer, and might leave her all to a cats' and dogs' home, so I didn't bank too much on it. Meanwhile, I rather pigged it. I had to be careful with money, one never knew what might happen, and I saved about a third of my allowance because I might need it. The way Mara took taxis, bought books, went to expensive places ... whatever she had was expensive. I thought with pleasure, though, that I had a rich friend. I did not know that she could walk out of money and comfort as easily as losing a handkerchief (and she was always losing handkerchiefs). She dazzled me a little, I had not been accustomed to this kind of spending.

From Mara's flat to Nancy's boarding-house I went back at night by bus and then trolley-bus up to Camden Town, a long, long way. Mara sometimes came with me. The statue of Cobden loomed in the darkness as if to bar the way. I'd never taken Mara beyond it. When we got there, we'd catch a bus and go all the way back to Mayfair.

'It's still a long way,' I told her one day when she said: 'How far from Cobden do you live, Red?' 'It's much farther, and there's no dinner for you at the end I'm afraid. You'll have to go home for it, and that'll mean my trotting back with you.' I said it half joking, half earnest, I didn't want her to see where I lived.

From Cobden there was another four hundred yards, a long, dismal row of houses, one of which was Nancy's. The houses were all alike, angular, spinsterish, narrow, an architecture whose dreary repetition became hallucinatory. Even on the brightest day they wore mute discouragement in every lineament of their façade. The windows were not conceived to admit light or air, so blindly forbidding their outward bleakness. All the houses must have smelt the same as Nancy's did, from the narrow hallway with the grime-worn lino, down the steps into the basement dining room, up the stairs to the rooms on the first and second floors and the attic, all smelt of stale cigarettes, cat, dirt, cabbage, and dustbins.

At Nancy's lived Edward, of course, the travelling salesman, who had been a keen Y.M.C.A. gym teacher. But he was blind as a bat, and the Forces didn't want him. He smelt of sweat even after a bath, and the bathroom smelt of sweat too because he used to do Swedish exercises in it, and then use the toilet. His conversation never left the topic of his muscles and his regular habits, no laxatives needed. Because of Edward I'd given up using the main bathroom in the morning, and took turns at the small W.C. at the top of the house. There was Andy, the son of a colonial bishop, doing medicine on a colonial medical scholarship because his father was a prelate in Singapore. He was not always present at our lino-covered festive board. His absences were the subject of elaborate and not at all obscure joking on the part of Edward and Nancy, the general idea being that Andy was a 'gay dog'; it was understood that he had been passionately loved by a White Russian, and was now pursued by a Free French woman, who would throw herself under the next trolley-bus for his sake. I didn't believe in her existence, and still don't, knowing Andy. Edward was Nancy's occasional lover, when she felt well enough between her fits of gastric acidity, deploring the war, and being upset over Winston the cat, who had been named thus under false pretences, and remained Winston after six litters because Nancy felt it unpatriotic to change. All of us boarders hated Winston, but we couldn't do anything about her, until one day Nancy fell suddenly with a loud cry on the floor after lifting the milk jug away from Winston's whisking tail. She had perforated her gastric ulcer. She was removed to St Thomas's because Andy took charge, was operated on, and was back in six weeks. During those six weeks we did for ourselves, in turn taking over the kitchen. That was when Andy had got at me, and I let him, we'd been doing the washing-up together, and then gone to the pub for some beer, and it seemed unsporting not to.

When Nancy came back, Winston came back too. We'd banished her during meals, but with Nancy's return she stalked among our plates, and once more cat-hair floated like scum on the morning milk jug.

That was where I lived. I was used to it, but I didn't want Mara to see it. Until now I'd liked my digs because they were dirt-cheap, but now that I saw how Mara lived I began to think of something better. A place where I could ask Mara. I could afford it.

Now I felt I must prove to Mara I wasn't too thrifty, as she had said. It made me feel bad too because of my great-aunt in the north, who was reputed to be a real miser, and I didn't want to become like her. And my step had always been at me, about hoarding things, because at one time I'd kept all the bits of string I could find, and tied them together in one long string.

I walked in Camden Town, back to my digs, and every time the smell in the corridor came to hit me in the face, I thought: I must find some other place. Where I can ask Mara to come.

*

One afternoon in mid-December it was milder, lighter. At four o'clock we walked away from the Horsham, dawdling as if it were spring.

'Let's have tea at Maggie's,' I suggested.

Maggie's was a small place off James Street. Before the war there had been wonderful buns and cakes, but now we only got some 'yellow perils', buns made with egg powder, with imitation caraway-seeds on top. I liked Maggie's because it was cosy, in spite of war. Maggie herself looked after the shop. She was a big woman, with a high, tired voice and large varicose knots in her legs. It was Louise who had taken me to Maggie's first, but now I took Mara and Louise didn't come with me any more.

We were early. There was no one yet at Maggie's, the office-workers hadn't come out of their offices. It was warm inside the small tea-shop, basking in almost green light, a liquid submarine glow from the bow window with its bottle-glass panes. It was wonderful to stretch one's legs, sitting beside Mara, as good as being in her flat with her: one felt submerged, enveloped, floating, tranquil as seaweed and as compliant. Here, in a sea-water absolution, with the stirring smell of hot buns, it might even be better than in Mara's flat, because here was no Karl entering, bringing unease with him, and a fear something might suddenly go bang, like a concealed gun with an unsure trigger.

'Afternoon, Maggie.'

'Nice day,' said Maggie, 'turned warm all of a sudden, like. Cold again tomorrow though, I shouldn't wonder.' Maggie dropped the subject and went back to get us tea. She had the gift of leaving people alone and comfortable with themselves. Her remarks about the weather she suspended in mid-air, take it or leave it. One didn't have to strike poses.

The radio was on, not too loud. There was a drone afar off, a buzz-bomb; I'd been doing some fire-watching the week before, and one had gone overhead and stopped quite a way off.

'There she blows,' said Maggie, putting down the tea-pot and two cups, and going back for buns. 'A doodle-bug last night near where I live. We spent half the night digging one bloke out, got himself cooped up in the basement. No other damage, I'm glad to say.'

This one was coming near. We lifted our heads. Very near now, it seemed just above us, and the vibration made the crockery rattle on the counter. Then the motor cut out.

'Mind your 'eads,' cried Maggie, diving under the counter.

Mara and I were both under our table when it fell, a whoosh so deafening it wasn't noise but a shaking and splintering and sucking of all the air round, then the instantaneous dust swirling eddies thick as cloth, making us cough and know we were alive.

Though the memory of that moment of terror is precise enough, I don't remember any particular, overwhelming fear at the instant when the buzz-bomb fell; only a stunned, nearly surprised joy and relief that I was still alive afterwards. Then Mara's face, thick with dust, featureless like one of those weather-worn statues in an old square. In the bronze blob the eyes began to move, ludicrously. I wanted to laugh with relief. We were both alive.

'Are you all right?' I said.

'Yes, I'm all right. Are you?'

'Yes.'

And then suddenly there were a lot of people, bringing with them a panic of emotions, terror, horror. We were picked up bodily, my legs now swaying under me and my heart racing, but there was also an enormous triumphant feeling in me as if I had just done something wonderful. People kept crowding round and asking if we were all right, and Mara and I were struggling not to be conveyed to stretchers, shaking our heads, slapping the dust away from our clothes, wiping our faces on towels that appeared. There was an ambulance, uniformed ambulance attendants, someone came up to me and asked if I wanted a shock injection, I said crossly: 'For God's sake, I'm all right I tell you.'

And now, the counter off, there also was Maggie. I think Mara saw her before I did, because she said: 'Oh –' very short, put a hand to her mouth. But it took me time after looking to see what was the matter, a lag between what I saw and heard and knowing what it was. There was some dark liquid on the floor, like coffee-grounds, which at first didn't make sense, then Maggie's sprawled legs with their disfiguring blue veins intact, and in her neck a jutting piece of green glass. The ambulance people had the blanket quick over her, head and all.

But death was only a word which I said to myself, a word without savour. Mara was clinging to me and saying: 'Red, let's go,' shaking my arm. She took my arm and turned me from looking at Maggie's stretcher, now heaved into the ambulance.

Though it must have been only minutes it seemed hours, giving our names, telling a lot of people we were quite all right, before we were out in the dark streets. And now there was another ambulance, and stretchers going up and down full or empty, and I remember saying, 'Can I help?' because that was the right thing to do, and

Mara whispering fiercely: 'NO, no, let's go. For God's sake, let's get away.'

And the A.R.P. man saying: 'Well, ducks, you've had quite enough, off with you,' and a man coming up again to say: 'Sure you don't need a shock injection?' and Mara saying again: 'Let's go home.'

I could see that the A.R.P. man thought Mara was a foreigner. He was immediately soothing, saying to me: 'You'd better take her home, she's had quite a shock.'

And Mara whispered. 'Let's go home, let's go home,' not a bit brave or anything.

I felt conspicuous because of Mara not being brave and not offering to help, so I said, 'O.K., pull yourself together, we're going.'

But the A.R.P. man said sharply: 'Now, don't fuss her, miss. Your friend's upset, can't you see?' And that was unfair to me, I thought.

Mara was silent till we got to the corner of her street. Then she tugged my hand, pulling me back, and said: 'I don't want to go there.' She began to walk away, and I had to follow her.

I said to her: 'You've been shouting "I want to go home," I see you home, then you don't want to go home. What *do* you want?'

She said: 'We'll go to your place. Where you live. Let's go there.'

Then I became angry, and frightened. I didn't want her to come to my place. What on earth for? I could have had such a nice bath in her place, and heaven knows I needed it. But at the same time, dimly, there was a kind of excitement in me as if I were shaking inside of myself; at the pit of my stomach tumult and clamour. I could hear my own voice being angry, but even as I spoke the anger went away into this uneasy excitement. I was now following Mara down the street, arguing with her. 'Look, Mara, what's come over you? Honest, Mara, it's so silly. My place isn't half as good as yours. You – we both need a clean-up. I'd like a good bath, my pet. Mara . . .'

She walked fast, I had to continue following her. A taxi was coming down the street, Mara stepped down in the road in front of it, waving her hand. The driver stopped, brakes crunching, leaned out and began to shout his annoyance. But she smiled at him, and he smiled back, mollified. She opened the door.

'Get in, Red,' she said. She gave the man my address.

'Now look here,' I began, 'now look here, you'll have to pay –'

But the taxi man was looking at me, and I am scared of scenes in public. Off we drove. I thought: it's no use Mara trying to bully me like that. When we get to the door I'll say good night. She'll have to go back alone, all the way to Mayfair. I'm damned if I'll see her home tonight.

As we turned sharply into Oxford Street the traffic hurtled its noise at us like the blast of the buzz-bomb, and all my anger swept out of me. I wanted to put my head down and weep. Maggie was dead, and here we were, driving in a taxi, and I could feel the dust in my hair, round my neck, between my fingers. But still it mattered that Mara shouldn't see my room, I was a fool not to have moved into a nice place before, even if I had to pay more. I *would* turn round and say goodbye at the door.

When we reached the door of Nancy's boarding-house Mara paid the taxi, and I pleaded: 'Mara, it's an awful place.' (The smell, the cat, Nancy, Andy. Mara would *never* want to see me again once she knew how I lived.)

'Let's go to your room and sit down.'

'O.K., if you insist. But you won't like it.'

Nancy was out (her coat wasn't hanging in the hall), which was a bit of luck. Nancy is rather a busybody, poking her face out of the basement dining room door and watching who is going up or down stairs.

'Upstairs, second floor,' I said.

We went up, treading lightly, her steps exactly in front of mine, mine timed to hers so that if anyone listened they would not hear two people going up at the same time. On the sixth step I used to kick the seventh for luck. Not this time. I opened the door of my room, turning the knob gently, slowly, feeling it turn. I pressed the light switch. The less noise, the better. Well, that was the worst that could happen.

'I like your room.'

The worst was over, and I couldn't help anything from now on.

She went to the deep armchair (the springs sagged, the cover was dirt-brown), and sat down.

'I'll put on the gas-fire.'

I felt her watching me as I took the match box, knelt to put a shilling in the gas-meter, a match to the hissing holes; with a pop the blue flames licked up. To face her I sat on the edge of the bed. Her coat was dusty, her face none too clean. 'We both look like wrecks,' I said.

'We are,' she replied.

Downstairs the gong sounded for supper. 'Call to the festive board,' I said.

'You go,' Mara said. 'I'll wait here.'

'I can't go looking like this,' I said, 'and I'm not hungry anyway.'

I didn't like going down, with Andy, Edward, and possibly Nancy back at the head of the table presiding over the soup. I leaned back on the bed. My hand fingered the blue tweed blanket which I kept on top. I told Mara: 'My Daddy gave me this blanket.'

'Did he, Red?'

'Yes.' I became a child, lapsing into near baby-talk. Mara was my mother, and I was drowsy, and telling her things I wanted to tell. 'I loved my Daddy. He was nice to me. Even when my step told him the most horrid things about me – that I should be psycho-analysed, that I was queer, that I collected bits of string and that showed I wasn't normal – even then he was nice to me. "Never mind," he would say, "you'll be all right. Daddy knows it. That's my girl," he used to say. I hate my step and she loathes me. I hope she dies of cancer, or something terrible happens to her. But my Daddy loved me, I know it.'

'I love you too, Red,' said Mara gently.

I did not answer.

'It is difficult, Red,' said Mara. 'I am a woman and you are a woman. I am a grown-up woman, with a husband, and I've always been what is called normal. I've never felt like this about ... about any other woman.'

I could hear Edward's booming laugh, and a clatter of crockery.

'When I say I love you, I mean, not like a friend.' Mara was speaking as if far from herself, level-voiced. 'This between us, can you call it friendship? I mean, do you think the other couples of women we see around us are only friends?'

'Yes, of course,' I burst out, 'definitely. You're wrong there, you're making up things in your mind. They're just crushes. It isn't what you mean. It isn't.'

'Perhaps you are right. Perhaps it is as you say. This is a funny time,' she mused. 'I get such a woman feeling, such a feminine, woman-world-only feeling here. Perhaps it's the war. It must be. Perhaps it's imagination. I don't know. But men seem effaced somehow ... they don't really exist, except when I walk in Piccadilly, where it's just rank with them. But I don't think I like men.'

'Don't imagine things, Mara. At the Horsham most of the girls you see going about in twos will get married, and they'll be quite all right. Even Louise.'

'Why even Louise?'

'Oh, I was at school with Louise,' I said. 'But she's quite all right, really. She'll hook a man and she'll be fine.'

I couldn't tell Mara about Louise. How Louise was one of my girls, in a way. She'd wanted it: made me hit her and kiss her and handle her breasts, while she uttered little cries and her big eyes rolled. But it wasn't really very serious. Mara was too clean for that, I felt. I didn't want her to know.

'Look,' I said, and tried to keep my voice from shaking, 'maybe some of us do do a bit of substitution. But it's mostly emotional. It's natural for a girl to have crushes on other girls, hold hands and all that.' I got angry. 'You've got the Continental viewpoint. Comes from marrying a Swiss. You look at everything from a sex point of view. It's not, I tell you. There isn't that much libido around.'

'I wouldn't know,' said Mara, 'where pure emotion, a crush as you say, stops and sex begins. Does anyone know? When does a feeling become a sin? When the body performs what is already formed in the mind? Tell me that, Red?'

'Quite the philosopher, aren't you?' I parried. So many things could be done, and if one didn't talk about them, didn't think about them, one could live with them, they would be quite all right. But when put in words they came barging into one's consciousness at all times, and one knew the foulness of deeds. But not before they'd been put in words. So the important thing was not to call things by their names. 'I wouldn't know,' I said, 'I'm not a psychologist, Mara.'

She said: 'I want to know why I have this feeling about you. I'm concerned to know what it is makes me want to be with you so much. I've never felt like this before, and I don't understand myself.'

'I don't know what you mean,' I lied, my voice trembling.

'You do know, Red. And I want to know.'

'Look,' I said, 'maybe I've had a hard time, see. Maybe you

131

haven't. You've always got everything you wanted, I suppose. You're older than I am, you've got experience, and you're rich. I don't want to start anything. I want to be normal. I am normal. I want to have men, I want to get married.'

She sat in profound attention, pondering, and with her next words things came into focus again: like looking down a microscope at a blur, then you turn a gadget and the proper focus comes on and everything is sharp and clear.

'Red,' she said, 'I don't want to *start* anything. That's why I'm asking you, why do I feel like this? I've never felt like this about a *woman* before.'

I lay back on the bed. Life was one great big treachery. Here I was back where I had not meant to be. Face to face with something I hadn't wanted to know. I looked up, and for the first time I noticed the ceiling of my room and the electric-light bulb with its round white shade suspended from the cord in the middle. Like an umbilical cord. I played for a moment with the idea that the lamp hanging like that in the middle of nothing from a string was a baby, and the baby was me. A small sprouting of life in the middle of nothing, tied to the womb of the past, tied by all the things that had been done and not said. And if you cut that cord, the lamp fell, the light went out.

And Mara said: 'This has happened to you before, Red, but not to me.'

How did she know? I'd never said anything.

'It was the games mistress, Mara. She'd been jilted by her young man. She took it out on me.' I raised myself on my elbow, acting flippant. 'It's always the games mistress or the English Lit. mistress, didn't you know? Or some senior girl. It's done in the best schools, m'dear.'

'Did you feel bad about it?'

'Not really.' Suddenly I saw her very clearly, Rhoda, my games mistress, fair curly hair cut short at the nape, pretty face, petulant mouth, blue frock with bosom-fitting lace. Now it seemed childish, ridiculous, yet dirty. That pouting mouth was stupid, that trick of hers of winking one eye at me which I had liked so much was stupid. Louise's eyes too were stupid. And I had called them blue interlopers when I was reading Shelley.

'Red, don't cry, please don't cry,' said Mara.

I was crying, I realized with astonishment. Tears ran down my face, my palm upon my face came off moist and shining like sweat under the lamplight.

She came over to the bed. 'Lie down,' she said, 'lie down. Lie down, my darling.'

'She said that she would be my mother. A mother to me. That's what she said.'

'She lied,' said Mara, 'but I'm not going to lie to you. I am not going to be your mother, Red. I just love you, that is all, and why I should love you I don't know.'

And somehow it was simple and right and beautiful and good this time when she put her arms round me and we were kissing, and could not stop though there was dust between our lips.

*

Christmas holidays meant Aunt Muriel. Aunt Muriel was my father's younger sister, and my nearest relative. I had spent Christmas holidays with Aunt Muriel for the past four years, nobody else seemed to want me, and in wartime there was no other place I could go to.

Aunt Muriel lived in Wiltshire, on a farm near the village of Abbots, seven miles outside Salisbury. She was on the station platform in her W.V.S. uniform, slapping her thigh with her riding-crop, when our train drew in. Almost as long as I can remember Aunt Muriel had a stick in her hand, using it to point at things on her farm, or to slap herself with; I think it gave her a sense of authority, of power. When I scrambled out of the train she looked at my shoes. She has a passion for highly-polished shoes, she thought mine weren't so good.

'Hallo, Aunt Muriel. My, how you've grown.'

She smiled. Aunt Muriel likes to be teased as if she were still a little girl in pigtails. 'Go on with you,' she said. 'Have you got your luggage down, dear? Good. Right, we'll go along then, I've got the station-wagon. It'll be a tight squeeze but you won't mind, will you?'

There were ten pairs of Wellington boots, a sack of chicken-feed, a saddle, two buckets, and on the front seat at the wheel, Rhoda. The last person I wanted to see. Of course, Aunt Muriel would ask Rhoda. She'd been there last Christmas, and the Christmas before that. That was my doing. I'd arranged it myself three years ago, and it had now become a fixture. Aunt Muriel thought a lot of Rhoda. She'd never known about Rhoda and me. She thought we were good friends, she'd thought that for years, ever since Rhoda, who's about ten years older than I am, was my games mistress at school. Aunt Muriel had come down to the school one Visitors' Day and Rhoda had rushed up to her and started telling her what an excellent sport, unspoilt and *healthy-minded* girl I was. That was music to Aunt Muriel's ears because she hated my step and my step had been telling her that I was abnormal and ought to be psycho-analysed. But now it was my step who was abnormal, taking up first Christian Science and then going on to spirit-mediumship, and now she kept on sending Aunt Muriel pamphlets about the dear departed. Aunt Muriel couldn't stand the idea of death, so anything that was against my step became all right with her. Aunt Muriel took to Rhoda, and after that Rhoda was asked to stay for Christmas. 'Rhoda's such a good influence on Bettina,' said Aunt Muriel to her friends.

'Well,' said Aunt Muriel jovially, 'shove in, Bettina. You sit between Rhoda and me, as you did last year, remember?'

'Bettina,' said Rhoda, with that healthy, fresh, and sparkling voice she used, which I'd thought wonderful and now was like a dose of Eno's fruit salts, 'so *good* to see you, m'dear.'

'Hallo, Rhoda,' I said. I sat down, hating the way she sat. I had to shove my arm in so that my coat sleeve touched hers, and even that was embarrassing. We had always been careful, casual in our greetings, taking pains not to notice each other, so people wouldn't get suspicious as they did about others I knew of. So it wasn't too difficult to turn away from Rhoda, talk to Aunt Muriel, find questions to ask about the farm, and the Poles and the evacuees in Abbots, since Aunt Muriel was head of the committee for the latter. Rhoda started the car. She drove, Aunt Muriel chattered on, I pretended to be terribly interested in all she said although I didn't hear half of it: Aunt Muriel can go on for hours about what interests her, so conversation is easy with her. All the time I thought: I hope Aunt Muriel doesn't put us in the same room, as last year.

But Aunt Muriel had put us in the same room, as she pointed out when we got to the house. 'You know the way, Bettina.'

I left my suitcase in the passage, and while Rhoda parked the car I tackled Aunt Muriel, who was already in the kitchen. 'Aunt Muriel?'

'Yes. What is it, Bettina?'

'I . . . it's . . . Aunt Muriel, I don't sleep very well, and I've got to swot. Exams next year, you know. I thought perhaps . . . d'you mind if I go in the spare room this year?'

'That's quite impossible, Bettina,' said Aunt Muriel. 'I thought I told you in the station-wagon about my new Polish help and her infant. They're in the spare bedroom. She's a D.P., a wonderful cook. I couldn't put her in the maid's room, it's much too small for the infant, and she'd leave me flat – you know how it is these days.'

'Well, can I have the maid's room, then?'

Aunt Muriel wasn't pleased. 'I'm afraid you can't. It's full of W.V.S. stores. I'm sure Rhoda won't make a fuss, even if you do study. And I'll give you one of my sleeping-pills.'

So there was nothing to be done, and I had to drag my suitcase into the room Rhoda and I would share, and start unpacking; and while I was at it Rhoda came in, smoking a cigarette. The room smelt of her. I pretended to be busy putting my things in a drawer.

Rhoda came and stood behind me. 'Bettybets,' she said, and put a hand on my shoulder, 'what's the matter? Having the grumpies?'

'There's nothing the matter,' I said, busily sorting my things into the drawer.

She kept her hand on my shoulder, and I couldn't go on keeping mine inside the drawer, so I closed the drawer slowly and turned round to my suitcase, and her hand dropped.

She walked to the bed and lay back on it, pulling on her cigarette and watching me. 'You didn't write much, last few weeks,' she said. 'I was expecting a letter from you.'

'I've been very busy,' I said.

'Red,' said Rhoda, 'don't act that way, darling. Please come and tell your Rho-Rho you're glad to see her.'

'Of course I am,' I said. 'But you know I'm going to be pretty busy now, I've got a lot of swotting to do.'

'Has anybody said anything?' said Rhoda, sitting up straight. 'Because it isn't true, Red. I mean, nobody else means anything to me.'

So there had been someone around. For a moment I thought it would be a good thing to act jealous. I'd been really jealous once about Rhoda. I shrugged my shoulders. 'Skip it,' I said. 'Of course one hears things.'

'Angela doesn't mean a thing to me,' said Rhoda. 'Not a thing, Red, you must believe me.'

'Well,' I said, still keeping that weary and worn look on my face, 'let's skip it, shall we? We've all got to grow up.'

I was breathing more easily now. I could even look at Rhoda sitting on the edge of the bed. There was a night-table between her bed and what would be mine.

'Red, you know no one else means . . . what you mean to me.'

She was plainly worried now. I could remember everything between Rhoda and me. I was sixteen, she was twenty-six, and something had just happened to her – she'd been jilted by her fiancé. I was big for my age, and lonely. She said she wanted to be a mother to me. Rhoda had used me, and taught me, and now I was what I was because of her. I wanted to shout at her, to hit her as she sat there looking at me out of her big blue eyes, afraid. She had on a blue dress, wool. I remembered the letters I'd written to her, and those she'd written to me, and that horrible June when I loved her and she loved someone else.

'You know jolly well,' she said, 'that I love you, Red. You and I, it's *different*, darling.'

I laughed, I couldn't help it. I remembered that summer when she no longer whispered: 'See you tonight.' No more little notes: 'The coast is clear.' Twice I'd gone to her room, knocking softly, lonely, sick at heart. The first time she made some tea, light conversation; then yawned: 'Well, nighty-night, darling, I'm so tired . . . such a hot, tiring day . . . see you soon.' A peck. No longer those deep, searching kisses that she had first taught me, that used to leave me shaken and spent. The second time she was annoyed: 'Darling, I'm sorry, I was sleeping. Come in if you wish, but we must be careful, you know.'

And on the following Sunday I saw her with a man, a red-faced, bull-necked fellow, walking in the woods near school. I'd been to the woods on my bicycle to pick flowers for her. She was wearing a blue frock with the lace frills round the bosom.

And now she wore blue, quite a nice dress, and I couldn't bring myself to think of touching her. Though I'd sobbed with happiness when she'd taken me back a couple of years ago. She'd sworn there was nothing, nothing between the man and her. Then she'd been quite sick for a while.

There'd been Louise, in an off-and-on way, but not really much: Louise was too bitchy, she just liked being hurt a bit. But there was Mara. And Mara was everything. I was in love, truly in love.

'Don't laugh, Red,' pleaded Rhoda, 'I do mean it.'

'Oh, for heaven's sake,' I said, 'don't be melodramatic.'

'You've *changed*, Red,' Rhoda said, like a bad line in a bad play.

'Of course I've changed,' I replied. 'I've grown up, I keep telling you.'

She crushed her cigarette then, she was going to cry, and I went on putting my things in the drawers.

'I see,' she said, and her voice was tired. 'You've grown. It's not me that's changed, it's you. Who's the lucky man? Do I know him?'

'No,' I said, enormously relieved that Rhoda had made it simple, 'I'm afraid you don't. I tell you, Rhoda, I've grown up.'

On the next day the local school had a carol service. Aunt Muriel, Rhoda, and I went to it, and I nearly fell asleep in the church. I hadn't slept much that night, Rhoda in the next bed, both of us not talking. I'd undressed in the bathroom, and all kinds of things kept cropping up in my memory, intensely disagreeable. Getting up, Rhoda had made morning tea (she always did for Aunt Muriel, and that was another reason why Aunt Muriel liked her so much: Rhoda really pulled her weight doing chores as a guest during the holidays).

'I've made tea for you, Red,' said Rhoda.

And I had to say: 'Thanks,' and jump out of bed quickly and get to the bathroom to stop any attempted conversation.

At church it was better. I thought of Mara and hoped there would be a letter the next day. I'd asked her to write to me. Before church we had done the chicken-feed, Rhoda and I, as we'd done in previous holidays. There were lamb chops for lunch, and chocolate fudge as a special treat, and Rhoda and I washed up. We didn't talk much to each other, but Aunt Muriel didn't notice, she was so glad she had helping hands to do the housework, especially over Christmas.

Rhoda was very good about things that morning, and apart from making conversation with Aunt Muriel of the do-you-remember kind and about how badly the Poles in the camp behaved, she didn't try anything woozily sentimental, so that by the time lunch was over the atmosphere was better. As long as one didn't linger on what had been and remember things, one could sound chummy and cosy, and that's how it was meant to be.

The telephone rang. Rhoda got up and said: 'I'll go, Aunt Muriel.' Taking care of phone-calls was Rhoda's job, and driving the station-wagon because Aunt Muriel said Rhoda was so economical with the petrol. Actually Aunt Muriel was a bit frightened of telephones and cars.

Rhoda came back from the passage where the telephone was. 'It's for you,' she said to me. She sat down without looking at me.

I got up, pretending to be surprised, with a who-on-earth-could-that-be look on my face. But I felt panicky and I knew I was blushing, so I turned my face quickly away, at the same time telling myself not to hurry too much or they might suspect; and though I wanted to run down the passage to the telephone because I was afraid the call might be disconnected, I forced myself to walk, my heart pounding because I knew, I was sure it was Mara.

It was Mara, all the way from London, of course it was. She alone would do a mad and wonderful thing like that, ringing me up. No one else ever did things like that for me. I always had had to do the ringing up and the asking, and going to people's rooms, always I was the one to ask for love.

'Bettina Jones?' said the operator. 'Call from London.'

'Hallo?' said Mara's voice. 'Is that you, Red?'

'Yes,' I replied, 'yes. Is that you, Mara?'

'Yes,' said Mara, 'it's me.'

I could see her hanging on to the telephone in London, just as I was here at Aunt Muriel's in Wiltshire, and it was absurd, we had nothing to say except: 'How are you?' and: 'Very well, and you?' I answered: 'Very well,' and she said: 'That's fine,' and I said: 'Are you all right?' I could have kicked myself for wasting the precious and irreplaceable time being inane.

She said: 'Did you have a good journey?'

And I said: 'Yes, it's nice out here. Lots of grub.'

Then there was another long pause, and I thought I could hear her breathe, then the instrument went pip pip pip, and the operator said: 'Have you finished, or do you want to extend the call?'

I heard Mara say: 'Extend.'

We hung on, and I said: 'How's London?' and she said: 'All right,' and I said: 'That's fine.'

And so another three minutes went by, and we spoke about the weather in London and in Salisbury, and again the instrument went pip pip pip, and again Mara's voice said: 'Extend,' and I said: 'This is getting terribly expensive, isn't it?' and she said: 'Red, do you read Blake?'

The telephone started to crackle.

'Read Blake?' I repeated. 'Why?'

'D'you know that thing of Blake's,' she said, '"Tiger, tiger, burning bright in the forests of the night"? That was a real live tiger, Red,' she said, 'lovely and striped with black and yellow, Red, a real tropical tiger.'

'What's that got to do with it?' I asked.

'With what?' she said.

'Oh, with everything,' I said. 'I don't understand.'

'It doesn't,' she said. 'That's why. It's just a way of saying how are you, talking of tigers. Perhaps one day we'll go to the jungles and see real tigers.'

'Listen,' I said, 'is this supposed to be funny? It isn't funny to pour money down the drain ringing me up long-distance to talk about tigers.'

'You mean, down the telephone,' she said. 'Don't you like tigers?'

'No,' I said, and suddenly I was angry and hurt. This wasn't at all what I had expected, but then what did I expect? Talking about tigers, and there I was, stuck with Rhoda stalking me. 'No,' I nearly shouted, 'I don't like tigers.'

Three pips.

'Time's up,' said the operator.

'Well, goodbye Red,' said Mara. 'See you soon.' And she hung up.

I swore under my breath, and I stayed there staring at the heartless black telephone on its hook. And now I wanted to say: come back, oh come back, only let me hear your voice again, your voice talking about tigers, beautiful tigers. But it was too late to tell Mara that I understood about tigers, or even elephants, that I would love a giraffe if she spoke about giraffes. And why had I become so angry suddenly? Perhaps because with Mara, or because of Mara, I was always being made to remember things that I thought I'd forgotten, or wanted to forget . . . like my mother. And now I knew. That afternoon in the Zoo, when I was five, or maybe six, my mother and a man talking to each other, in front of the tigers' cage, and I, beribboned, with mittens, I wanted to pee, and I was scared of the terrible smell of the tigers; and there was my mother laughing, her face rosy under a big hat, with that man whose face I would never remember because I hated him so much, his hand tugging at her gloved hand.

When I came back Rhoda was sitting with her back quite rigid, and Aunt Muriel said comfortably: 'Who was it, dear?'

I said: 'Just a friend, wanting some of my Organic notes.' That was enough for Aunt Muriel, and as for Rhoda I didn't care. She won't try anything, I told myself. I took Blake's *Complete Works* down from the book-shelves where Aunt Muriel had it along with other Complete Works.

I went round all afternoon in anguished happiness, then as it grew dark I became unhappy and restless, repeating tiger, tiger. So many days before I could see Mara again. Why, yielding to habit, had I come to Aunt Muriel's instead of staying a few more days in London? It was only the twentieth, five days to Christmas. Couldn't I have come, say, on the twenty-third? That would have been three days, three days more with Mara. I could have done it, it wouldn't have hurt anybody, I could have told Aunt Muriel that I was busy swotting. She wouldn't have minded too much. I hadn't thought of it that way before leaving London. Aunt Muriel was my relative, she'd be leaving me all her money, I should be nice to the old girl, give her a bit of my young time and company in the holidays, which meant doing the chickens and washing the dishes and helping clean the house, and doing the fires on alternate days. So I'd come on the twentieth as usual, sheer force of habit. Sometimes I had to remember that Aunt Muriel also *liked* me, and didn't only ask me to help out on the farm. It wasn't fair to think of it that way. There was a war on. Before supper I went down to the kitchen to help the Polish girl peel potatoes and do the sprouts, and later I shut up the chickens. And all the time I longed for Mara so much I felt quite ill.

After dinner, with the blackout curtains carefully drawn, we sat round the fire. Rhoda did *The Times* crossword puzzle while Aunt Muriel did the W.V.S. accounts. I wanted to go up to the bedroom and write to Mara, but it was jolly cold upstairs, the other two might suspect, or Rhoda might say something catty about me to Aunt. By leaving the room I would break up the picture of cosiness, of us three women peaceful round the hearth, each doing her bit for the country. So I sat on, pretending to read my physiology notes (I made a show of having to swot). By pretending to read, keeping a book open in my hands, I needn't talk, I could dream to my heart's content. And so I sat, lost in a dream of Mara, and I didn't know what was happening around me until I heard Aunt Muriel's voice saying: 'What are you smiling at, Bettina? Is it a novel?' Aunt Muriel thinks all novels should contain some passage funny enough to smile at, though naturally never coarse.

I was brought back to the present, to Rhoda watching me with narrowed eyes. I felt Rhoda knew I had lied to her, that she was wondering about the phone-call. Perhaps if you've loved someone and they've loved you, some telepathic understanding remains, so that she was aware I hadn't told the truth, just as I was aware that she knew it. Anyway, I found myself going red, and I said: 'I was half asleep. Think I'll toddle off to bed now. 'Night, Aunt Muriel. 'Night, Rhoda.'

If Rhoda didn't come up too soon, but stayed downstairs with Aunt Muriel, I would have some time alone, some time to dream of Mara.

*

The next morning Mara's telegram was phoned through by the Post Office, but I didn't know it as I was with the chickens. It was Rhoda who took the message over the telephone, and I didn't get it until an hour later. Of course she did that purposely. It happened that she was in the house and heard the phone ring when I'd already gone down to the chicken-run. Instead of coming to tell me about the message, she disappeared; one hour later, when I went upstairs to wash my hands, I found the piece of paper in the bedroom with Mara's message: 'Arriving eleven-twenty train tomorrow Mara.'

I was furious. That was a rotten thing to do to me, and of course Rhoda had done it purposely, and now she knew I'd lied to her and that it wasn't a man. I leapt to the telephone and rang up the Post Office. They told me that the telegram had been sent the night before from London, so 'tomorrow' on the message meant today, meant now. Of course it was just like Mara to write a vague tomorrow instead of putting the date.

She would be arriving by the eleven-twenty from London, which got into Salisbury at two o'clock. I looked at my watch. It was eleven thirty-five. The morning bus passing our village went at ten. The afternoon bus left the village at two, and got to Salisbury Market Place at three-seventeen because it detoured through a lot of little places before swinging towards the town. By three-seventeen Mara would have been in Salisbury Station for one hour seventeen minutes, and God knows what she would think of me.

I tried ringing up Salisbury Station to leave a message for her, but they were damn rude to me on the telephone. 'Don't you know there's a war on?' they said. I was in a stew, I felt myself sweating all over, visualizing Mara arriving and finding nobody, and maybe taking the next train back. And then she'd never speak to me again. She'd think I'd let her down.

I dashed into the living room, then to the kitchen. 'Where's Miss Jones?' I asked the Polish girl, meaning Aunt Muriel.

'Miss Jones? She go with Miss Rhoda, in the station-wagon,' she said. 'They come back to lunch.'

That didn't help. I hated Rhoda for doing this to me. And one time she'd said – oh, so many things, about loving me, and wanting me to be happy. I was choking as I thought how beastly it was of Rhoda. I got into my best flannel slacks, my green Braemar twin set, buckled my coat around me. I would have to walk the seven miles to Salisbury. I was a good walker, averaging three miles an hour. With luck, and maybe getting a lift on the way, I could do it.

It was ten minutes past two when I reached Salisbury Station, and I ran into it and started looking for the right platform, which took another three minutes. But when I got there the train hadn't come in yet.

'It's twenty minutes late,' a guard told me, 'Christmas rush.' I never felt more relieved. I sat on a bench opposite the gate of the platform at which the train would arrive, as if looking might make the train come earlier.

And at last it came: the engine, with its round black face like the head of a worm, belching noise and heat and smoke, and then the disgorging sideways of so many people. I was so afraid of missing her. Another gate was opened to let the travellers through more quickly, so with two gates to watch, time and again I thought it was her, and it was not. And suddenly I panicked that perhaps I would not remember her face clearly, and she had slipped past me and was searching for me. Such a flood of people streaming past, and I stared and searched for her face among all those faces.

Then I saw her, and she was not alone. Behind her but obviously attached to her, for she was turning her head to speak to him, was a man in uniform. I stood there, and it was Mara who said: 'Red!' and came to me. She had on a wonderful coat, I thought: deep brown, soft, and a red pixie cap, and of course lipstick, and she looked so utterly different from all the drab, untidy females the war had made of us, it took one's breath away. It was no wonder the officer couldn't stop looking.

'Red,' she said, 'I want you to meet Captain Felton. He very kindly gave me his seat. The train was so full.'

The young man looked pleased. He stared at Mara as if he was going to eat her up, and I thought: he looks like a dog who's going to wag his tail and beg at any moment now. We shook hands, and he said to Mara:

'I'm so sorry I can't give you a lift as I'm going straight on to Bulford in the truck. I'll ring you up, may I, tonight? I might be back in Salisbury in a couple of days. I'd like to show you round, if I may.'

He was all eager beaver, I could see he was quite ready to throw himself at Mara's feet; but she wasn't looking at him, she was looking up in my face, smiling.

She said: 'I'm afraid I'll be busy, I shan't be staying long in Salisbury. I'll be staying with friends.'

She took her suitcase from him. He let go slowly, as if it stuck to his palm. I took the suitcase from her and we walked off. After a few paces I turned. He was still watching her. I felt awkward now, carrying Mara's suitcase. The pleasure of seeing her was over, she was here with me, securely here, and I became cross. Because of that chap, because of Rhoda, because I was very hungry. I had walked seven miles on an empty stomach, and Mara wasn't a bit grateful. She seemed to take my presence there as a matter of course; walked on, swinging her little red handbag and smiling to herself.

'I wonder,' she said, 'if we can get a taxi to the Black Swan? I booked a room there by telephone. You'll stay and have dinner with me, won't you, Red?'

'Considering I haven't had lunch yet, and I must get back to shut up the chickens, I'd better catch the five o'clock bus back.' I added: 'You don't need *me* to look after you.'

'You haven't had lunch?' said Mara. 'Why not?'

'Because, you dumb cluck,' I said, 'if I had had lunch I wouldn't be here now. I've walked seven miles to get here in time. Do you know that? Honestly, I wouldn't do it for anybody else.'

'Oh Red, we must get you something to eat, right away,' she said, 'or you'll faint or something. I do when I don't eat, I pass out.'

'It's all right. I won't pass out.'

But she dragged me to the station buffet and ordered some dried-egg sandwiches, which were pretty grim. I ate some, but there were lots left, and again I felt conspicuous, and irritated with Mara because always something like that would happen when we were together: if it wasn't the bomb it was her husband, or Daphne coming along to have a bath too, or this young chap carrying her suitcase, or people looking at us because she was so different. Always something extra, untoward, out of place. And I hated to be different from other people. I wanted to be approved of, in an unremarkable, unnoticed way. But that could not be with Mara. I couldn't remember how excited I'd been to hear her voice on the telephone yesterday afternoon, how wonderful it had been walking, walking as I had never walked before to get here in time to meet her. Now I resented her, the bondage of love upon me, for I had not learnt that in love there is also bondage, that resentment is always a part of love.

I drank the lukewarm tea, stirred with the spoon tied by a string to the counter, and looked at Mara. Now, because I had eaten and was no longer hungry, I rediscovered her beauty: my irritation went. I wanted to go on sitting in this buffet, looking at her, becoming slowly more and more happy.

She said: 'I've been told that the Black Swan is the best hotel in Salisbury, and the food is good, even for wartime.'

'Why didn't you tell me yesterday on the phone that you were coming, Mara, instead of sending a telegram?'

'Because I hadn't decided to come then, I only decided after I'd put the phone down. You'll stay with me, Red, won't you?' she said.

'What about Karl?' I said. Karl had been away when I'd left London.

'Karl may be back tomorrow, so I shall have to return to London tomorrow.'

'It's hardly worth it then,' I said, 'coming just for the day.'

But she said: 'Of course it's worth it.' And I was so happy I could have walked another seven miles there and then. 'Ring up Aunt Muriel,' suggested Mara. 'Tell her you have a friend in Salisbury, and are staying the night.'

Again I felt myself pushed into something I wanted, yet I was afraid to do it because it was upsetting a routine. I liked it, but at the same time I protested: 'I can't, Mara. I can't do this to Aunt Muriel, she'll be hurt.'

'She won't,' said Mara. '*I'll* ring her up. Let's go to the Black Swan.' And of course we did.

They were very nice at the Black Swan. Mara had a way of getting things done simply by looking so sure, and her clothes were always so right. They gave her a lovely double room. We both signed our names. No one seemed to mind at all.

'Now you can stay with me,' said Mara.

I said: 'I hope people won't think things.' I felt more conspicuous than in London: Aunt Muriel was well-known in Salisbury, a lot of people knew me as her niece and heir. But I wanted so much to stay, look at Mara, hold her in my arms again as I had done, feeling whole and peaceful and happy. How much better, I thought, to be in love with Mara than with anyone else, for with Mara until now there had been nothing but this holding of each other and kissing her soft and beautiful mouth, and it seemed quite enough, it seemed all I wanted, for hours and hours. At that time I was pleased that the physical (as I thought) played such a small part in the sum of our feelings, and I thought it would remain like that; and yet, at the same time, already I knew it couldn't.

Mara picked up the telephone and rang Aunt Muriel. Sitting opposite her I could hear Aunt Muriel's voice, and it all seemed so simple and natural that I wondered why I'd been frightened. Mara said she was a friend of mine, passing through Salisbury, and that I'd been good enough to come to the station to meet her and show her round, and could I please stay with her as we had so much to talk about. We were at the Black Swan.

Aunt Muriel was a bit surprised, but she too responded to the upper-class touch in Mara's voice, and of course Mara's voice assured that it would be perfectly all right, and so it was.

Then we were both very happy and hugged each other, and I said,

'Oh, Mara, I missed you so,' even though I had left London only two days before.

Mara had come because of me. Rung up, sent a telegram, come all the way because of me, me, Bettina Jones. Nobody else had done so much for me. Always people had asked me for things, but they'd never *given* me anything; at least, not sought me out and made me feel like Mara did. I'll never forget it, I thought. This is true love. At that moment I'd have died for Mara.

I helped her unpack, hang her clothes as if she were going to stay for ever, already dreading, as I hung them up, the gesture of to-morrow which would take them down.

*

I was braced for a lot of questions from Aunt Muriel when I got back to the farm after breakfast the next day, but the old girl was worried about something else. The Polish cook had had a haemorrhage the night before. It was a threatened abortion. Whether she'd tried to bring it on herself or not, she wouldn't say. I got down to work at once, and Aunt Muriel was so relieved to see me back that she didn't ask any questions.

We ate some cold pie and baked potatoes prepared by Rhoda, and Aunt Muriel said what a blessing Rhoda was. I knew she was a bit peeved at my not being there, because she thought I might have done something to help out. I asked whether the doctor had seen the girl.

'Of course,' said Aunt Muriel sharply, 'Dr Sanders has been. Couldn't let her bleed to death, could we?'

So we didn't talk about my being away, we discussed how to go about getting a substitute, and after lunch Aunt Muriel whisked off with Rhoda in the station-wagon to see some friend of hers in the village who might know of someone to help. But there was a woman-power shortage with the war, and she didn't think anyone could come except old Mrs Wood, seventy-four and a bit, and with rheumatism, possibly just to get lunch going, but no washing up afterwards.

I washed up the dishes alone, then popped upstairs to see the Polish girl. She was looking quite all right, fat and healthy, she had her toddler playing on the bed. In a way I was glad, because with the Polish girl out of action there'd be more to do, and Aunt Muriel probably wouldn't have the heart to ask a lot of questions about Mara. I had a feeling Aunt Muriel might be wiser than she let on; she needed both Rhoda and me to carry on during the Christmas festivities, and somehow I think she might have twigged that Rhoda and I weren't as chummy as before, because she hadn't said things like: 'What've you two been up to now?' when we'd done the chickens or brought the coal in for the furnace together; it was a very small point, but I noticed it: she never used the words 'you two' this time.

The next two days we all had to work hard, the conversation was all on dusting and sweeping and doing the vegs and food, and mash for the chickens, and we were so tired at night that it was easy for me to fall asleep and forget Rhoda in the next bed. Rhoda always got up first while I was still asleep, or pretending to be. And all the time I thought of Mara, and of that night in Salisbury, and the thought was like a flame glowing in me; I ticked off the days on the calendar, wanting to be back in London with Mara.

Aunt Muriel decided to hold the usual Christmas Eve evacuees' tea-party. 'They'd be so disappointed if I didn't.' She was expected to anyway, as chairman of the committee. That meant more work. We rushed round, Mrs Wood came in to help, someone baked buns, I cut the bread and made fish-paste and cheese sandwiches. After lunch Rhoda and I started decorating the room for the tea-party. I pushed the furniture back and removed all the valuable things and put them in Aunt Muriel's own bedroom, just as I'd done the year before. I rolled up the carpets and put them in my bedroom. Aunt Muriel was in the kitchen, the Polish girl had now got up; she hadn't lost the pregnancy after all, and the bleeding had stopped, so she was making trifles with some tinned fruit that had been sent to Aunt Muriel from America for her evacuees. Aunt Muriel wasn't going to ask her who the father was, of course, because that might make her leave; and after all, what with so few men about, and the birth-rate going up anyway, and ATS and WAAFS jumping over the walls at night and tramping miles to Bulford and other men's camps, even Aunt Muriel knew there was such a thing as sex, and not only for cats and dogs and chickens.

Rhoda stood on a step-ladder, winding coloured streamers round the lamp-shades and festooning the walls with the paper chains we'd stored from last Christmas. I didn't know what to do next after pushing the furniture back and rolling up the carpets, and it was awkward asking Rhoda. I thought I'd better start on the Christmas tree, which Rhoda had brought in a few minutes before. So I dragged it in its big flower-pot into the middle of the room, got out the tinsel and glass balls, the stars and the cotton-wool snow, kept in a big box in one of the cupboards in the passage, and I started on the tree.

Then Rhoda came down from the step-ladder, and stood behind me until I had to look at her. She was furious. Her mouth was working, and her hands. 'How dare you,' she said, 'that's my tree. I bought it for Aunt Muriel, don't you dare touch it. I'm going to do it.'

That made me angry. 'Go ahead,' I said, 'I won't touch your bloody tree. In fact, you can do the whole lot from now on, if you like.'

'Oh no you don't,' said Rhoda. 'You stay right here and help, or I'll tell Aunt Muriel.'

'Tell what?' I said. 'My dear Rhoda, aren't you making a prize fool of yourself?'

'I'll tell her about you and that married woman with her painted nails, that Mrs Daniels,' said Rhoda. 'You lied to me. A man, you said.' She spat the word. 'Fancy *you* getting a man. Why, you'll never be able to get a man.'

I said: 'You've no right to talk to me like that.'

'I have every right,' said Rhoda. 'I won't let you get entangled with that woman. She's all painted up and she's older than you, and she's just making use of you, can't you see?'

'So did you,' I said, '*you* also made use of me, and you're also older than me, *much* older.'

She stared at me, dumb with fury. I walked towards her, forcing her to step back. I wanted to hit her, slap her, and in other ways too, hit her with words, make her suffer for all she had done, all the things she had taken from me, the feelings that I'd given fresh and that would never be quite so sincere again.

'You!' I said. 'You, why you've got no right to be in this house! If Aunt Muriel knew the truth about you, you'd be out this very moment on your ear.'

'Red,' she said, 'Red, don't speak to me like that. I love you, and I need you.'

I gave a laugh. 'Tell that to Aunt Muriel,' I said. 'Tell Aunt Muriel how you started on me because I was lonely, how you talked about being a mother to me, remember? And then one night you cried and told me all about the man who'd let you down, remember?'

She leaned against the sofa, sobbing. I hadn't expected her to crumple so quickly.

'Red,' she said, 'Red, please, I didn't use you, I really love you. Why can't we be as we were before? We were so happy.'

'You're ten years older than I am,' I said. 'Ten years. And you've had men. More than one. You've even had a baby and an abortion, or so you told me once, though afterwards you denied it. And it's because that man let you down that you said you hated men and came to me. You started it. You took advantage of me.'

'My God,' said Rhoda, 'you're cruel, aren't you? Well, I can tell you that she'll make use of you too, she's taking advantage of you right now. I bet she's unhappy with her husband, and you're just a filler-in. Because she damn well knows you'll never get a man on your own. She'll throw you away when she's finished with you and has got herself another male. I know her kind. She's a man's woman, she's not your type. She's just fooling around with you between two men, that's all.'

I dug my hands in my pockets. 'That's none of your business, Rhoda. I can take care of myself.'

'All right,' she cried. 'Carry on with that blasted tree. I'm going.' She rushed out of the room.

I stood for a while with my hands in my pockets, then I took my hands out and started again on the Christmas tree. They were shaking, I hated the shaking and I hated them. Rhoda must have been spying on us, I thought. She must have seen us at the Black Swan, perhaps when Mara and I were having dinner together in the restaurant. 'You'll never get a man, you'll never get a man.' Well, I didn't *want* a man, Mara loved me and she was worth a thousand men.

'You're a beast, Rhoda,' I said out loud.

*

The evacuee children's party was rather a strain. I didn't feel I was there, and all this frightful jollity and pretending to enjoy the party games made me sick. In the middle of blind-man's-buff the Polish cook started bleeding again, and Dr Sanders was very annoyed when he came.

'I thought I'd told you she was to stay in bed for a week.' He glared at Aunt Muriel.

Aunt Muriel didn't tell him about the trifles. The Polish girl was weeping out loud and screaming as if she'd die any minute. The kids were kicking each other, somebody's nose bled, so there was human gore all over the place, and Aunt Muriel said she'd never give a party again, it was a waste of time and effort and money. And people were so ungrateful nowadays.

The sight of all this and the noise of children screaming set off something in Rhoda, she sobbed in her pillow that night. I pretended I didn't hear, and after a while she fell asleep.

As I was dozing off I remembered the chickens. I hadn't shut them up, and I bet Rhoda hadn't either. But rather than ask her and hear her snivel, I put on my things and took my torch and went down. Sure enough, nobody had bothered. So that was one more thing I had against Rhoda. It was so cold I shivered all the way back to bed.

Rhoda left the day after Boxing Day, to Aunt Muriel's consternation. She said she'd had an urgent letter from a cousin of hers in Gloucester who wasn't well, and she must go and look after the cousin's children.

'My dear, you're *too* kind,' murmured Aunt Muriel to her, but when she'd left Aunt Muriel said this was most inconsiderate of Rhoda.

'Never heard Rhoda *mention* cousins in Gloucester before,' said Aunt Muriel. I could see her speculating whether Rhoda would be back for the next Christmas holidays. 'Perhaps I'd better find out whether Eunice can come,' said Aunt Muriel, thinking of the chickens. 'She's such a nice girl, so fond of the country, don't you think? I do hope she's got over her conversion by now.'

Eunice was a very distant relation of Aunt Muriel's. She was about twenty-five, and had gone around for years with a girl called Jean. They were so always together that the men students at the Agricultural College all made fun of them. Jean would pull Eunice's hair and scream if she only looked at someone else. Then Eunice became a Roman Catholic. At first Jean didn't seem to mind. But when Eunice became a Child of the Holy Grail League, Jean got quite annoyed. And then Eunice stopped being so much with her, and prayed for her, and Jean became more and more depressed and one day took a heavy dose of sleeping-tablets, and that was that. Eunice now went round with an angelic look and was sweet to everybody. Which is why Aunt Muriel thought of her for the chickens and other chores on the farm.

Then the holidays were over, and there I was with my suitcase packed and some eggs in a carton, pecking Aunt Muriel's cheek and waving goodbye from the train compartment.

When I got to Waterloo I took a taxi from the station and went to Maybury Street. I had written and told Mara I would be back, and the train time, and half expected her at the station. But I knew Karl might be around, and Mara hadn't written to me, or rung up again. But now, Karl or no Karl, I had to go and see her, if only to see the house, to stare at her windows. Then when I was halfway there I got scared that Karl might be there too, and he might think it odd that I'd come with a suitcase. I'd have to leave the suitcase downstairs.

The porter said he didn't know whether Mrs Daniels was in or out, could I go up and try the door? He gave me a haughty nod, and went back to his newspaper. The lift sighed its way up. I stood outside the flat and pressed the bell. I pressed again. Again, and yet once more. No one came.

After a time I went down again in the lift. The streets seemed all changed, empty. My suitcase (the chap looked as if he expected a tip for looking after it) was heavy. I dragged it with me to the corner of the street, and suddenly there she was, walking towards me, and then running, running towards me, and I ran towards her, suitcase and all, and we met; and I could hear her pant and gasp.

'Red, Red, I had to go to the station to see Karl off, and I missed you by about ten minutes.'

We stood looking at each other, laughing, and then I walked back with her to her flat. Karl had been there most of the holidays, he'd gone just today. That was a blessing. We were very happy about it.

'It's been quite a strain,' she said, and again that pinched look came into her face.

But we didn't want to talk about Karl. That day we decided to have our own place. Mara actually had already arranged it. She'd found a big, clean, double bed-sit in quite a nice house in Blooms-bury, and she said we would share it. Even though it was much better than Nancy's, Mara looked out of place there; but it wasn't too far for her, and she could stay with me when Karl was away and go back to the flat when he was around. It was better than anything else.

The room was pleasant and we had a small kitchenette so that we could cook our own breakfast, or anything else we wanted. Every day Mara went back to her own flat in case Karl had returned – 'Though he always lets me know in advance when he's coming' – to collect the post and the milk, and so that the porter wouldn't become too suspicious. So we managed to be together a lot more.

I bought a little blue notebook for our common expenses, and wrote down our purchases: coffee for breakfast, vegetables, whatever we bought together.

Now I was really happy. I was living with Mara. We never stayed the night at her flat, though I often went there with her in the after-noon after the Horsham and we had baths there. She mussed up the flat a bit too, pretending she'd been sleeping in, and sometimes we'd buy a few things to cook, and eat in her flat before returning home to our bed-sit. Or we'd go to a restaurant, though I was a bit worried about that, although Mara always laughed and said: 'I like to eat something better.' She wouldn't let me share the restaurant bill ever.

Then Karl came back suddenly, without telling her, and luckily it was an afternoon I'd come with her to the flat, and the major-domo downstairs was grinning and said to Mara, 'Mr Daniels is just back, madam, I've just let him in.' So I let her go up alone. And I had a feeling that the chap downstairs knew about us, and it made me very uncomfortable.

I tried not to mind too much. I told myself as soon as Karl left she would be back at night with me, but it was horrid, horrid that night, and the next days and nights. We couldn't speak about it at the Horsham, we pretended there wasn't anything, but we clung fiercely together in our bed-sit, clutching each other, before I let her go, and I saw her to her street corner, as I used to do – but I didn't go to her flat with her, and she didn't ask me. I knew that something would have shown. Then Karl went away again, and we were together once more.

We bought things because it made us feel more together: a second-hand bookcase, which we spent an evening sandpapering and re-painting, a coffee-pot in a junk shop, some pictures. Mara brought a wireless because she knew I liked to have it turned on and listen to music or to anything that was going while I was working. She herself didn't like it, and never turned it on of her own accord. Always when we came in, and even before removing my coat, I would walk to the radio and switch it on; but then I always wanted to know what was going on, and Mara never did.

'You don't seem to care a bit about what's going on,' I used to say to her. 'The war might end, and you wouldn't know anything about it.'

'I do care,' said Mara, 'that's why I don't want to know.'

And I loved this in her, it seemed to me then a superiority, some-thing very grand, to care so much she couldn't bear to listen to the radio.

Towards February Daphne started wearing an engagement ring, and simpering that he was a missionary doctor. They'd be going out to work at his mission school and hospital in Africa as soon as the war was over.

'Congrats,' I said, 'hope all your troubles are little ones.'

And she said: 'Oh Red, you're sweet,' but she said it as if I were a boy, and somehow I didn't like it, and going home with Mara that night I was restless.

I turned on the radio, then went to the mirror and looked at myself, Bettina Jones. I was wearing a brown skirt, and I pulled it up to look at my legs.

'You've got very nice legs, Red,' said Mara's voice. She also was in the mirror, behind the leg I extended to look at in profile. I could see her just above my shin bone.

'I'm just wondering what that soppy Daphne's got that I haven't got?'

'Oh Red,' said Mara, 'she's such a soppy little thing, as you say. You're really very beautiful, darling, if only you'd do your hair and get yourself some clothes.'

Mara had already tried getting me some clothes as I had spare coupons, and doing my hair some other way. But I'd always turned round and kissed her and said: 'Not for me, darling, it's you who're the booful one.' But now I looked at myself, came nearer to the mirror to look at eyes, eyebrows, nose, mouth; I rubbed my cheek.

My skin had been rather pimply, but since knowing Mara and eating better and being happy, it had become quite good.

Mara came behind me and lifted my hair. 'You ought to cut it,' she said, 'and have a fringe in front, like that. Here, let me show you.'

She twisted it a bit off my face, gathering the bulk behind so I could see the effect.

'You cut it for me,' I said, 'you do yours so well, Mara.'

We twisted a towel round my neck, and she cut away while I watched. I looked different when she'd done it, but it wasn't quite what either of us expected.

'It'd be better if you went to a proper hairdresser,' said Mara.

'It's fine,' I said, and fingered and twisted it. It did look a bit odd.

'Oh Red,' said Mara pitifully, 'I can do mine, but somehow I can't do yours so well.'

'It's lovely,' I said, but I wasn't happy.

The next day she made me go to a hairdresser in Bond Street, and they fixed it and chopped it a bit more, but my face did not look right to me and it cost me a lot of money, twelve shillings.

Then I got some clothes. But in the shops I felt awkward, trying on things. Finally I bought a nice checked dress with a leather belt, but I never wore it much. It was as Mara said: she knew what suited her, but it simply did not look the same on me. And the saleswomen were no help. At Harrods a snooty woman in black brought us things with frills and bows, expensive and reserved, not utility. 'Modom needs something *feminine*,' she said.

'Bitch,' I muttered when her back had turned.

Most of the time we were terribly happy. It seemed to us that what had happened was so different and new, we did not tire of its wonder, we believed that no one else had ever felt the same way, except the poets and they had written just for us. I had no qualms, none of the torturings that had been mine with Rhoda, I was sure this was the real thing at last. I ceased to question the past, and we both dreamed of the future, all we would do together later on. For of that there was little doubt, that Mara and I belonged together, for years and years. That's what we both said.

Karl was again back from Europe, but again he came back unannounced, as if he suspected something. Luckily it wasn't at night, it was the evening and Mara hadn't left the flat yet when he turned up. I hadn't gone with her, I'd gone home to get supper ready. I waited and waited for her, and she did not turn up. I rang then, and he answered the telephone, saying: 'Karl Daniels here,' so I muttered: 'Wrong number,' in a muffled voice, and put the telephone down.

Again it was a terrible night, and Mara looked dreadful the next morning. 'I don't think I can go on like that,' she said.

'What did he say?' I asked.

'Nothing, nothing at all,' she said.

But he didn't stay very long, only a few days, then he was gone again. And meanwhile she must have allayed his suspicions, because he told her he wouldn't be back for a month or so. I suspected a trap, but Mara said no, he seemed quite happy. And then she cried a lot at night, but wouldn't tell me why.

It made us both nervous, and sometimes Mara would stay a night in the flat, just on a hunch.

'Wouldn't it be wonderful if we could really get married and live together?' she said.

'Yes,' I said.

We really *felt* married, we felt we belonged together. When Karl was not there.

As March began we took long walks in the evening. We walked along the river, and in Hyde Park. We wandered in the streets in the long-spanned twilight, and one night, pushed by a human flux going the same way, walked to Piccadilly Circus. There, against the walls of the buildings or leaning in the doorways against the closed doors of shops, stood many soldiers, Free French, Poles, but mostly G.I.s. Converging upon them, until each upstanding man was surrounded, lapped like a rock by waves, were women, women of all ages and sizes and descriptions, like a great washing tide, flushing up and down and round and round. And more and more were coming, in that same movement that had pushed us there, until the Circus seemed filled with them, four, five, perhaps more to each man. Mara and I strolled round, circling the Eros which had gone, fascinated and horrified because, not understanding in our own bodies the hunger of others, it appeared strange, alien, abnormal to us, degrading yet gripping in an ugly way which we had escaped, were glad to have escaped. We hovered beyond the lurching groups, went home like cats walking away, superior and free, leaving the milling women and the murmurings and laughter behind us, and did not turn our heads.

On our way home we talked about it, wondering that such things should be, wondering verbally, as people talk who feel detached from their topic.

'I suppose that's what's called normal,' said Mara. 'It's we who are abnormal, Red.'

'I don't know,' I replied. I didn't like the word 'abnormal'.

'I suppose we are what are called lesbians,' said Mara.

'If we are, I suppose we must have been born that way,' I said, 'both of us.'

'I wasn't born that way,' said Mara. 'At least, I don't think so. But now, Red, I don't want to be any way other than I am.'

'Nor me,' I said.

Our little world of trust and tenderness, world enough. Everything and everybody else receded, hazy ghosts in a shadowy play we watched, but nothing they did or said really concerned us. We were happy, and people left us alone.

Mara was convinced that she would never love a man again. 'I thought I was in love with Karl when I married him,' she said. 'But he's horrible, and so are all men. I don't think I would let one touch me again ever.'

We wrapped ourselves closer in our love for each other and felt protected, safe from that other hunger which drove the women to Piccadilly Circus and to the G.I.s. Yet it was when we felt most immune to change that change came.

Until then we had not made love to each other: not in the sense in which two women together enact the ritual gestures of pro-creation and fulfilment, one the giver, the other the receiver. I don't know why it was so; but there had been always between us restraint and a kind of shyness which was gentle and tender, a deep emotion which kept us from physical exploration. But now we were too much together, the evenings longer, drawn out and restless with lingering, unfinished light. Desire was with us, and Mara was ardent but, I thought, ignorant, and I did not, could not accomplish the realizable if limited caresses that might fulfil her: perhaps my experiences with Rhoda had left a sourness upon me, a too-conscious knowledge I was unwilling to repeat.

I shut my eyes against the erupting past, recollections devoid of meaning now and therefore become ridiculous and obscene. Gestures, strokings, actions which at the time of their performance seemed exalted, even holy; at least exciting and pleasurable. It hurt me to know that some of these gestures and actions I would now repeat with Mara, because although my mind protested that it wasn't the same thing, it wasn't the same at all, yet the deepest part of me knew that sometimes before her mouth, her closed eyes, a taste of Rhoda would come falling upon me, and I was afraid. Even that early, even before we had begun, there was the taint of what had been: the shock of repetition lay between her and me. What I wanted unique bore thus an occasional, hastily crushed resemblance to a memory now rejected. I shook these things away. I firmly shut the door on Rhoda, finishing her off with a final explanation:

'Anyway, Rhoda's a friend of Aunt Muriel's, and she's been staying with us for the hols, but somehow I outgrew her even before I met you. I went off to London and started at the Horsham, and then there was Andy.'

I'd told Mara about Andy because he didn't matter at all, because I didn't want to pretend I didn't know about men.

'But you didn't like Andy, did you? You never did. And you liked Rhoda,' she said one day out of the blue. 'But maybe you'll come to prefer Andy to me in time.'

'Oh, hell no,' I said. 'If there's one thing I know, it's that Andy doesn't mean a thing to me, and never will.'

She slipped by my side, and again I felt protective and protected; we were each other's shelter against all that had been. But this was not to last. In a little while the peace between us was too much for me. I became irritable, angry that at all times our actions and our words fell short of a consummation which we could dream but not perpetrate.

And thus I realized that with Mara it would not be possible for me to pretend to a masculinity which I lacked, certainly not with the artifices which were the lot and the condemnation of such people as we deemed ourselves to be. With Mara, in front of her clear eyes, there could be no such counterfeits or rigmaroles of lust. And her frightened whisper: 'No, no,' stopped me.

One lacerated night when I was frayed and crying: 'For God's sake, oh, for God's sake,' kicking the sheets with frustration, she rose and she whispered: 'Lie down.' And then suddenly it was not the way it had always been, but the reverse, for until now I had always given and as a lover, with hands and mouth and the apings of domination; but now it was not so, it was I who was the woman. I do not know from what innocence or instinct Mara acted, but I know that I was loved and that I knew myself a woman and desirable then. 'Oh Mara,' I said, 'Mara.'

But she would not let me make love to her in the same way. And we were for ever pursued, as all half-hearted things pursue us, with lingering irritation.

But it was a shortcoming so slight, so easily laid by compared with all the rest: the emotional peace, apart from the near but not altogether achieved physical fulfilment; the security and the trust; the sense of caring and being cared for. Tenderness, which made our inadequate loving better than anything we had had so far, made us shrink from desiring more, from desiring too much. These would only be explorations in the physical realms of satisfaction; disgust and satiety would follow, and then we would have doomed ourselves. Therefore we thought we had enough.

*

Then it was suddenly spring, warm, the 8th of May and VE Day, with an enormous exhilaration which began rather artificially with the radio and the newspapers making it distant instead of near, and suddenly real and intense and joyful when one went out into the mad, shouting streets, with its delirious joys and exuberant displays.

It was with Andy, Andy who had bothered to look me up at the Horsham and knew where I now lived, and a mob of students from St Thomas's and Bart's, that I danced in Piccadilly Circus, blew whistles and cheered buses and sang myself hoarse, and finally got dragged into an all-night pub-crawl and came home with a terrible headache, beating back Andy at the end and locking myself in – Andy, who was saying lots of things about the end of the war, and asking me not to be a spoil-sport and a medieval prig. And the room was empty of Mara, and I threw myself on her bed, breathing in the smell of her hair on her pillow, and cried myself into a drunken sleep.

Mara was not there because Karl was back. She wasn't there that day, or the next, or the next.

The next afternoon Andy came up and apologized, and we had a cup of coffee together. We went to the Everyman to see Anton Walbrook. We had some sandwiches after the film, then I rushed home because I was afraid that Mara might have returned. But she wasn't there, and I was so overwhelmed with loneliness my legs were weak beneath me. Then I went to Nancy's place, and there was Nancy wiping the lino on the table, and the cat walking among the dirty plates and cups and saucers, and Edward with his pipe, and Andy, who gave a shout as he thought I'd come to see him. But I hadn't, I was just lonely for Mara. We sat round and had tea, and Nancy opened a tin of peaches in syrup she'd been hoarding ever since 1942. And later we all had beer, and Nancy got very drunk and began to utter little shrieks as Edward put his hand down her blouse. Soon they'd gone off together. Then somehow Andy was with me in his room, and calling me old thing and using words which were dirty but also exciting in a way; and I was trying to push him away but I had no strength left, and, while he was heaving himself over me and afterwards, my heart kept crying Mara, Mara, Mara, and I didn't feel anything, not a thing.

*

At Mara's return I tried to hurt her as much as her absence had hurt me. When people suffer they take it out on the object of their love, because the object of their love is in their possession. They cannot stop themselves. This goes back to Adam taking it out on Eve, telling God it was her fault; and all our lives we must rend and tear and warp our love to reproduce the primal agony of birth, which is love and hate, joy and suffering, indissoluble together. What I did to Mara then I do to Andy now, but differently because I do not care for him, he only belongs to me. In the ways of wives, I keep him in doubt of himself as a man by making him feel small, by nagging him about his being late for meals, and by rationing him where bed is concerned. Really I don't care at all, but it's a way of passing the time, it affirms the security of my marriage, it is a tug on the chain he wears, reassuring him too that he is safely imprisoned by me. Mara had hurt me; she had been with Karl for three days. There was no security with her, only the constant fear of losing her, and the bright satin heart of love gets frayed perhaps sooner, shows wear more quickly, than the hempen ropes of marriage.

'Well, stranger?' I said, when she came in breathless on the fourth day, watching the joy wipe itself out, uncertainty creep into the smile on her face; but then she decided that it was affection, I was always a bit abrupt, and she took it as it truly was, a mark of having missed her. Of course it was, but she had no idea how much I would make her pay for having missed her.

She was hugging me when I gave her the second shot: 'Had a good time with Karl?'

'Oh, Red.' She buried her face in my sweater, moving her head against it like a cat rubbing itself, plaintive, placatory. 'Don't let's talk about it, Red. You know it's horrible. I'm back now, that's all that matters.'

But I wouldn't let her push the horror away, I wouldn't give her the tenderness and the peace she wanted, though I could see how thin she was after three days with him, with black shadows under her eyes. Now I can scarcely bring myself to face my own cruelty, it is my punishment, to be borne: how I held her back from me, holding her shoulders, forcing her to look at me, saying: 'What did he do to you *this* time? Tell me' – adding – 'he's a man, isn't he, that precious husband of yours?'

And of course it was horrible because she accepted the cruelty, she wept. She thought she deserved it because I was hurt, she thought I was so hurt in my love for her that I had to hit her with the memories she ran away from. And thus, as Rhoda had done, Mara gave me an excuse for being cruel to her, and it eased my pain to hurt her, it was nearly joy; and after that it became impossible for me to change, to stop hurting her, on and off. It was impossible to go back and acknowledge to her that it was because of what had happened to me the night before, with Andy, that I wanted her to tell me about Karl. I went on pretending it was a kind of pure jealousy, due to my love for her. It was easy, because Mara accepted it at once. She had an essential simplicity where feelings were concerned, too readily she accepted that she was to blame, she could not imagine my double-dealing in my own emotions. If only she'd stopped me then, if only she'd stood up to me . . . but she did not. She wept, and tried to console me, though she was the one that was hurt, and even now I marvel that Mara should have been so naïve, like a child in her belief that there was never any ulterior motive or intent in what I said and did where she was concerned. She cried, and of course she told me, whispering in my arms, shivering and sobbing great heart-rending sobs, how much she hated Karl, and I felt such a sensation of triumph and of power as I'd never had before.

'I'm going to finish it,' she said. 'You'll see.'

'How?' I said.

'I can't tell you yet, darling, but I'm arranging things, so we can be free, and together, for ever.'

Of course I didn't believe a word of it, it's not easy to get rid of a husband. 'You'll never get rid of Karl,' I said. But I was happy again, in that extraordinary and foolish way in which happiness seems solid, for ever, when it is already rotting in our grasp, when we ourselves have dealt out its death.

It was a couple of days after that, I think (my memory hesitates, perhaps I do not wish to remember), that I gouged out of Mara the recollection of her relationship with Karl.

One thing follows another; the runnels of rainwater bite deeper as they go. It was easy now that Mara had sobbed once to make her sob again, once a week or so. Easy, and queerly satisfying. Some glamour had gone out of my image of her, washed away with her tears. Disappointed that she was vulnerable, that I could make her weep, I made her weep again.

'Tell me,' I said, 'you've got to tell me. I can't go on like that,' putting a desperate, brusque note in my voice, sitting up straight in bed. I didn't feel a thing, yet I did become angry, so that I nearly believed myself when I shook her and said: 'I want to know about Karl and you, d'you hear? I can't bear this kind of thing any more.'

'Oh, Red,' she said (crying, of course), 'you hurt me, Red.'

'And what d'you think you're doing to me?'

I sounded so phoney to myself, how could she not hear it? If she'd turned round, said coldly: 'Don't be silly, Red, stop acting,' I would ... would have been enchanted, ravished with love again, once again her devoted slave, as when she was beautiful and un-attainable and wore little gold rings in her ears. She was still beautiful, but she was gentle and tender, and now I was irritated by her beauty. I looked such a wreck when I went out with her, and my hair kept on not being right for my face.

'What d'you think you're doing, trotting up and down whenever Karl returns? How do I know that you don't get on well with him? I've got to know.'

And so it came out of her. And now I am ashamed, though when she had finished telling me, I lay back looking into the black night ceiling, coldly: 'Is that all?'

She did not answer, there was only her faint breath, held in long pauses. Soon I was asleep. Perhaps I have the excuse that I did not understand, did not know. To understand one must undergo, and I was not imaginative enough, the capacity to love had been wrung out of me quite early, as it is out of many of us. I slept, and when I woke up next morning I remember I felt pleased and excited, and more cheerful than I had felt for a long time.

Now I can scarcely bear to write this down: boomeranging comes the suffering I did not feel then, alive as it never was. I hope that Mara in time forgot, did not feel this as I do now. I hope she has forgiven me; that in the telling which hurt her she was eased, and did not keep this pain inside her, like a child to be born, through the years as I do.

Some of us are brought up to disfigure love into obscenity. Many of us are twisted to ugliness in thought and deed because we have been made afraid. We do not trust to tenderness any more, and without tenderness towards the other human being little is left but a sad and vicious performance of emotions or contact. Karl, like many others, only knew love, or what he called love, as a domination, an imposition of will, preferably if the imposition was of something slightly tainted and repulsive, like the aroma of high game to bolster appetite. To engender unwillingness, and crush it, and thus enhance authority, that is how we slake our stifled hates. Karl too did this, not because he was evil, but because as with so many of us sex was to him the way out of his weakness; a villainy to be perpetrated like murder, but unlike murder to be got away with unpunished.

Now I understand all this because of Mara, because of Andy. I go through this embarrassed struggle, quickly done; I too am bent back into myself and can make do with non-feeling, with revenge instead of generosity. So long as the radio is turned on loud I don't have to think about it. I can take it. I can. I think of tomorrow's lunch, and what I'll try to get at Harrods for the kid. And when Andy's done, I hate him calmly and feel superior, and rush off to the bathroom to wash myself clean – clean. And I can think up ways of nagging him so that his manhood will be shorn from him, little by little, so that all that's left of him is a preening body, still pretending to maleness, but getting it over quickly now, getting flabby and coming quickly, and the quicker the better for me. He's really getting impotent; I know, and he knows, but we never talk about it, and I keep an eye on him so he won't stray, and he's scared of me I know. If he'll only do the usual hole-and-corner stuff and if I catch him at it, I'll make him pay for it. Pay and pay. I've got Andy taped.

But Mara couldn't tape anybody. She couldn't let Karl perform his gym exercises and give her mind a wander-off, she couldn't forget about it, or pretend it was all right really. She wanted love to be an open, day thing, clean and tender, not belonging to the murky half-sleep that we all burrow into, eyes shut.

I can give it back to Andy by making him feel he's a louse that's got to be forgiven for doing this. But Mara couldn't give it back to Karl, because she did not know what was to be forgiven. And Karl must have hated her, precisely because she could not giggle when he leered; because she could not provoke rapture by murmuring the dirty words he wanted to hear; and when, in the middle of the honeymoon, drunk for courage to perform on a Mara already shrunk within herself, pitiful and afraid and bewildered, he produced those obscene postcards, bought in Paris, and stuck them round the large bed, and acted them all, one by one, upon her, then she thought she knew that love of man was a beastly thing, the extermination of beauty and tenderness.

'Is that all?' I said.

I do not know what horror I had awaited to thrill me. I was disappointed, and fell asleep. Perhaps Mara, who wanted to be blind because she loved me, told herself that I was trying to alleviate her dread, that out of tenderness and love I had said: 'Is that all?' Why else were we so gay next day? For Mara loved me, I think. What Karl had not valued she tried to give to me. But, alas, I too belonged to that dread company that fills the world, in whom body and mind have been sundered to rage at each other, and love lies to be slobbered over, unextricate from shame.

*

We laughed a lot that week, nearly a hectic happiness. We went to see a Chaplin revival, *City Lights*; walked in the park, and the ducks with their little round, boot-button eyes made us roar. I talked flippantly about Rhoda, learnedly about the opportunities in a girl's boarding school. We agreed that each human being was both male and female, and anyone who denied both sides in themselves was lying. I analysed myself. 'Expect I was unhappy and lonely – unwanted child, wicked step, all that sort of thing. Then segregation, during the most vulnerable years, exposed to adults who take out their own sexual frustrations upon us youngsters.'

It sounded clever, detached, scientific. A new tranquillity, since I could talk about these things objectively. As if I'd stuck my past in formalin, this scientific approach made it as safe as pieces in a museum.

Mara told me about her family. Mara's father had died when she was young, and all the money had gone to her mother. Her mother was twenty years younger than her father. 'She was just eighteen when she had me, Red, that explains why she's never felt like a mother.' Mara had been brought up mostly in posh boarding schools on the Continent, taken for the holidays to large, rich houses with gay parties and all kinds of idle, rich society people. 'My mother's very gay and beautiful. She's married again, of course, two or three times, but somehow these men never made any difference to her, she's always gay and pretty and having a lovely time and she always has lots of men hanging round. Karl was one of them. I don't really know her well, she's a stranger to me. She's always been very generous. Lots of lovely toys and clothes, but I didn't see much of her. I think that's why I married Karl at nineteen, I wanted to love, to be loved. Karl is rich, but I haven't got anything, not in my own name. Anyway, I've written to my mother (she's in America now, her latest husband is American), told her I want to leave Karl and I want some of my father's money. She's my mother, after all. She's got to help me out.'

And then she said: 'I'm leaving Karl, I'll never go back to him.'

And since Karl was not there, I didn't say anything. I hoped there wouldn't be scenes.

*

But it didn't work out that way. One afternoon Mara got a letter from some lawyer in Zürich. The gist of it was that Mara's mother was too busy to write herself, but that she was shocked to hear that Mara was going to leave Karl, she advised strongly against it. She felt that giving Mara any money to help her was unjustifiable in the circumstances. It was all in the kind of language lawyers use, but it was quite plain.

Mara was sitting on the bed, looking at me reading the letter she'd passed to me. 'Well, Red,' she said, 'it doesn't really matter. I'm leaving Karl anyway.'

What could I say? It was so difficult. I loved Mara. Of course. I missed her terribly when she was away. I was sure I loved her. But I didn't know what to say. Of course I wanted her to leave Karl, it was awful when she was with him, but if she left him and there was no money who was going to foot the bills? We went fifty-fifty, except that Mara was extravagant and often bought things to eat and brought them and forgot to enter them in our budget book. I kept the accounts because with Mara we'd never have known how much we spent. There were so many things we did together, and all this I'd have missed so much. But on the other hand, if Mara couldn't get any money from her mother and left Karl flat, then it would be a bit awkward for the bills. I couldn't be expected to foot all the expenses. So I didn't quite know what to say. I said: 'You must do what you think best.'

'Oh, Red, darling,' she said, jumping up and coming to hug me, 'I knew you'd say that. You're so wonderful, really.'

'I'm not.'

'Yes, you are.'

'Look, don't do anything rashly,' I said. 'Think it over carefully. I wouldn't like you to be sorry for whatever you did. I wouldn't want to feel I pushed you into anything.'

She looked at me out of eyes crinkled with happiness.

A few days passed, and nothing happened. She still went back to the flat every day (Karl wasn't there), and now she'd arranged with the chap downstairs to ring her in case he came back unexpectedly. We didn't have a phone in our flat, but there was one in the flat downstairs which belonged to some other people who were obliging and didn't mind an occasional call; in return we got tit-bits for their cat. If ever Karl was to crop up suddenly during the day the chap could ring up either at the College or home. If he came at night then he was to ring, but not after midnight when he was to say that Mara was staying with a friend; in that case he was to ring at seven-thirty in the morning (the people below got up at seven) so she'd be warned.

'But it doesn't really matter now, does it?' said Mara. 'I mean, whether he gets furious or not.'

'What d'you mean, it doesn't matter?'

'Well, I'm going to tell him I don't want to go on with him,' said Mara. 'I've made up my mind, Red. I am not going back to him.'

'Of course. But I wouldn't do anything rash. I mean, don't give the enemy any ammunition, darling. Better have it out quietly.'

She laughed every time I said that. I could see she was gathering up courage for a show-down; but at the same time I knew she wasn't practical, and she might put herself in the wrong, and then it would all be very tricky. Of course it didn't matter if she stayed with me without paying for anything for a few months or so, but it couldn't be for ever, and I didn't know what would happen in the future if she didn't fix things properly. I do hate insecurity and fecklessness, I mean I do want to be able to look a little ahead, and Mara never seemed to look ahead.

Then Aunt Muriel wrote to me that my great-aunt up north had died. 'You know she was a bit strange in her last years,' wrote Aunt Muriel, who had been called to the death-bed. 'Most of the rooms in the house were locked. They were full of trunks and suitcases, all locked too. I had to open them, with the solicitor. They were full of old clothes, old newspapers, pieces of string and tins of food – tins and tins she'd kept, some over twenty years. Your poor aunt was always too careful.'

She'd left thirty thousand pounds, to be divided equally between Aunt Muriel and myself.

'Quite a windfall for you, my dear Bettina, and since you'll be twenty-one soon there won't be any trouble about your getting the money. I'm sure Mr Thurston' – that was Aunt Muriel's lawyer – 'will be only too glad to advise you on the matter of investing it safely and well. He also wishes to tell you about your father's legacy.' I'd have to go up to Thurston's office in Wigmore Street and sign some papers and things, and have the will read to me. In two months' time I would be twenty-one, all the money would come to me: Father's, and my share in my great-aunt's money.

Mara thought I was a bit cut up about my great-aunt because I did suddenly shed a few tears. I was upset, but it was a far-off upset, it wasn't really me getting the letter and crying a bit, it was someone else I could watch doing all this. I told Mara I was getting some money.

'Oh Red, you're an heiress!' said Mara.

'Of course not,' I told her. 'The old girl didn't leave much, and what with death-duties I doubt whether there'll be anything left.'

I went to Mr Thurston's office the next afternoon, and of course Aunt Muriel was already there, in brown tweeds, with a big bag, and a small feather in her hat.

'Well, dear,' said Aunt Muriel after I'd kissed her, 'you do look well. Like your new rooms?'

'They're spiffing,' I said. Aunt Muriel winced, then smiled. I asked about the farm, the chickens, the evacuees. Aunt Muriel was quite happy talking about the farm. The evacuees had gone, but the Polish cook had had her baby and was staying on.

'Bless my soul,' said Aunt Muriel, 'it seems the father may even marry her now. I do hope she'll stay on for a while, though.' I could see Aunt Muriel didn't like the idea of the cook being made into an honest woman and then leaving her.

When Mr Thurston had read the will, and we'd signed papers and things, Aunt Muriel said jocularly: 'Well, it's earlier than expected. How about a cup of tea at your place? I'd love to see it.'

So I had to take her back to our bed-sit, and hope for the best.

'How very cosy,' exclaimed Aunt Muriel, looking at everything. 'You say you are sharing it with . . .?'

'Mara Daniels,' I said.

'Ah,' said Aunt Muriel, 'the gal who met you in Salisbury last Christmas?'

'Yes.'

'Is she a widow?' said Aunt Muriel.

'No. I mean, I don't quite know. We don't really ask each other too many questions, you know, Aunt Muriel. She shares this place with me, but of course I don't know much about her. I mean, one doesn't ask questions.' I was floundering a bit, but Aunt Muriel didn't seem to notice.

'Well, I'm sure that's a very good policy,' she said. 'It is *rather* a pity when people get *too* involved with each other, don't you think, dear? Now dear Eunice, such a *nice* girl, but she does get so emotional about people. She's now trying to convert the Polish girl, you know.'

'I thought all Poles were Catholics?'

'This one isn't,' said Aunt Muriel, 'or says she isn't. Dear Eunice is trying to get the man to marry her. I *do* think people ought not to meddle,' said Aunt Muriel, sighing. 'I mean, she might be more unhappy than she is now, don't you think? The baby is perfectly sweet, so good. You must come down at Christmas, and perhaps you can have a chat with Eunice and see whether you can help her a bit. She does get so involved, poor thing.'

She prattled on, and after a time got up and I saw her into a taxi.

I was glad Mara hadn't been in the flat while Aunt Muriel was there. I straightened out the tea things, and when Mara came back I told her about the lawyer, and Aunt Muriel, making it all sound an awful bore.

*

Then Karl came back. And he came to our flat.

How did he know? At first I thought he must have had Mara watched. It would be quite easy to follow her. But it was simpler.

It must have been about nine-thirty, a warm July twilight. I'd just looked at the clock on the mantelpiece, a rather pretty clock Mara had brought from her flat; I always compared it with my watch to see if it kept time.

There was a ring at the door, and Mara went to open. I wondered who it could be, and somehow (I don't know why) I thought at first it was Andy. At the door stood the outline of a man in a coat with a scarf and no hat. But Mara said: 'Karl –' and Karl came in, and he didn't have his spectacles on.

What a difference that made. Karl without his spectacles had soft, furtive eyes, not like an arrogant human being but something brow-beaten; sleepy eyes like a doctored cat. He came in, but didn't look round because he couldn't see, obviously.

'Karl,' she said, and there was a tremor in her voice, 'how . . . how did you come here?'

'By taxi.' His hand went into his pocket, brought out the frame of his glasses; one of the lenses was cracked and a piece missing. 'Just as I was getting out they fell. I trod on them.' His voice was annoyed. 'The people downstairs guided me here.'

There was quite a silence, and I said: 'Won't you sit down?'

'Thank you,' he said. 'I must say . . . Mara, what is all this about?' Suddenly he turned towards where she stood, with the oversatined certainty of the half-blind. 'I'm told you're staying here now. Your mother wrote to me that you wanted to leave me. What is all this foolishness?'

'It's true,' said Mara. 'I . . . I just don't like being married to you, that's all.'

'You don't like being married, that's all. Is there someone else you're interested in, may I ask?'

By his tone of voice I could tell he was quite incredulous. He even looked at me quickly as if to say: isn't this a joke?

'I want to leave you,' said Mara. 'I'd like a divorce, so I can be free.'

Karl turned round to me, laughing. 'I'm sorry this domestic scene has to happen here, Miss . . . Miss . . .?' He'd forgotten my name. Then suddenly he got angry, began to shout, making a kind of grab towards Mara. 'Mara, you cannot do this. You are crazy, crazy. You are a child. I will not let you do this to me, do you hear? You are out of your mind.'

I was up on my feet, but Mara did not understand.

'Bettina,' she said, 'don't.'

Of course I wasn't going to do anything. Just say, if you'll excuse me, and go out. I'd walk about a bit while they were having it out. There was nothing I could do, just standing there.

'Leave us, Bettina,' said Mara.

And I said: 'Righto. I'm going round the corner, got a phone call to make.'

I went down, and on to the street. I did make a phone call, though my hand shook a lot putting the coins in. I called Nancy's place and asked if Andy was there. But he was out.

I walked round for about half an hour, and then suddenly I got terribly frightened. Suppose that man was dragging Mara away, I'd never see her again. Suppose . . . but suddenly I couldn't see him except as a weak man, and I was even sorry for him. I went back and stood outside the door of the flat, but everything was quiet. I opened it and it was dark inside, and I thought for a horrible moment that Mara had gone. But she hadn't, she was just lying down on the bed, flat on her face.

'Well,' I said, 'Karl gone?'

'Yes,' said Mara. 'I've promised to go over to the flat tomorrow and talk it over.'

'Did he . . .?' I began.

'No,' said Mara. 'It never crossed his mind. Another man yes, but not you. I think he was reassured, seeing it was only you.'

169

So that was all right. 'We'll have to be a bit careful. Karl might turn quite ugly, you know, it would be rather unpleasant.'

'He's got to accept things,' said Mara. 'I'm never going to be his wife again.'

We went to bed on that, but it was some time before I could sleep. I was less frightened, and at the same time something in me smouldered, a burning core of resentment. 'Only you,' Mara had said. Karl hadn't even looked at me as a person. Suddenly I hated them both, Karl and Mara, together.

Then followed days in which Mara wasn't home except late at night. Every day she seemed to be away talking to Karl, and this time I didn't feel too unhappy. We were just beginning our summer vacs, and now the war was nearly over everybody wanted to go somewhere, or spoke of going somewhere for holidays. Mara didn't talk about what Karl was saying to her, and she to him. But when Saturday came round and I was doing the week's expenses, there was no money forthcoming from Mara.

'I couldn't take anything from Karl. Not at this moment.'

'Well,' I said, 'that's O.K. I do understand.'

Another week, and Karl went away. Mara didn't tell me anything much about her talks with Karl, but as the days had gone on she seemed more and more sure of herself. 'He's promised to let me think things over for a couple of months. Karl was worried that it might be another man, and I've told him there isn't one, it's just me, I want to be alone. He asked about you, but I sounded off-hand.'

'He doesn't say anything about me?' I said.

'He seems to take it for granted that you're a friend I'm staying with. I gave our address to my mother. That's how he got to know where I was. She wrote to him. I think,' she said, mouth twisting, 'that Karl and my mother really get on together better than I ever did with either.'

'Nothing doing that side, then,' I said, thinking of the future.

Karl had tried to give her fifty pounds before he left, insisting she take it, but she hadn't and so I was paying for everything now. And then Mara decided we should go for a holiday. Now I want to make it clear that I didn't pick going to Wales. She did. She chose the place, the house, and the people. Seeing it now, it looks like too much coincidence that we should have landed just there, but that's how it did happen.

'Peaceful Holiday in beautiful Welsh valley. Excellent food, mod. cons., easy train and transport.' That's what the ad said in *The Times*, and Mara said: 'Let's go there.'

I protested, but she said: 'Oh Red, say yes for a change. And next year,' she added, 'when things are normal again, we'll go round the world.'

'Thanks,' I said, 'I want to get me a job first.'

Mara sent a telegram to the place in Wales, and received a letter back, signed Adelaide Fox, promising home cooking, fresh veg, and butter and eggs 'from the farm', and giving directions. We wired the hour of our train arrival, asking for a taxi to meet us. We took the Paddington train, arrived at Carmarthen round three in the afternoon, changed for Llanfolen. Llanfolen turned out to be a minute little station entirely occupied by an enormous, ramshackle Austin, with straw sticking out of its floor, and a man in a peaked cap and a moustache standing next to it looking with strenuous attention at our train.

'You'll be the paying guests for Talybeck Manor, I expect?' the man said to us.

I nodded.

Mara looked at me happily, as if to say: How exciting! She gazed raptly at the Austin.

'Eighteen shillings,' said the man. 'It's a good hour over the hill and into Talybeck. Eighteen shillings you'll owe me for the fare.' He stood there until I had produced the eighteen shillings.

We went over the hill and into a valley, which was Talybeck valley, along a road which wound in lazy long arcs of circle, with woods on one side and deep-folding hills beyond, soft with late afternoon light turning blue. It was a gentle landscape with no bare rock protruding, remote as if withdrawing from contact. I'm not the kind of person who sets out for the Great Unknown and enjoys roughing it without access to the amenities of life, food at the proper time, buses, telephone. As we plunged along the looping road, never meeting any other taxi or car, I became worried thinking how far we had to go; I would have preferred something more accessible, more houses around me, people on the roads. But Mara seemed happy, and I suddenly thought what a bad time she must have had with Karl the last few days, she looked so thin now. But she was full of courage and sureness. And she didn't seem to hate Karl at all now.

She spoke quite naturally of him, as if it was already settled. But that was because she already felt free. Marriage has a built-in hypocrisy about it that's so tremendous it keeps the partners together better than love could, but you feel the tension all the time.

So I felt a sudden great love for Mara, and was also sad for both of us. Here we were, carried into an unknown place in a ramshackle taxi – there was something symbolic about it, it was a bit like the future that was coming, so uncertain, and I wanted to put my arms round Mara and say: beloved, tell me that we love each other, tell me not to worry about anything, tell me to be like you, certain and clear and not too practical. But I didn't do it, and the mood wore off, and I became hungry.

The more uncomfortable I was, the bluer and deeper the shades of the woods, the more Mara seemed happy, and finally that happiness without rhyme or reason made me irritable.

The taxi driver unbent and started telling her about Talybeck. 'You'll be staying no doubt with the English ladies who have taken over the Manor,' he said. 'It's a big place.'

'Any other guests?'

'Not that I know of. I haven't taken anybody else this way. The ladies now, they don't know much about the countryside themselves. All these folk down from the cities, they don't find it too easy.'

'I suppose it's the rationing,' I said to the taxi man. 'Where do they shop at Talybeck?'

'Rationing now don't bother us,' said the taxi man. 'There's not much to miss in Talybeck valley. Government doesn't come down here often, so we don't have to bother about rationing. Mind you, it does strike us in the tea, can't have as much tea nor as good quality as before. But you'll be all right anywhere in the valley for food, except for the ladies of Talybeck Manor.'

'Oh?' I said, and glanced at Mara.

'They *buy* their bread, and everything else,' said the taxi man. 'To town they go for it.'

'Oh, look,' cried Mara, 'how beautiful.'

The sun had burst its last slanting gold between two hills, and all the valley glowed. In a few minutes it was gone.

'Did you see, Red, how beautiful that was?'

I said: 'Yes, but we can't live just on sunbeams. I don't like the sound of Talybeck Manor.'

'Then we'll go somewhere else,' said Mara airily.

'But I'll have paid a whole week in advance.' That had been the stipulation, one whole week in advance. 'I wonder if I can get my money back?'

'Oh, Red,' said Mara, 'don't worry about such things now, it's too beautiful to worry.'

The road took a dip, we were on a gravel drive in an unkempt garden, a long drive overshadowed by yews leading to a pile of masonry and brick with window shutters badly in need of paint, and a crowd of children in the most extraordinary, ragged clothes, worse than Aunt Muriel's evacuees, sprawling on the broad steps leading up to the open front door. They now abandoned the steps to gather round the taxi, pushing and shoving each other, and although there were only six of them it looked like a mob. They yelled, too.

'My God,' I said, 'd'you mean to say these kids live here?'

'They're the Talybeck Manor children of the ladies from London,' said the taxi man, clambering out of his machine.

We got out, stood looking at the children, and being stared back at. The oldest couldn't have been more than twelve years old, and the youngest, about three, had his legs in iron calipers.

'Where's your mam?' said the taxi man to the oldest.

'Feeding the baby,' replied the twelve-year-old, and she turned to bawl: 'Ma! Ma!' and all the children took it up. 'Mam! Mam!' they shouted.

'Coming,' said a voice from inside, and with a baby in her arms out hurried a little brown woman, dark-haired, brown-eyed, with gold rings in her ears, in faded red corduroy slacks with a scarf round her head.

'Oh,' she said, 'you'll be the guests, I expect. Did you have a nice trip down?'

'Quite nice, thank you,' I said.

The little brown woman seemed taken aback. Mara wasn't participating, just looking round with a dreamy look upon her face. The brown woman shifted the baby on to her other arm, and said: 'I expect you'll want to see your room, it's facing the front, so you've got a nice view of the valley.' She said it quickly as if afraid that we might leave on the spot.

'We'd like some tea,' I said, 'if you don't mind. It's rather late.'

'Oh, certainly,' said the little woman, 'I'll get Mrs Fox to make

you some tea right away. She's the kitchen department, you know.'
She gave a kind of wheezy laugh. 'She's a very good cook. And I
suppose you'll want some sandwiches with your tea?'

'Yes,' I said, 'I think we'd like sandwiches, if you have any.'

She gave me another frightened look, and padded away in front
of us. Mara and I followed her up a dark staircase to the first floor,
and into a large room which didn't look at all bad, with twin beds
and a nice high ceiling, a carpet on the floor.

It was true that the view was lovely from here, the valley running
before us and the hills seeming to run beside it, like flocks of scamper-
ing ponies, and Mara of course would immediately say: 'Oh, how
beautiful,' which was quite the wrong thing, because the nut-brown
woman said eagerly: 'Yes, it's well worth the trip, isn't it?'

I said: 'We would like our tea fairly soon, please,' just to put her
back in her place.

'Oh, yes,' she said, 'and I'll have your luggage sent up immediately.'

'Where's the bathroom?' I asked.

'Oh, the bathroom,' she said. 'Oh, well, we're using the well water
at the moment. Something's gone wrong with the pipes. It's only
temporary.'

'It said mod. cons. in the advertisement,' I pointed out.

'Oh, Red –' said Mara.

The little brown woman gave me another of her scared looks, and
said: 'Mrs Fox is getting someone from the village to fix the pipes.
I expect it will be *quite* all right by tomorrow. Meanwhile, would you
like a jug of water sent up?'

'Hot water,' I said, and she gave me another terrified stare and
scuttled out, still clutching the baby to her breast.

I was furious. 'Look what you've done,' I said to Mara. 'Got us
into this hole, no water, no mod. cons., a battlefield of children
including one with infantile paralysis.'

'Red,' said Mara, 'you do look funny when you're bad-tempered.'

'It isn't funny,' I retorted. 'We're going to have a bloody awful
time, and it's my only holiday of the year. I don't know what
possessed you to pick this place. It's miles from anywhere, and just
the train fare cost the earth.'

Then Mara was unhappy too. I had broken her happy mood, and
she sat on the edge of one of the twin beds, a bit hunched as if to
comfort herself.

I said: 'I suppose we'd better unpack, we can't go anywhere to-night.' I started unpacking.

The tea came, a teapot and a plate of sandwiches, the bread not too well cut and rather stale, but there was lots of milk and sugar, and after tea I felt better.

Then the brown woman brought us two pails of water, luke-warm, and we washed ourselves in the bathroom, which had a tremendous number of rusty pipes protruding from the walls and a lavatory which didn't work. We came back to our room and sat down.

'Thank goodness there's electric light,' said I, turning on the switch.

Later we went to dinner in a downstairs room, the dining-room, which was very beautiful with curved walls and an oval rosewood table to seat about twelve.

The brown woman, who told us her name was Lena Bradford, served us with soup out of a tin, boiled gammon with brussels sprouts and boiled potatoes, not too new, and then a kind of semolina pudding.

'Honestly,' I said to Mara, 'it's exactly the same food as Nancy's, though there are no cat's whiskers here, it's the only difference.'

Then Mrs Fox came in, wiping hands on the apron tied round her middle. She was a short, tough-looking woman, with tough, dry, yellow hair and she was in slacks. Her eyes flickered from Mara to me, and then back again to Mara, while Lena Bradford hovered around her with little exclamations, saying: 'I was just telling Miss Jones that we were getting a man from the village to come to fix the pipes,' and 'Do let us know what you'd like to have for lunch, we've got masses of eggs, but the vegetables are a bit of a trial . . .'

Mrs Fox didn't speak much at all.

We got back to our room and sank into our beds, and, by God, if the sheets weren't damp! Mara looked exhausted.

'It's a hell of a place,' I shouted at Mara. 'It's awful. Why the hell did we come here?'

I heard a sound as if she were giggling, then I found that she wasn't giggling, she was crying; and then I knew what a bitch I'd been to her, and how I'd made everything so ugly, when it was her holiday too. And I came over and soothed her, and my heart burst with remorse, and I stopped saying harsh things to her, and soon she slept, and I lay staring at the ceiling thinking how I'd never do it again,

175

I'd never try to make Mara cry again. Why was I like this to her? After all, we'd decided to stay together, we loved each other. Why then did I do this to her? But, then, why did she cry? Why didn't she stand up and give me back something? She could do it to others. But with me she cried too easily.

*

We woke to a sun streaming in through the windows, to the howls of children, to a breakfast of three eggs each with bacon, served by the silent Mrs Fox still in the same slacks and sweater. She had a stumpy figure, curiously tight and hard, except for her breasts which sagged the sweater into a flabby oblong from the clavicles to just above the stomach. Her hair looked dyed; from the tangle at the back, straggling loose on her sweater, individual hairs fell upon her back, making me think of Nancy's cat.

Lena came in, holding two children by the hand, and told us the pipes were nearly fixed and now we could use the lavatory flush without having to ladle water out of the pail.

I don't like remembering that morning's discomfort. Mara escaped what I could not, the exacerbation of details of living. But then she had never been really uncomfortable, she wasn't frightened of discomfort because she hadn't really known it. She could soar above it all, be with the sun and with the extending valley, it was all a game to her, and that was intensely aggravating to me. Look here, I wanted to say to her, I've pigged it at Nancy's and elsewhere, not because I had to, but because my step put me to boarding-school early, and I've not known how to enjoy myself, and I certainly don't enjoy paying to be uncomfortable all over again. Like Lenora Stanton with her caravan trips, I can't see any point in being uncomfortable unless you can't afford better. But I couldn't say that, because I could have afforded better than Nancy's place, and I didn't. I didn't because I was scared of spending too much, one never knows what one may need. But I paid quite a bit at Talybeck, and it wasn't worth my money and I felt cheated. That's why I was cross, but I couldn't say all this to Mara, and we both spent the morning pretending everything was all right; but we didn't talk much. Small, trivial things to get upset about – but at the time I felt bruised all over. Mara was all wrong, I didn't like the place, expensive and bad, nor the people, and we would be stuck there for two weeks. It was like being married, for we could not detach ourselves from each other, we couldn't leave each other, we were mentally dragging each other around. Mara was far-away, going away into her own mind for a few minutes at a time, then coming back to me with an effort; we smiled at each other, and made small talk. And we were miserable, yet neither would show it to the other.

Then just before lunch Mara went into the bedroom, reappeared with crayons and a sketch pad, settled on the porch and began to draw the kids. It was a kind of act she put on: go on, sulk, I don't care, she seemed to say to me. There was about her shoulders and her silence a passive, non-committal acceptance of being buffeted about, but also cutting me out, a tranquil defiance as if she had made herself free of me now, and was absorbed in sketching. I knew those decisions in her, like taking my hand after the bomb and bringing me home, ringing me up on the telephone at Salisbury, coming to Salisbury. But this time it was against me, and it hurt.

And then I began to love her once more, slowly flooded with love of her thin shoulders, her hand with the pencils, her going away from me, and this grew to include the children. But I could not tell her this.

After lunch we walked into the garden and along the gravel drive. It was a bad bit of walking because the gravel was slippery green with mould in places under trees. But as soon as we were out of the gates it was different, open country with sun, and Mara began to loiter, and I fell into her rhythm. We climbed a little hill, walking away from irritation into a vagueness of mind, and I let myself go, unclutching myself (though making a note to remember the way back, Mara couldn't be trusted to remember it and I didn't want to get lost). We walked and Mara led the way though it did not look as if she did, just as if there was a way that she knew, and climbed among pines, and then another hill where we sat on the top among small boulders protruding like bumps under skin, and about us all the hills humped their backs, smooth and round. Everything was clear as far as I could see, except way out on the horizon where there was a little wad of mist like blotting-paper sitting untidily halfway up what looked like higher crests. I looked at my watch to see the time. And then I caught Mara looking at my watch. She'd seen it many times. She never wore a watch. She had an obsession about *not* wanting to know precisely the time.

She said: 'What a nice watch you have, Red. It's just right for you.'

That pleased me. 'Isn't it?' I said. 'Do you know how I got it?'

'No,' she said, 'tell me.'

I told her. My watch is an excellent chronometer watch. I first saw it in the shop window of a jeweller's off the King's Road, a window wedged between two narrow houses. A little Jewish watch-maker sat all day behind this glass pane, little wider than he. The door was very narrow and began immediately where the window left off. The watch had been left in pawn with him by an American G.I. going to war. One day I looked in the window and saw it. I went in, tried it on and it just fitted my wrist. It would hurt me a lot if I lost it, because it not only gives me the time, but a feeling: the feeling of continuity with the me walking down the King's Road then, with the Jewish watch-maker behind his little glass pane, with the American G.I. leaving the watch for a time as he thought; but it turned out to be for always, the jeweller told me he had been killed in the war.

'It'll go on working for years,' the jeweller had said.

Tick-tick, tick-tick, the watch went on peacefully counting minutes and hours. Security is what I feel as I look at its round placid face, solid, resting on my wrist. It's never gone wrong. The Jewish watch-maker who sold it to me is dead too. We had become friends, and he told me he had an ulcer and I suggested he go to the hospital. I told Andy, and Andy persuaded him to go, so at last he went. They gave him a barium meal and X-rayed him; it wasn't an ulcer, but cancer; they opened him up, and he died.

And Mara now said: 'How terrible,' in a dreamy, drowsy voice, as if it didn't matter. Thinking it over, perhaps that moment was very important – who knows? She didn't show her feelings in the same way as I did. With her everything meant something other than it appeared to me. One couldn't tell. Perhaps she judged me then, judged me and found me wanting.

That afternoon we were happy lying in the sun warming ourselves, being healed in our breach, and I felt I loved her more than ever. Again, as always happens when it is quiet, I was transported back in a tide of remembering. I remembered my mother again. I do this in fits and starts: in Mara's flat the first time I went, a vision of warmth and tenderness which I did not know I possessed until it caught me there; but other visions not so nice, vicious fragments, came back on the Welsh hill. Of the time when my mother ran away from my father with that man (I never could find out whether it was the man at the Zoo or someone else). She took me along, and I saw again the hotel room, with the big double-bed in its middle, so big the room became a three-sided low corridor round it. The smell of damp, similar to the mouldy drive of Talybeck Manor, the soggy grey feel of the sheets, the curtains at the window, badly drawn with a most irritating gap where they wouldn't meet, some kind of brownish-pink material, one corner torn; I remembered my mother wiping my shoes with a corner of the window curtains one afternoon, doing it brusquely, all the time her mouth working, talking angrily with the man whose face I couldn't see even in memory; it had worried me, the ragged edge of the curtain dipping towards the floor, and my mother made the tear worse wiping my shoes. Then I was in a cot with bars; at night, awake, wanting to tell my mother about the curtain, and I stood up in my cot to tell her; but I couldn't see her, only the big bed, the blankets, a big humped mass.

Another memory, another time; perhaps another hotel room, my mother crying, sitting on the edge of another bed, while I stood, holding something, perhaps a doll, staring at her, and then she lifted her skirt and showed me a big bruise, blue-black on her thigh. That man had done it to her. Or was it another man? I remembered again waking up, looking at blankets, looking at the mounds in the bed, like these low hills in Wales, scarcely out of earth. I couldn't see my mother's face at all, nor her hair.

And then, one day, Aunt Muriel in a brown tweed suit and a hat. There had been some shouting and crying, and then I was in a train with Aunt Muriel. I hadn't seen my mother again, and no one mentioned her to me until I was about ten and my step-mother told me she was dead. I'd been at boarding school, and in the holidays back with father in a dim, big house, but he was very busy. I didn't see much of my father, he seemed to travel so much, but I saw quite a lot of my stepmother, she seemed to have appeared suddenly when I was seven or so. I remember her saying to someone one day: 'Of course, the child's mother was low class.' I remember how she tore up in front of me a lot of photographs from a big album that was lying on a top shelf in a wardrobe in a spare room. I knew they were my mother's. I pretended I hadn't seen her do it. Then I wore black back to boarding school; then home again to see my father, terribly ill in bed. I was taken to see him in his bedroom, but I wasn't allowed to stay near him, then one night they woke me up saying: 'Your Daddy wants to see you.'

There was a faint night-light on the table, and his head on the pillow showed two hollows at the temples and two more under the cheek-bones. And suddenly blood began to pour out of his mouth, and my stepmother was sobbing, and I was taken back to bed and I fell asleep.

On the hill in Wales all this came back, but strangely without pain, without this terrible burning inside which made me go out and want to hit somebody. It hurt so little that I could even tell Mara some bits of it, as the memories came. Then Mara gave me her hand, her face was very beautiful, and we walked back again to the house. I thought: now she knows all about me, now she'll know what to do with me. She'll know. She'll know why I am as I am. She'll take me in hand.

*

At Talybeck we were miles out of anywhere. Mornings and afternoons we tramped the hills. We went to bed early; I aired the sheets myself. We saw the children, and heard them, but they didn't interfere much with us. Mara sketched the children, and gave the sketches to Mrs Bradford. I thought some of them very good, and told her so, but she said they weren't. I was a bit bored. There was little to read. I listened to the radio in the evenings. Perhaps we really were tired after a hard year at the College, and Karl, and this was right for us.

About the end of the first week Lena Bradford's friendliness became bolder, more pronounced. She lingered after meals trying to talk. She stayed longer and longer with us over coffee, and since there was nothing to do we couldn't push her off. I wasn't anxious to know her or her children, or anything: I didn't want to get involved with anybody. Only a lack of curiosity about others could entrench us in the safety of our mutual world. I felt we must not take on anything or anybody else. People are so damn inquisitive.

But one day, when I'd gone down by myself to the small village about one and a half miles away to fetch some shoes that I'd had re-soled, while Mara was sketching the twelve-year-old, Lena tackled Mara; I found them sitting together on the front-door steps with the children round them. Lena was talking, talking, talking. That is how we got involved with Lena Bradford and Adelaide Fox; not too much, but still emotionally to an extent that wouldn't have happened had I been there that morning and taken Mara away. And once again I ask myself: didn't this, later on, influence us? Is it not partly because of that lovely and wretched holiday that Mara and I did what we did? I keep puzzling over it, but I'll never know.

'Poor Lena,' said Mara to me in our room before lunch, 'she's had an awful time with her husband. He's a terrible man. I'm glad I haven't any children. He just used to make her pregnant all the time, did it to tie her down, to destroy her.'

'That's what *she* says,' I replied.

'But it's true, Red, and she's quite young. She ran away when he tried to make her pregnant again. She says it's jealousy. He's a painter and she wants to write. That's why he's jealous, because she is good at what she does, better than he is. So he found this way to keep her down, married her and gave her lots of children.'

'That sounds a bit like blarney to me,' I answered. 'No woman need have children if she doesn't want them. Perhaps she's a masochist.'

But Mara's sympathy went out to Lena Bradford. 'She's awfully brave,' she said.

'Darling,' I said to her, 'haven't you got enough on your hands with Karl?'

'But that's different,' said Mara. 'I love you and I don't love Karl, and so I have left him. It's all very straightforward.'

'Well, I hope Karl will see it that way. Your mother isn't much help.'

'Oh, Red,' she said, 'nothing matters, so long as I know my own mind. I'm not going back to Karl, come what may.'

Well, there in Wales it sounded obvious, simple, and easy. And I thought: of course, even if Karl doesn't give her any money, I've really got enough for both of us, and next year we'll both take jobs or something . . . I stopped worrying.

The next morning Lena hovered round with more tales of woe; — I left Mara for a little while alone and ambled round the garden. The children came round, over-friendly like their mother, with beasties and flowers in their hands. I don't really like children in the mass, but they were so friendly it was difficult to push them away.

That evening both Lena and Adelaide Fox came and sat with us after dinner, after asking us if we'd mind. Of course we had to say we didn't mind. It was a regular session. Lena did most of the talking, and Adelaide Fox sat back and nodded. It developed that Lena thought we might be able to help her by giving witness that her health was ruined, or something to that effect. She thought we were medical students. I suppose this kind of entanglement often happens to doctors, they always get brought into other people's lives; but they know how to disinvolve themselves. But Mara was all for trying to help, perhaps by lending money so that Lena could go and visit a competent doctor, but I said: 'For heaven's sake, don't *you* get into this thing. It won't do any good. She's making quite enough money out of me as it is.'

'Oh Red, but we must help.'

'Why?' I said. 'Am I my brother's keeper? I can't be mixed up with other people's lives, you and I have got our own problems.'

Willy-nilly however we *were* involved. Whenever we met Lena Bradford and Adie Fox, they'd talk about their problem, and their problem was Lena's husband and how he *didn't* provide for his family, and how both of them with the children had to stay here, miles from anywhere, and everything was so difficult because he didn't give his wife any money. Or so they said.

They talked and talked, and Adie analysed Lena's husband too (his name was Henry), described him with the kind of sentences found in psychoanalytical books for the layman: they said he was quite abnormal, and it must be because he'd had such a strict upbringing. Lena hinted at all kinds of things, but somehow it only made me think of Mara, and of myself. Men are odd, there's no doubt about it. They get all kinds of notions. Even Andy. Only I put my foot down; I mean, if I'd let him, he'd just be at it at any old time, even in the kitchen. Lena's talk embarrassed me, and I think it also embarrassed Mara: it brought Karl to her, and it also brought up how I'd made Mara tell me about Karl. And now I feel ashamed of myself, more ashamed of what I'd done than thinking back to what Karl did, because after all men are like that.

Lena said she'd have died of another baby, and she was dead tired, sick of men, she'd never go back to her husband again.

And then a couple of days later, late in the afternoon, a chap with a mac and a fair moustache and his hair all over the place, and lots of battered luggage, arrived in the same taxi we had taken. The children looked at him shyly as he sprang out of the vehicle, and he sort of slobbered over them, saying: 'My dear, dear children,' and grabbed one of them in his arms, and I'm glad to say the kid started howling the place down.

Mara and I stood there looking at the chap going through his father act and saying to the rooted kids: 'Where's your Mum, eh? Let's find your Mum,' looking a bit apprehensively around him, but hugging the kids over and over, calling them 'darlings'. Then he saw us and said: 'Can you tell me where Mrs Bradford is? I'm her husband. My name is Henry Bradford.'

'Come on,' I whispered to Mara, 'let's get out. There's going to be weeping and wailing round here.'

But without waiting for an answer Henry walked round the house, dropping the howling kid. The others ran inside shouting: 'Mam, Mam, Dad's here.'

We went to our room, and I locked the door.

'Damn it,' I said, 'I suppose there will be no dinner cooked tonight.'

We heard voices raised downstairs, and Lena Bradford's loud sobs, and Henry's voice.

'I do hope he doesn't bash her about,' I said. 'I'd hate to be a witness, but if there is any trouble I'll say I didn't hear anything.'

Mara looked at me coldly and said: 'Why are you so afraid of being involved, Red?'

'Because it isn't my business,' I said. 'It's damn stupid, all this, silly people doing silly things. Let them mind their business and I'll mind mine.'

The shouts were getting louder, footsteps came running up the stairs, there was a thumping at our door and Lena shouted: 'Mara, Mara, please open the door and let me in.'

'Don't open,' I said. 'Let them stew in their own juice.'

But of course, like a fool, Mara had already gone to the door and opened it. I had forgotten to put the key in my pocket, I'd left it in the lock.

Lena came hurtling through into our room, and behind her was that man, still in his mac, saying: 'For God's sake listen to me, Lena darling, please!' And then Lena was in Mara's arms, sobbing so loud one couldn't hear oneself speak. The thing that made me most angry was Lena calling Mara by her Christian name, rushing up to her as if they were intimate friends.

Everyone was trying to talk at once, and it ended by me shepherding Lena out and putting her to bed in her bedroom. When I came back to our room there was the chap sitting on my bed talking to Mara.

'It's that woman,' he kept on saying, 'that vicious, pernicious Adelaide Fox. She's a devil. It's she, Mrs Daniels, who's lured my wife from me. I love my wife, I really love her, and my children too, I adore them. They're splendid. She's a splendid wife, and they are wonderful children. There's nothing in the world I wouldn't do for them, and we were so happy, all of us, so happy till that woman came and blasted all my happiness to pieces. She's a wicked woman, Mrs Daniels, wicked and abnormal. We were so sorry for her, Lena and I. Lena took her in, and I never dreamed she'd do this to us. How could I ever dream that my wife, a perfectly normal woman with children and a happy home, would go and fall for that woman's lies? But Lena was like putty in her hands. Of course I knew it was hard on Lena having so many children, and she had always wanted to express herself – she writes *quite* well, you know – but of course I never meant to keep her down, that's a beastly lie. I did all I could to help her, but she herself lost interest in writing. I often asked her: why don't you write any more? And she used to say: "Oh, Henry, haven't got the urge to, these days." Then Mrs Fox came along, and after a while I knew she was plotting against me because Lena refused to sleep with me. She organized a camp-bed for herself. And one night when I came back late I found that she'd moved her bed in with that woman. She'd made up a bed for me in the sitting-room, and they were both in the bedroom. Of course there was a row. Naturally I lost my temper, but I've always loved my wife,' he repeated as an incantation, 'and all I want is for her and my children to come back to me.'

The sap, I thought. What saps men always are, and so incredibly selfish with all their man-made ideas of what women think and how a woman ought to be happy just to be with them. And it isn't quite true, it never is wholly true, women aren't happy just being married and having kids and doing the housework, they want something else too. But we're so unsure of ourselves, we've always been so dependent on their approval, we feel guilty if we're not happy as

184

they tell us we ought to be. How few of us really try to find out what we're like, really, inside?

I didn't like Lena, but I could sympathize with her, hearing that man blab about his Love for her and for his children and how happy their home was. I could picture him making love to her, aah-ing and breathing all over, and she just worried about not getting pregnant and not wanting it, but tired of saying no, and the poor sap couldn't even think of using a cap so's not to get her in trouble; and Lena gradually hating to be touched. I'd get that way with Andy if it wasn't that he is bothering me less and less. But this guy Henry, he must have thought it was like the Holy Sacraments, what he was doing. And now the poor sap started crying, actually crying, and Mara looked unhappy for him and tried to say soothing things.

Henry left our room at last. Mara lay on the bed, face downwards, not looking at me. She had a headache, she told me, and I said no wonder. She put her face in the pillow so that I couldn't see it, and I went out and got some cold water and wrung my handkerchief in it and put it on her forehead.

A little later the oldest girl came to the door to tell us dinner was ready, cold meat and salad, cheese afterwards. Nobody had bothered to cook anything, and it was all on the table. We saw neither Adie nor Lena. There was a hush all over the house, so we went to bed, Mara and I, and lay apart, away from each other, but we spoke about Henry and I told Mara how soppy he was and what I felt about him and Lena. But we didn't discuss Adie. It was difficult going to sleep.

Next morning was a stiff-upper-lip sort of morning, everyone going round holding their feelings in check and being awfully polite. Henry had breakfast with us, then went on with the father act, playing with his children in the garden, wiping their faces with his handkerchief, giving the smaller ones a piggy-back. He must have felt lonely, and suggested we go out for a walk together.

Mara said: 'No thank you, perhaps some other time.'

Then of course he settled down by her, and began to talk of his troubles again. He was at our table again for lunch, sitting at the top of the oval, with Mara on his right and me at his left, and a great big bunch of flowers with sprays of leaves arranged in the middle. He'd picked them early in the morning, he said, and started telling Mara all about the flowers. He felt that he'd added tremendously to the place, picking these flowers, while no doubt Lena and Adie slaved away in the kitchen.

Lena, looking defiant, came in with the soup plates, and Henry sprang up as I'm sure he never had done in his happy home and tried to take the plates from her, and said: 'Please, Lena, won't you sit down?'

And she said: 'Please don't bother.'

He followed her out, and came back later looking like a dog who's been beaten. He was very quiet and ate his soup in audible silence, but he made a heroic effort with the mutton chop and started talking about painting and exhibitions and Continental painters he knew.

'If he's going to be with us at meals from now on,' I said afterwards to Mara, 'we might as well go home right now.'

But there were still three days of our second week to go, and I don't suppose they would have given me back my money, so we might as well stick it out for three more days. And Mara laughed, a bitter little sound, and said: 'We might as well sit it out and see what happens.'

In the afternoon when we came back from a walk for tea, we could hear their voices arguing, this time from the kitchen. There was an awfully oppressive atmosphere. If only we'd kept clear of it from the beginning it would have been much better, we could have ignored the whole thing. Lena and her husband telling us their woes had involved us. We all hung in the same suspense. I blamed Mara for this, though I didn't say anything to her directly. Suddenly on our walk she had begun to be interested in flowers. Since that talk with Henry about painting, and flowers and flowering shrubs on Welsh hills, she looked at the hedges, along the paths, paying attention to what she saw. I wasn't going to hurt Mara any more, even though she picked some leaves and some small flowers and said: 'Yes, that is what he was telling me about,' with a kind of stupid satisfaction, so I didn't say anything. I thought then she was malleable stuff, easily swayed, with not much mind of her own. With terror I thought: why, she's weak, she's influenceable, she doesn't harden herself against things as I do. And for a fleeting panicky moment I thought how easy it would be to lose her. To someone else. A man, for instance. Look at that Henry. The way he spoke to her. If Lena hadn't been around I bet he would have tried, sooner or later. But he never looked at me.

The next morning everything had changed. The first thing was, our breakfast came late, with Adelaide Fox serving us, her hair more in a mess than ever, her face terrible to see, swollen and her lips quivering. Out in the garden Henry and Lena were talking, we could see them through the window.

'They've had a reconciliation,' I said to Mara. 'It's all over now for poor Adie.'

It was pathetic, and yet funny in an uncomfortable way, to see Adie going about looking like death warmed up, not saying a word.

In the afternoon Lena and Henry, like cooing doves, went off with their children, the ideal picture of a Happy Family; they came back with masses of leafage in their arms, and Henry insisted on draping it all over the place.

After tea Henry knocked at our door and came into our room, looking blissful, and started thanking Mara, for what I don't know. Then Lena came in her turn and hugged us both. That night there were more alarums and excursions, with Adie bursting in just as we were going to bed, wearing a purple flannel dressing-gown, with her hair done up in two ridiculous plaits stiffly sticking out from either side of her head behind the ears, her face ploughed up with wrinkles from weeping, and of course she too went straight to Mara and started howling and blubbering.

'He's got her back,' she kept on saying. 'All he had to do was just show himself and she's gone back to him, and what'll he do but give her another kid, and so on till she dies. And she's a much better artist than he is. I know, she's a *real* artist, and he's lousy.'

Poor girl, she looked so awful with that face, those plaits, those sagging breasts.

'I'm sorry,' she said, 'I didn't really want to worry you with all my troubles, but you see how it is.' She gave us a miserable smile-through-tears look. 'You know,' she said, 'if Lena leaves me, I'll just kill myself, that's all. I won't be able to live without her.'

Of course we didn't believe her. There was nothing we could say to her one way or the other, her grief seemed unreal. I was sleepy and couldn't stop yawning, and we were both relieved when she left. That's how tragedy occurs: most of the time it doesn't make one feel anything, it's always more real when it's acted than lived.

The next day at lunch Adie was gone. She must have gone while we were having our usual morning tramp. There was only Lena rushing around looking distrait, laughing a little too much, and Henry smoking a pipe, already installed back in his happy family. He had set up an easel in the garden near the steps, and with a pipe in his mouth, and Lena running round with cups of coffee for him and the children being told to keep quiet, their father was working, everything was coming back to normal.

He told us he would paint the valley. 'Wonderful perspective,' he said.

The next day we went back to London.

It was a few days afterwards that I found it in *The Times*, under the 'Hatches, Matches, and Dispatches', which I always read.

FOX. – On August 29th, 1945, suddenly, at York, Adelaide Emily Fox, formerly of Fareham, Hants, dear sister of Charlotte Fox.

There was a paragraph on an inner page about her being found in her room dead from an overdose of sleeping pills. Verdict, accidental death. Her sister vowed she had nothing on her mind at all, was healthy, cheerful, had just taken a job as a nurse-companion to an old gentleman. That's where it had happened. I didn't show the paper to Mara, or tell her about it. I don't think she ever knew.

★

In September we went back to the Horsham for the final year. Karl hadn't given any sign of life for over six weeks, and no money came in, but Mara didn't seem to worry at all.

Poor Lenora Stanton hadn't got through the exams, so she wasn't with us, she was doing second year all over again. She had got married and produced a baby about six months after the wedding. She brought the baby to classes, and when it was feeding time unfolded a screen around herself and said, in that frightfully gay and coy manner of hers: 'Now, now! If you want to look, girls, there's nothing to be ashamed of!' She even fed the baby during Eggie's quiz talks, if they happened to coincide with the baby's feeding schedule, and Eggie couldn't say a thing because Lenora said it was biological and natural. Anyway Eggie suddenly seemed much happier, and then rumours began to go round that she was leaving the Horsham and getting married, which we all said was incredible. But the rumours persisted.

I had a party for my twenty-first birthday, a small party with

Nancy and Andy, both of whom turned up, a couple of other girls, and Mara. I asked Andy to bring another man, and he brought an Egyptian. Andy had scraped through his exams and was now doing a housemanship. Of all things he'd been offered a job in Singapore, if he got his Tropical Medicine degree in a year's time after that, because his father the bishop had lots of friends there and could pull strings; the salary scale in Singapore was something stupendously high, and he said he longed to find out if it was all true about Eastern girls, so he'd probably go to Singapore. All I knew about Singapore was that the Japs had sunk some of our ships there, and it was on the equator. At the time I was sad to think Andy might go away, but it wouldn't be for another eighteen months, and by then Mara and I would be qualified and have jobs too.

The Egyptian lost his temper over something Nancy said about winning the war, and he said of course the next century would be in Asia and in Africa, and he got awfully excited about colonialism. And Andy said: 'Have a drink, old boy,' and he got even more angry and left soon afterwards.

'I forgot he's a Muslim. They don't drink,' said Andy.

The party was also in the nature of an anniversary for Mara and me, because the year previously we'd met about a week before my birthday, only I hadn't celebrated it that year: just got the usual card from Aunt Muriel and a present from Rhoda, and also a small present from Nancy. But this year I was twenty-one, I was coming into some money of my own, my great-aunt's legacy and my father's, all together about twenty thousand pounds. Of course, I know it sounds like an awful lot of money, but one never knows, and anyway I wasn't going to squander it, but I need not feel so insecure about the future now. Even if Mara didn't get anything from her mother, we might manage; we'd have to be very careful of course, and the sooner there would be jobs for both of us the better. Mara gave me a beautiful hand-painted Italian box, and Aunt Muriel sent some pearls, a pearl necklace which had belonged to her mother and which she'd had restrung for me.

Then a week later of course it all happened, everything came together, like a big wave toppling upon us. I should have realized it would happen, but I didn't, and maybe because everything happened so quickly I panicked and said and did things that finished us. Yet I still believe Mara should have known better, she should have taken things in her hands, as she had done before . . . after all, she knew about me. But she didn't do anything, it was left to me.

On Monday afternoon we came back from the Horsham, and I found the letter from Aunt Muriel. When I began to understand what I was reading I had to sit down. Mara was in the kitchen putting the kettle on to boil. When she came back I still had the letter in my hand. I was afraid she might notice, so I went to the W.C. with it and read it again, and then tore it up and flushed it away.

My dear Bettina,

I have been most disturbed by the visit yesterday of a certain Mr Karl Daniels who says he is the husband of your friend. He came un-announced and of course I was quite surprised. He has told me a story which I cannot bring myself to believe to be true. I need not tell you what a shock such a visit is to me at my age, and though it is difficult for me to travel nowadays, as I have had practically no help on the farm and neither you nor Rhoda could manage to come and give a hand this summer, even for a week or so, I shall take the train up to London on Wednesday, the 12.45. I would come earlier, but that I have two committee meetings tomorrow and Tuesday and I must pay a visit to my lawyer. I feel the matter is serious, and I must ask you to meet me at my usual hotel, the Caduceus, for a talk on the matter as soon as you can after your classes that afternoon.

Your affectionate aunt,
MURIEL JONES

'Oh, Christ,' I swore. I went into our bed-sit and drank a cup of tea and tried to look natural. Mara had put her glasses on (she was a little short-sighted) and settled down with a book. I remember it had a blue cover. She looked so placid and calm, she didn't know anything, so I began:

'Well, Mara,' I said, 'the fun's over, I'm afraid.'

She looked up, surprised. 'What is it, Red?' And I saw the quick alarm on her face. She had learnt to be frightened of me. Why should she be scared of me? I was going to pay for all this, wasn't I?

'Your Karl, dear. Your husband. He's gone to Aunt Muriel and poured out a tale of woe. God knows what he's said, but the old girl's coming up the day after tomorrow to have a chat with me. God, what a mess.'

'Was that the letter you were reading?' said Mara, very calmly.

'What do you think?' I hadn't the letter now, I wish I'd kept it to show her. She was so calm, she had no feelings at all. 'The old girl's hopping mad. She'll probably disinherit me now. These things always happen to me,' I said, bitter and flippant. 'Oh, hell.' I stumped away into the kitchen but couldn't do anything there, so came back and threw myself on my bed.

Well, Mara didn't say a word. She just went on reading her book, very calmly. Then we prepared supper. Then we went to bed, saying good night, and she seemed asleep in a moment.

The next day we went to the Horsham as usual. And neither she nor I could speak about Aunt Muriel or Karl. You can say I was unfair, or crafty, or ruthless. You can say what you like. You can say: why didn't you say anything? What could I say? Mara should have spoken, she should have broken this wall of silence between us. She just did not say a word. And now I feel . . . sometimes I feel . . . perhaps *she* wanted an opportunity to go away from me, perhaps she had stopped loving me before I stopped loving her.

Then I can't explain my next move, which was to call up Andy during recess hour, and sound sweet and breezy on the telephone, thanking him once again for my birthday present (a little Indian ivory elephant, quite awful really), and he asked me out straight away that evening, as Tuesday happened to be his afternoon and night off till 6 a.m. Maybe I didn't know what I was doing, but I made all the moves, and yet it seemed they just happened. I dressed that evening in a new bronze-coloured dress which suited me (Mara and I had bought it on our return from Wales), I brushed my teeth carefully because when I get too excited sometimes my breath goes bad. I told Mara I'd been asked out by Andy. I said:

'It just slipped my memory. He asked me at my birthday party, as a matter of fact, I forgot to tell you.'

Then all the explaining seemed superfluous because she just nodded, she was reading a book and I noticed it was the same book as yesterday; now I think, I have a feeling, that she didn't turn the pages of that book, just kept it in her hand – but I can't really remember. All this time I never looked at her face, her lovely face, and now I miss it so, and she hasn't left a photograph, not one.

Perhaps I wanted to find Mara gone when I came back that night. I ask myself again, but I no longer know. When I came back late, with Andy kissing and pawing me on the front doorstep, and let myself in, I think I would have howled with misery if she had not been there. But she was there, an immobile and silent lump in bed. She turned when I came in, as if she'd just woken up, and said:

'Had a good time?'

And I said: 'Yes, thanks,' and described the film we'd seen; and we made small talk for a decent interval, then said good night.

All of us double-cross ourselves, pretending, because we can't face all, all the contradictoriness. It makes me laugh now when I hear Andy talking pompously of how concerned he is about the fate of Africans or the spiritual freedom of the Chinese, or one thing or another: because he really doesn't care, it's just a pose, but it makes him feel good that he should have such noble feelings. Well, I'm a double-crosser too, but I feel better because I've owned up to my own other self. While I was breaking up my love for Mara, I could at the same time weep for what I was destroying, and wish it all different; wish myself different from what I was. But of course it could not be.

*

There isn't much more to say, but I must put it down.

I went to the Caduceus quite early on Wednesday afternoon. Aunt Muriel was waiting. We chatted about the farm and the Polish cook (she wasn't married yet). Aunt Muriel was wearing her best tweeds, I mean the kind she wears for church, with a grey silk blouse and her amethyst necklace, and that was a bad omen. It meant lawyers and things like family quarrels: she'd worn tweeds to take me away from my mother, and again when once she had a row with my step. It was quite impressive, if I hadn't had something to say I would have been very frightened. There was an awkward silence while Aunt Muriel rang for tea to be served, though it wasn't four yet, but 'they do take ages to serve tea, we might as well ask them slightly earlier,' she said. Then tea came and we filled up the silences between the chink of china on the tray with questions and answers about my studies, then Aunt Muriel took a deep breath and plunged in:

'I suppose you received my letter, Bettina.'

Obviously I had, since I was here. 'I did, Aunt Muriel.'

Aunt Muriel began to redden slowly. 'I need not tell you,' she said, her voice muffled, 'what a shock, how I felt . . . I would like to think the man is mad, Bettina.' She put her cup down. Her hands were shaking. She was obviously very upset.

'Honestly, Aunt Muriel, it's been a shock to me too. Very uncalled for.'

She was breathing a bit better, I must have said that well.

'I'm relieved to hear you say so, Bettina. But this situation must end. It seems to have given rise to considerable misunderstanding, at least in the mind of *one* person. It is really quite thoughtless of Mrs Daniels to leave her home for such long intervals and to stay with you. It might look odd to some people. Very odd. A married woman does not usually leave her home, especially when she is well provided for, to engage in studies, especially prolonged studies. And then to stay with you, to share a residence with another person when she has a perfectly good home of her own . . .' she breathed heavily. 'I told this man that I was convinced there was nothing to it but a very normal friendship. I said you were completely innocent, and probably had never thought of any complications. But you can see, can't you Bettina, what an unpleasant position has arisen? This Mr Daniels seemed quite ready to run to extremes. He is a foreigner, and seems quite highly strung. He even spoke of legal redress, Bettina. I must beg you, for my sake, to stop this friendship of yours at once.'

'But, Auntie, seeing as how I'm engaged to Andy I really don't feel people can misunderstand anything.'

'Don't say "seeing as how", Bettina,' said Aunt Muriel sharply. 'Really, Bettina, I don't understand how you young people can think it's smart to talk that way. And who's Andy, may I ask? I don't think I know the name.'

I explained about Andrew Morton being the son of a bishop and himself a doctor now doing his housemanship; how I'd known him for years but had waited till I was twenty-one, which was just a week ago. 'Of course, we're not quite officially engaged, Aunt Muriel, because I told him I wanted him to be vetted by you first. But he asked me on my birthday as a matter of fact, and I told him that if . . . well, if he came through with you it would be all right with me.'

Aunt Muriel was now so overcome with relief I thought I'd over-done it. She turned purple, then pink, slowly sank back in her chair. Then she gave me a long, long look, and the look went right through me. At that moment I felt sure, absolutely sure, that Aunt Muriel knew everything: I mean, everything about Rhoda, and Mara. I felt she had really always known, but like so many people of her class she was superb at *not* seeing or hearing or knowing things that were unpleasant. And in that flash of intuition I felt nearer to Aunt Muriel than I'd ever been, really close, really of the same flesh and bone, kith and kin. And then I could see her make up her mind that that was the way it was going to be, and she'd decided to see it my way. After all, it was Aunt Muriel who'd come to take me away from my mother, not my own daddy; it was Aunt Muriel who'd fought for me with my step. She knew me through and through.

I wore my best skirt and blouse, and I had her pearls on too, the necklace that she had given me.

'Well,' said Aunt Muriel, 'of course I told the man he was ridiculous, making mountains out of a molehill. But he's a foreigner, that explains his attitude ... they're not very *balanced*, are they? I mean, he was probably rather cruel to his wife and she doesn't like him, and it just happens that you've got yourself involved ... I think you've been rather *careless*, dear. After all, you're an inexperienced young gal, and it never struck you how odd it all *might* look.' Here she took a big gulp: I-may-as-well-say-so sort of thing. 'I didn't really like the idea of this er ... friendship. I blame myself for not saying something about it when I heard she and you were now sharing a ... er ... rooms.' Aunt Muriel couldn't bring herself to say digs.

'Well, Auntie,' I said, 'I can't throw Mrs Daniels out, can I? It's not my fault if she and her husband don't get on, is it?'

Aunt Muriel frowned. 'You could tell Mrs Daniels that I'm very concerned,' she said firmly. 'Meanwhile I could write to this ... to Mr Daniels and tell him that I've had a talk with you and I'm absolutely *convinced* that not only is there nothing to confirm his suspicions, but that should he be so rash as to take certain steps he might find it very difficult ... Of course, it would be most unpleasant, most unpleasant if he did take any legal action, as he threatened to, but he probably wasn't too sure of his ground since he came down to see me first. He said that he had had his wife followed for some time now.' Aunt Muriel's lips curled with dislike. 'At first he thought it was another man, then he found out she was staying with you. Then he gathered that his wife had gone down to visit you in Salisbury last Christmas, then ... well, then he thought it was all very *odd*, especially when his wife said she'd never go back to him. Then you both went off to Wales together. Of course, I'm sure it was quite innocent on your part, but you do see, don't you, what some people might make out of it? Especially in a court of law. I . . . actually thought of seeing my lawyer about it, but then I decided I'd see you first . . . but you *do* understand that all this must stop at once, don't you? For my sake, Bettina. You must explain the position to Mrs Daniels, and she must leave immediately, or you must.'

Precipitately all was changing, just as if a sudden shrill storm had blown up, obliterating the landscape before me. I was feeling quite sick. Mara, I thought, Mara. What was I doing here? I wanted to shout to Aunt Muriel: 'To hell with Karl, and your money, and everything. I love Mara and she loves me.'

I said: 'I can't ask Mara just to go like that, Aunt Muriel.'

'I'm afraid you'll have to,' said Aunt Muriel sharply. 'I am your guardian, Bettina. You've had a very unhappy start to your life, my dear, and I've always made it a point to look after you to the best of my ability. I don't consider this relationship a healthy one for you. If you do not take steps, I cannot do anything but wash my hands of the whole business since you're now of age. Needless to say I shall consider that I have wasted a good part of my life on someone who does not repay the care and attention I have tried to give, and I shall have to be guided in the future disposal of whatever I may possess by other considerations. I am not saying this as a threat to you, Bettina, but simply because it is the truth. I am an old woman, my dear, and I have had to cope in the past with some very painful situations. I cannot, at my age, be dragged into *another* scandal.'

She's talking of my mother, I thought. It must have been an awful scandal at that time, my mother running away with a man, having lovers, my father divorcing her, my step . . . My mother low-class, not good enough for my daddy, everyone against her . . . Aunt Muriel had never mentioned it before. Nobody ever spoke to me of my mother, they'd all kept it from me. But Aunt Muriel must have felt it all these years. It must have been in the newspapers, shame for all to see.

I said: 'I'll try to arrange it, Aunt Muriel, though of course it's difficult when we're both studying.'

Aunt Muriel got up. She pecked me on the forehead, and her eyes were troubled and brimming with tears. I knew she knew I was lying and I think she did not like me for it. She twisted her amethyst necklace and looked straight into space.

'Bettina, my dear,' she said, 'we all have to do . . . certain things. Believe me. I can assure you that . . .' Then she flushed scarlet and her lips tightened. 'Let me know soon . . . within a week.'

She wasn't going to let this thing go. She was going to make sure.

So I had to go back, and now it was horrible, horrible; in the bus, like a dim, growling hurricane all round me, my ears filled with the storm wind of what I had done. What had I done, what had I done? What could be done? Mara, Mara, they're trying to break you and me, they're doing this, Mara. Mara, I have to choose. Help me. I was running, running up my street, our street, through thick fog, only there wasn't any fog, but people round me like shadows flitting, turning surprised that I ran, dark against the dark evening, it was so very dark, or so it seemed to me then.

The light was on, the radio too, loud. Mara, Mara, just on the other side of the door. I turned the key, I would see her, I would say: I love you, Mara, to hell with Aunt Muriel and the newspapers and the scandal. I love you. Help me. I would see her lovely face.

'Andy, what are you doing here?'

There he was, the slob, spread out on the bed with a conquering hero sort of air, the radio on, just as if he were in his own digs.

'Get your feet off my bed,' I said, 'I won't have filth all over it.' We'd just had the bedspreads laundered, Mara and I. Mara, oh Mara . . . a dead hand squeezing me inside, horrible, horrible pain. 'Where's Mara?' I asked.

Andy had got to his feet, looking sheepish and silly, and was sweeping his hand over the bedspread.

'Who?' he said. 'Oh, Mara? She was going out just as I came up. Met her on the stairs. Fact is, she opened the door for me.'

'Did she say where she was going?'

'Not to me,' said Andy. 'Just said "Bettina won't be long, please come in and sit down." Nice girl,' said Andy. 'Real little woman. Nice shape and hair. Needs a man though, I can see that. Though I prefer the long, lean type . . .' He moved forward, hands foraging; he liked to pinch and tickle, but now I've broken him of that habit.

'Oh, for heaven's sake,' I said.

'C'mon,' he said, 'c'mon, Red, how about some more like last night, eh?' He clucked his tongue. 'Boy, that was good last night.'

Oh God, he was so pleased with himself. Because for once I'd put on a show as if I couldn't resist him any more, as if he was a hell of a guy. All the time I felt like being sick.

'No, thanks. And besides, Mara might come back at any moment.'

'No, thanks,' mimicked Andy. 'Goodness, Red, you say that again and I won't be able to control myself. We'll lock the door.' He winked. 'Won't be long. After all,' he said, 'you might as well get used to it, you know. I'm warning you.' He rolled his eyes again, winking and pinching, irresistible he thought.

'Oh Christ,' I said, 'leave me alone. Not now.'

That made him angry, and he said some nasty things. 'Why, what's the matter? Trying to play me up, or what?' Then he took my hand quick and put it on his trousers, to show me, thinking perhaps that might do it, and started trying to push my skirt up. And now I was scared if I refused he'd back out or something. After all, it hadn't been easy the night before getting him to say: 'I'd marry you if I could, old girl,' and me saying: 'Oh, Andy, but you can,' and artlessly telling him about my twenty thousand pounds. Not shoving it at him, of course, but . . . I know what it's like, I know about Andy. The bishop is not well-off, Andy was on a clerical scholarship and always short of money. I knew how he'd react. So I let him, after locking the door, and lay there and thought: God, I'll have to get rid of him, I'm not going to put up with this all my life, night after night. I was so scared Mara would come in I kept my eyes on the door. And the radio played loud, louder, which was good, I'd turned it even higher so I could always say I hadn't heard her knock. Then I got frightened I might not hear her knock – oh, would he never be done? Then I realized something was wrong.

'Hell,' I said, 'what happens if I get pregnant?'

'Eh?' he said. He looked like dropping off to sleep.

But I didn't let him. 'Get up,' I said, 'get out. I don't want Mara to find you here. And I've got to wash. Quick.' I was in a frenzy, and he did go away, thank God, I got him out quick. Then I ran to the bathroom and cleaned myself up, cleaned myself. That would be the worst ever, if I got pregnant.

Then I looked round everywhere, and I felt better, Mara hadn't taken anything, just coat and handbag, everything was here, her dresses, her books, everything. I went to the kitty where we kept the flat money, and there it was, so she couldn't have had any money with her at all, she had no money from Karl. She must have gone for a walk.

I lay down and tried to sleep. I dozed a bit, then I woke up, waiting for her. Then I looked at my watch, dressed, and went out, went to the cinema hoping, absurdly, that she might have gone there. It was just closing time, but she wasn't in the crowd coming out. And of course she had no money. I went back and waited. The night went away and Mara did not come back.

It's better now, it will probably get better as time goes on, I know I keep telling myself it's better. I tell myself. I don't seem able to do otherwise than stammer the same words: like the pain that keeps on coming, on and on. At first it was so awful, so terrible, all over again like waking up and seeing the big hump, the colossal mountain of silence and indifference that was my mother and her lover in the bed; night and the face of my father in bed with a driblet of blood between his lips; the little Jew who died of cancer; all, they all came out at me, in and out, all the time, and Mara wasn't there. I cried out for her, oh how I cried out for her. But her face . . . I could not even get her face back in front of my eyes. Her face is entirely gone from me. And I haven't got a picture of her. Not one. I could say: her nose was straight and small, her eyes were brown, but there is nothing I can take hold of, grasp solidly. Her face is gone from me, as she is gone.

I went to the Horsham. Mara did not come. I waited, every moment thought I could see her. If I just shut my eyes for a moment, then opened them, she'd be there, at my side. But she did not come. The day after there was sunlight coming through the windows, specks of dust dancing in the sunlight, and I wanted to scream: God, her little gold ear-rings. I ran home and ransacked through all her things, her dresses, her extra coat, her books. I found the ear-rings, and kept them in my hand all night: if only I held them in my hand, she might come. She hadn't even taken her pyjamas. Nothing. There was her smell, her perfume, though lately she hadn't been using much; Karl had not brought her any more perfume, and of course I couldn't buy any. For days I lived at night, holding her things in my hands, packing and unpacking them, laying them carefully in the drawers. In the day time I went to the Horsham. Queer, no one came to ask me about Mara. No one mentioned her to me. Not even Louise. One evening, about three days later, the phone rang and I jumped to it, thinking it was Mara, but it was only Andy. I said I was ill with flu.

*

After nearly a week I couldn't bear it. Mara. I'd written letters to her, left them about the room in case she came back, torn them up in the morning. One night when I was already in bed I got up and put on my slacks and my mac on top (the old mac, the one that I had when I first saw Mara) and I went to Maybury Street. I thought I would ring the bell, and, Karl or no Karl, I'd take Mara away. I would say: 'Come, Mara, come with me. I love you, and neither of us need be frightened of anything because we love each other.' We'd be together, walk together, hand in hand, under the London sky with winter closing in, closing in like a cold tent but the only house we knew. We would be together.

On the way to Maybury Street I suddenly thought: she might be dead, maybe Karl has killed her. I couldn't get my mind off that. Otherwise she would have telephoned, or written. Maybury Street was still some way off, so I hailed a taxi, but when it drew up I couldn't make up my mind, and the driver said: 'Well, I can't wait here all day, lass,' so I said: 'Maybury Street,' and got in.

Maybury Street was awfully quiet, empty. I made him stop past the house. I went walking slowly back, looked up. Her windows were dark. I didn't dare to go in. I stood looking, hoping, willing her to come to a window and look out. Surely, surely, she would hear me, hear me straining to reach her; would wake up, I wanted her so much to wake up and see me. I prayed standing there: 'Oh God, if you are, please make Mara come and look out of the window. No, not even that, just let me see her face, only once more, once more. You see,' I said to God, 'I've forgotten what her face looks like, and that is the worst of all, the worst. Why can't I remember her face? Soon it will all go away from me, like water, like sand washed under one's feet in the tide. I'll have lost all of her, everything, everything of my love, my love . . .' And even as I stood there I could feel it going away from me, wearily, weary as an old woman hobbling away. Perhaps I had suffered so much I was worn out and I couldn't feel any more that night.

The next morning I went to see the Secretary at the Horsham, the one who keeps track of our addresses. I said Mara had been unwell for a few days now and had gone down to the country, and did they have her address there? And the Secretary looked at me surprised and said no, they had no news of Mrs Daniels, only the address in Maybury Street. Then she looked concerned and said I must let her know how Mrs Daniels was, if she'd be back soon. I thanked her. And at that moment in came Eggie, and she too was concerned that Mara had missed coming for a week. Eggie had a new suit and looked quite smart. She said:

'Mrs Daniels is *such* an attractive woman, isn't she? I hope she'll get well soon.' Then she looked at me and said: 'You don't look too well yourself?'

Lots of people had colds and flu these days, so I said I wasn't feeling well.

And then on Saturday I got quite a shock, for outside my digs, there on the pavement, stood Karl. He was waiting, looking . . . just as I must have looked at his flat in Maybury Street. He came striding towards me. I pretended I hadn't seen him, but he could not be avoided.

'Miss Jones,' he said, 'where is Mara?'

'I don't know,' I said.

I kept on walking, but he was at my side, and it wouldn't do, so I stopped. We faced each other. He had his glasses on, they gleamed a bit.

'You don't know,' he said. 'I don't believe it. I'm warning you.'

'It's true. You can have me followed, you can ask anyone. She went away a week ago. I thought she was with you.'

So it had been in vain, waiting in Maybury Street, she wasn't there. And all this time Karl must have been watching me, and realized Mara wasn't with me any more, or he wouldn't have asked. So now we believed each other.

'Where is she?' said Karl. 'Where is she, then?'

'I don't know,' I said.

He turned and left me. I wanted to run after him and say: Look, don't go away, perhaps if we talk a bit we might find her, we might . . . But it was too late. He wasn't interested in me at all.

That night I wrote another letter to Mara, upbraiding her for going away. 'Don't you see, darling,' I wrote, 'it was just pretending. I was just pretending to get engaged to Andy, and then you could have gone back to Karl for a bit, but we could still have met each other ...' Then when I'd written this I realized it wouldn't have worked at all, it could never have been like that. Anyway, Mara had said she wouldn't go back to Karl. She had not gone back. Then where was she?

I've even gone through the 'Dispatches' in *The Times*, all the way back to that day, in case. Nothing. About ten days after she'd gone I made a discovery. I found her key to the Maybury flat and her key to our door. Both together in a small work-basket she had where she kept her thread and needles and things.

*

Well, Andy and I got married in June when I finished at the Horsham. Honeymoon, we went to Belgium, it rained a lot and I was glad to get back. He didn't get his Tropical Medicine degree, so we're staying in England, and he'll have another shot at it in a year or so. Aunt Muriel is talking about a practice in Salisbury for Andy, but what with National Health coming in and the huge pay one gets abroad, Andy says there's a packet to be made in the colonies. And anyway, with my money, and Aunt Muriel's, we can afford to look around a bit before settling down. We've been staying in London, and I haven't done anything much. No point in looking for a job, since I got pregnant on my honeymoon or before. We've got quite a decent flat, plenty of hot water. When Andy isn't there I take walks. I walk and walk around in the streets, and I know what I'm looking for. There are lots of women in the streets, I look at them, sometimes they look back at me. Sometimes one of them looks like Mara, I think it is Mara ... but it never is. I even went to Piccadilly Circus several times, in my slacks and old mac: the same as ever, busy, not so many soldiers now, but still lots of women.

Looking for something. Even her name grows faint as an echo at times, at others it's very clear. Perhaps I'll have to go on all my life like this, really searching for her, doing and saying things I don't want to do and to say, always knowing just beyond reach there is something marvellous, unreachable. Well, I am what I am, and did what I did. Who knows, if I'd given up everything for Mara, who knows where we'd be now? Or if it wouldn't have become impossible. Even if there is something else that could have been done or said, it did not happen, it was beyond me to make it happen differently.

And Mara was wrong. She should not have accepted so tamely, have bowed down to my will, or whatever it was that made me do what I did; accepted it and been pushed by it into the night, into going away out of my life, out of life . . . If she really loved me, she shouldn't have walked out on me. I wake up at night dreaming she is somewhere and I cannot reach her. Sometimes I *wish* she were dead. Then I would stop worrying. She should have been herself with courage, told me what to do. It was she the prime mover, propelling me forward. Why did she give up so easily? Why? Was it because she got tired of loving me? This is what I cannot face: that really she went away because she did not care any more . . .

So I write to her, and tear up: rant and rave and tell her that it is her fault, her fault. She should have stopped me. She should not, so easily, have walked out with only her handbag and nothing in it, into the night, disappeared as over the edge of a precipice. I walk the streets looking for her face, like a pearl in the darkness, luminous as I remembered it. And once, coming out of a restaurant, I saw that man, Felton, the chap who had carried her suitcase in Salisbury, talking and laughing with a woman with dark hair down her back. For one crazy moment I was sure it was Mara.

If someone tells me that all my life will be like this, listening to the radio and sleeping and eating with Andy, getting up in the morning and bed at night, I'll kill myself.

Sometimes I pretend that I'm on a hill in Wales, and Mara by my side, the sun dancing on her skin, a little cloud like a blotter on the mountain beyond. I even tried finding those people in Wales, the Bradfords. Perhaps, perhaps, they knew where Mara was. But I couldn't find them.

And so I go on, to go on, as autumn deepens, and darkness draws in to another constricting winter, towards a cold so cold, short days so short you must turn on the lights by four in the afternoon; so I turn on the lights, and the radio loud, and draw the curtains against the night.

Some other Penguin books by Han Suyin
are described on the following pages

Destination Chungking

Han Suyin

This sensitive autobiography, 'written piecemeal by oil light in what was left of the room after a day's bombing', is by a Chinese woman born and bred in Peking, but trained in England for her medical calling. It is a statement of belief in living, throwing compassionate light on a place and time all too unfamiliar to English readers – China, struggling against Japanese aggression. The book combines the absorbing realistic interest of a good documentary with the appeal of the story of the author's love and marriage. Han Suyin conveys horror with the stoical restraint one would be tempted to call Chinese if it were not also an English characteristic. Her heart is with her own people; her wit and perception are universally feminine. This evocation of China at war as the setting for an individual's life helps its readers to bridge the immense, more than geographical, gap between East and West.

... And The Rain My Drink

Han Suyin

In the hands of a more pedestrian writer this might have been a factual and laborious report on the conflict in Malaya. But the exotic style and leaping imagination of the author of *A Many-Splendoured Thing* weave a vast human tapestry from the varied strands of politics. *... And The Rain My Drink* becomes an epic prose-poem of Malaya's darkest hour.

'A book of great richness, a very full canvas but not a congested one, and one that is often quietly, unforcedly, but profoundly moving' – *Daily Telegraph*

NOT FOR SALE IN THE U.S.A.

The Mountain is Young

Han Suyin

And the wildest dreams of Kew
Are the facts of Khatmandu Kipling

When Han Suyin attended the coronation of the King of Nepal she found the inspiration for this sun-washed portrait of the 'Land of the Gods' in the toils of Western 'Aid'. As in *A Many-Splendoured Thing* love pours colour and meaning into the life of Anne Ford, but here a cast of Ranas, Maharanis, doctors, priests, poets, missionaries, and soldiers, with a chorus of tourists, gives us a Nepal which at times is reminiscent of Nepenthe in Douglas's *South Wind*.

'A long story in which the magic of the background – Khatmandu, its mountains, people, and customs, all vividly brought to life – supersedes the lovers in interest' – *Sunday Times*

'This lovely and moving book . . . it is difficult briefly to convey the flavour of this rare novel . . . in which wit and humour are combined with a wise tolerance' – *Daily Telegraph*

'Desperately readable, witty, edgy' – *Daily Express*

A Many-Splendoured Thing

Han Suyin

'With her unfaltering honesty, fine balance and astonishing feel for the English language she has written an outstanding love story. That the story is her own, that physical love and dependence did not come easily to her, that she was irrevocably separated from the Englishman whom she loved, make her book all the more remarkable. But while she never loses the thread of her heart's theme, she weaves it into the hectic, over-crowded background of post-war Hongkong, where she worked until "as a Chinese and a doctor", not as a Communist, she could return to China. Whenever she moved in this shifting world of rich and poor Chinese refugees, of European big-business men, of idealists and realists of both continents, she brought away her own keen-edged impressions. In this sense her book is brilliantly topical but it is far more than that, for she handles an eternal theme with power, insight, and unfailing artistry' – *Sunday Times*

'This is one of the loveliest books I've read for a very long time' – Alan Melville on the B.B.C.

For a complete list of books available please write to Penguin Books whose address can be found on the back of the title page